DEATH DO US PART

A PAGE-TURNING CRIME THRILLER WITH A
STUNNING TWIST

JAMES D MORTAIN

BOOKS BY JAMES D MORTAIN

DETECTIVE DEANS SERIES
1. STORM LOG-0505
2. DEAD BY DESIGN
3. THE BONE HILL

DI CHILCOTT SERIES
1. DEAD RINGER
2. DEATH DO US PART
3. A WHISPER OF EVIL

DETECTIVE DEANS PREQUEL
THE NIGHT SHIFT
(Visit www.jamesdmortain.com to download a free and
exclusive copy)

DEATH DO US PART

A DI CHILCOTT MYSTERY
BOOK TWO

Cover Design © Manvers Publishing
Images: SSokolov/Shutterstock.com
Casther /Shutterstock.com
Edited by Debz Hobbs-Wyatt
ISBN: 978-1-9160084-7-2

Dedicated to Rich, my lifelong and closest friend. Thank you for being a brother to me all these years!

PROLOGUE

Friday August 13th

7:02 p.m.

'Permission to board,' came a voice from the jetty.

Jane Hicks looked out from the cabin and saw a smiling Debbie Baxter standing at the edge of the walkway, holding a "token" bottle of something white in her hands. Her husband, Walter, stood flaccidly at her side, but he was anything but smiling.

'Please do,' Jane said, coming towards them with an outstretched arm to help the glamorous younger woman step across from the wooden jetty and onto the open-plan stern of her boat. She took the bottle of wine with a polite smile and an 'Ah, that's sweet of you', but she didn't bother to look at the label. Turning to Walter, she extended a thin, measured smile, but instead of offering her arm in the same manner she had to his wife, Jane simply turned her back and made towards the inside with Debbie's arm looped inside her own.

'Well, if it isn't our fun-loving neighbours,' the other host, Trevor Hicks, boomed with dramatic gusto as he joined them on the deck from within the cabin of his plush, forty-five-foot Princess cruiser. He gave Debbie a welcoming wink and extended an upward nod to Walter, who didn't reciprocate any form of greeting of his own. Trevor had with him a customary glass of champagne sloshing inside a tall crystal flute.

'Ah, that's… kind of you,' he said, taking the bottle of gifted wine from Jane in his free hand. 'Can I offer either of you a glass of fizz to help get the party started?'

'That would be lovely,' Debbie said. 'Thank you so much.'

'I'll have one glass of *that* wine, please,' Walter replied with an upturned lip, referring to the donated bottle in Trevor's left hand.

'One glass of fizz and one…', Trevor made a point of bringing the bottle to his face for a closer inspection of the label, '… Chilean Chardonnay.' He caught Jane with a mischievous glint of the eye, and he grinned insincerely at Walter.

'Coming right up, sir,' he said with a subservient bow.

Stopping at the sliding cabin doors, he turned. 'Are you sure I can't tempt you with a vintage Dom Pérignon, Walter? It's rather nice, you know. Who knows, it might even help you relax?'

'So I see from your empties on the jetty. I assume they will be gone by the morning.'

'Of course, dear Walter – ever the environmentalist.'

Trevor winked at his wife; the wind-up had begun.

'No,' Walter answered. 'One glass of Chardonnay will be adequate. Thank you.'

Trevor beamed a broad smile, his bleached white teeth catching the fading light of the dropping sunset. He shot a final glance at his wife and stepped back into the cabin, party music and laughter escaping from the open doors.

'Well,' Jane said. 'Shall we join the others inside?'

'Who else is here?' Debbie asked with apparent interest.

Walter cast her a dour stare.

'We've got *Gekko*, *Master and Commander*, *Stainer*, *The Captain*, oh, and their better halves, of course.' She giggled, and Debbie joined in her amusement.

'Quite a gathering,' Walter commented just as the immediately recognisable and penetratingly high-pitched laughter of *Gekko's* wife – Rosemary Collins – escaped through the gap left in the door by Trevor who had just announced the arrival of the latest guests.

'Why must Trevor give everyone nicknames?' Walter asked.

Jane just smiled. *Wait until you hear yours*. She was pretty sure Walter had no idea he was widely known in this tight-knit marina community as, *The Serial Killer*.

Seeing a mark of recognition in Debbie's eye, it seemed apparent that she was also "in" on the joke.

It was Trevor's passion to have as much fun in life as possible, and if that meant upsetting a few people along the way with his wicked yet priceless sense of humour, then so be it.

Jane prized the doors wider for them all to pass through, and the ambient, soothing rhythms of a *Chilled Ibiza* classic greeted them.

'Here you go, Debs. Enjoy that, my love,' Trevor said, bounding towards her with a brimming flute of lively, top-end champagne.

'Walter,' he said in sad contrast and handed Walter a yellow plastic beaker containing his tepid Chardonnay. 'Can't be too careful.'

Walter peered down disapprovingly at his alternative drinking vessel, setting Rosemary into further fits of hysterics at his expense, but Trevor hadn't quite finished with him yet.

'They always say you have to watch the quiet ones... don't they, Walter?'

Walter looked back at his host with utter disdain and the blatant, unapologetic hatred he had for the man.

The Hicks' lived a lavish lifestyle. Their boat was by no means the most expensive on the marina, but their passion for life couldn't be matched. *Generosity* was a noun that came nowhere near describing their unparalleled hospitality levels. Eight unopened bottles of vintage Dom Pérignon champagne chilled inside individual ice buckets on the side of the galley. They would probably only go through half that amount tonight, but it was the thought that counted for their valued friends.

Trevor lowered the music volume and stepped into the middle of the lounge area.

'So, now we're all here,' he roared, holding his glass aloft. 'Here's to the end of summer, and may we all enjoy calm waters and distant horizons.'

'Calm waters and distant horizons,' everyone except Walter repeated as they joined Trevor in a lofty toast of their glasses.

'So,' Trevor said playfully to Debbie. 'We're all putting our keys into the pot later. You up for a little fun tonight?'

'I'm game for anything,' Debbie giggled, giving Trevor a gentle prod in the ribs with the point of her elbow.

'We'll be doing no such thing,' Walter said.

'It's okay, Walter,' Jane said. 'He's only joking. Ignore him. You know what he's like.'

'Yeah, we don't need keys – none of us is driving,' Trevor roared, clinking glasses with several of the other guests, including Debbie.

'Are you still enjoying marina life here?' Tim Collins, also known as *Gekko* after the character *Gordon Gekko* in the film *Wall Street*, asked Debbie as she took a seat on the crescent-shaped cream leather sofa beside him.

Tim was a retired City banker of almost thirty-five years, hence the nickname. He and his wife had always planned to spend their twilight years beside the ocean.

'I love it, thank you.' She glanced around the room and caught the smiles and welcomes of other guests.

'How long's it been now?' Tim quizzed. 'Since you both first pitched up here?'

Debbie looked across the cramped saloon towards her husband, standing by himself close to the outer doors.

'It's been nearly fourteen months now.'

'And I understand the sale of your house in Pensford went through?'

'Yes. In fact, it was faultless.'

'Blimey! Just as well Stainer wasn't handling it; you'd still be there at Christmas.'

Ben Staines was a local property agent and had quite an impressive portfolio of premises, but he also came with a reputation as a bit of a shit magnet. If anything could go wrong in Ben's world, it generally did.

'I heard that, *Gekko*,' Ben replied from across the room and balled a playful fist in Tim's direction.

'He's only jealous,' Tim whispered, grabbing Debbie's partially empty glass from in front of her in one smooth motion. 'I'm sure he just wants to sit next to the most beautiful woman on the marina… instead of me.'

'Aww,' Debbie cooed and knocked his arm playfully with the back of her hand. 'You're just saying that to be nice to me.'

'Debs is ready for a top-up,' Tim called out to Trevor, holding out the champagne flute in an outstretched arm towards the host.

'Oh… no really, I'd… I'd better not.'

Trevor dutifully came to Debbie's side and, barely taking his eyes away from hers, he skilfully filled the glass, treating every drop of the champagne with reverend respect.

'Ooh, thanks. But I really can't get—'

'It's no crime to live a little,' Trevor replied, handing her the refilled crystal glass flute.

Across the room, Walter was watching her with the eyes of a hawk, a miserable one at that.

Trevor navigated the guests with the bottle of champagne until he was opposite Walter. Trevor took pride in his hosting skills, and Walter's disconnection with the rest of the party was glaringly apparent and at odds with what Trevor would have desired.

'So, what did you say you did for a living before retiring?' Trevor asked Walter to engage and include him in the party.

'I didn't.'

Trevor stepped back in a theatrical display of defensiveness.

'Okay,' he said, holding up his hands, one containing the nearly full bottle of Don Pérignon, the other his glass flute. 'Then pray do tell us, Walter, what did you do for a living? How can you afford that beautiful yacht of yours?'

Walter's eyes tracked Trevor's without deviation. The rest of the guests hushed to near silence. All they could hear now were the relaxed tones of *Café del Mar* playing softly in the background.

'I worked for the Ministry of Defence.'

'Ah, a *James Bond-type*, I bet?' Trevor jested. 'Quiet and mysterious. Got your licence to kill and all that?' He beamed broadly to his audience, much to the delight of Rosemary, who was well on her way to a serious hangover in the morning.

Walter didn't reply and kept his eyes trained on his much younger host, who appeared to be deriding much comedic mileage at his expense.

'He was a draughtsman,' Debbie whispered to Tim. 'He worked in the drawing office.'

'I won't tell anyone if you don't?' Tim reassured her.

She giggled softly and sipped from her glass.

'Nibbles anyone?' Jane asked, producing a large silver platter of prepared canapés, fresh peeled prawns, dressed crab, and savoury snacks. The warm smell of samosas filled the saloon. 'We've got meat and veggie options,' she said, taking a bite from the first delicious-looking morsel nearest to her. Years of corporate and private entertainment had shown her this was the best way to break the ice when it came to eating at parties – scoff something first yourself. And after all, she'd spent four hours of the day making the stuff, so the last thing she wanted was for everyone to stand around politely staring at the plate of food while waiting for someone else to make the first move. Sure enough, Rosemary stepped forward, took a dish from the stack on the side and took one of everything on offer.

'Top-up anyone?' Trevor asked, holding the freshly-opened bottle of champagne aloft, before heading directly for Rosemary and topping up her glass to the brim, even though she hadn't answered.

'Anyone else?' he asked, catching Walter's disapproving frown from across the room. He lowered the bottle and quietly walked over to him.

'Come on, Walter,' he said gently. 'Just one little glass of fizz? No one wants to see you alone here tonight.'

'I'm not alone. I'm with my wife.'

Trevor twitched a brow and looked back over to where Debbie was surrounded by all the other men on the small half-moon sofa.

'We've got a busy day tomorrow, and I want to be compos mentis,' Walter said.

'Ooh, that sounds interesting. What are you up to tomorrow then?'

Walter didn't answer immediately. He peered at Trevor with a dubious mistrust.

'We're picking up a new boat,' Debbie shouted from across the way. 'We can't wait. It's wonderful.' She looked at her husband's disapproving glare and then ducked down as if hiding behind her glass.

Trevor turned back to Walter, whose facial expression hadn't altered.

'So I see,' Trevor said. 'Walter looks positively gripped with excitement.'

Walter narrowed his gaze.

'Where are you picking the new boat up from, Walter?' Trevor asked.

'Salcombe Marina.'

'Salcombe? That's a beautiful location but a long way to go for a boat. Are you transporting it by land?'

'No, we're sailing.'

'You're sailing to Salcombe! What about the predicted winds over the next few days? I've heard it's going to get pretty messy out there.'

'You don't need to worry about me.'

Trevor scratched the side of his temple. 'I'm not.' He turned back towards the half-moon sofa. 'But Debs, on the other hand.'

'You don't need to be concerned about my wife either.'

'Okay,' Trevor said, holding his hands up in submission and taking a step or two further backwards. 'I was just trying to be helpful.'

'Are you causing problems again, Trevor?' Ben called over playfully from the sofa.

'Not me… not me.'

Trevor turned his back on Walter. 'I think I need a top-up.'

'Tell me about this trip of yours tomorrow,' Tim asked Debbie. 'What boat are you getting?'

'It's a new *Amel Sixty*.'

'New?'

Debbie nodded.

'My god! What's that… one point four, one point five million?'

'Something like that. I leave Walter to do the negotiating.'

She took a moment to catch the eye of her husband and smiled across to him.

'What are you doing with your existing yacht?'

'It's already traded. We arrive at Salcombe, do a hand-over, and then return on *Death Do Us Part*.'

Tim almost spat his drink across the table as he reacted to the new boat's name.

'That's an interesting choice of name. Don't you think that could be tempting the fate of the Sea Gods? You know what they say?'

'I chose the name. I think it's perfect.'

'Well, then who am I to disagree? What time are you planning to leave? The tides are early tomorrow.'

'We're heading off by seven-thirty at the latest and plan to make a late stop-over somewhere in Cornwall. We'll then do the final stretch to Salcombe, probably arriving late on Sunday.'

'Have you seen the forecast? Have you been on a trip in weather like that before?'

'Yes, I used to work as crew on large commercial yachts. And Walter and I have sailed to the Channel Islands and France numerous times, so this should be fairly straight forward.'

'When do you think you'll be back in your swish new boat?'

'Possibly next weekend, weather permitting. We are going to spend a few days in Salcombe. I love it there; it's just so beautiful on a summer's day.' Debbie sipped from her glass and glanced at her husband. He was paying her undivided attention from across the room.

'Just keep a close eye on that weather,' Tim suggested, like a father to his daughter. 'It's due to change late on tomorrow with a front moving in from the west.'

Noticing her concerned frown, he quickly backtracked. 'Uh… but you never know with the English weather.' He smiled and finished his glass of champagne.

'Your wife seems to be enjoying herself,' Debbie commented as she looked over to Rosemary, who was fussing over spillage of champagne on the sheepskin rug.

'Oh, she's never long without a glass in her hand. She must have thought all her Christmases had come at once when Trevor and Jane pitched up next to us three years ago.'

'They do like a party, don't they?'

'Every weekend, and most days in between. They're still young enough to enjoy life while they can.'

He looked over conspiratorially at Trevor, who "playing down" Rosemary's little drinks accident.

'I do wish they'd give it a rest sometimes, though. It would be nice to come down here occasionally and enjoy the peace and tranquillity, which is why we bought the boat in the first place.'

'How long have you lived here full-time?' Debbie asked.

'We started visiting at weekends and then gradually built up to living here permanently around two years ago; once we got to know a few people around the marina – you know how it goes.'

'Yes, I know what you mean. Walter lives here full-time, and I do try to be here as much as possible, but I sometimes also stay away with friends.'

'Yes, I've seen you coming and going.' He gave Debbie a knowing lift of the eyebrow.

She flashed a smile and then covered her mouth with her glass and glanced sideways at her husband.

'I'm going to check up on Rosemary. Good luck with your voyage tomorrow.' Tim touched the top of her arm and then slid his legs away from under the table to join his increasingly tipsy wife.

Debbie wasn't alone for long. Dave Reynolds approached and took the recently vacated and still warm seat alongside her. He waited for Walter to look away in another direction before speaking.

'Hi Debs, how are you doing?'

'I'm good.'

'So, it's tomorrow?'

She nodded and looked down gingerly.

'That's great.'

Her eyes darted up and around his face. 'Yes... yes, it is.'

The rugged, thirty-one-year-old heir to a multi-million-pound fortune looked anxiously towards Walter, who was fending off the attentions of an increasingly amorous Rosemary Collins.

'I can't wait,' he said quickly in hushed tones.

'Me either.'

'Okay, you two?' Trevor said, bounding over towards them with another opened bottle of champagne. 'Who's ready for a top-up?'

Dave put a hand over the top of his glass. 'I think I may go onto the brandies, Trev. Too much of this, and I'll be anyone's.' He looked sideways at Debbie, who recoiled with blushing coyness.

'I think I'll join you in that, Dave,' Trevor said as he refilled Debbie's flute with bubbly.

'Let that be the last one,' a stern voice came from across the table. Walter was now standing just feet away from Debbie with his arms firmly folded.

'Hello, Walter,' Dave said. 'I hear you are off to collect your new boat in the morning.'

'Only if *she* stops drinking.'

'Oh, she's just having—'

'Just having what?'

'I was just going to say… Debs is enjoying a couple of drinks, that all. She's not coming to any harm.'

Walter moved towards his wife in a determined fashion. 'Well, then maybe it's time I put an end to that.'

Dave quickly turned towards Debs. She was curled up on the seat beside him.

Instinctively, he reached out and pulled at Walter's arm. 'I'm sure Debs is old enough to decide for herself.'

'Get your fucking hand off me.'

Time, sound and movement stopped in an instant.

Walter's face was tight with fury.

'Come on,' he shouted, shooting out a hand and taking a fist full of Debbie's white blouse. 'It's time to go.'

He yanked her towards him, thrusting Debbie's body forwards against the table.

'Hey, watch it, you prick,' Dave yelled, reaching out for Debbie's arm.

Walter clamped eyes on the younger man while still holding Debbie by a balled fist of material.

'Stay out of my business,' he seethed through gritted teeth.

Dave swung his legs out from beneath the table and fronted up to Baxter toe-to-toe as Tim and others attempted to claw him back from the confrontation.

'I said watch it,' Dave replied, taking hold of Walter's wrist in a firm and uncompromising grip.

'You'd better let go, son,' Walter said, looking down at Dave's hand. 'You can't afford to be up on charges of assault.'

Dave hesitated for a second and then released his grip.

'Walter,' Trevor called out as he came back up to the saloon from the toilets. 'Where are you going? You've only just turned up. We haven't sorted out the wife-swap yet.'

Jane prodded Trevor in the ribs with her elbow and silenced him.

All background chatter had ceased, and eyes were trained on Walter and his wife.

'I'm sorry, Walter,' Trevor backtracked. 'I was only joking about the wife-swap.'

'Yes, that's all you do,' Walter spat as he pulled Debbie closer towards him with considerable force.

'Go easy,' Dave shouted, bouncing his chest off Walter's shoulder.

Walter pointed a rigid finger towards him. 'You keep your bloody nose out of our business, and I'll keep mine out of yours.'

He twisted the strap of Debbie's handbag, slung over a shoulder, and dragged her behind him towards the exit like he was leading a donkey.

Everyone watched him, rooted to the spot.

He turned around at the exit. 'Thank you for the…' He looked around at the stunned faces peering back at him and paused on Trevor's gawking face. '…hospitality.'

He led the way through the sliding doors with an uncomplaining Debbie still connected by her bag strap. Dave tried to follow, but Tim stopped him.

'Don't get involved, son.'

'But he can't do that.'

'Bloody hell,' Trevor cussed. 'What an obnoxious little shit. He's only gone and ruined the party.'

'Do you think we should check if Debs is okay?' Rosemary slurred to her husband.

'We'll leave soon,' Tim said. 'We're moored close to them. We'll hear if anything else happens and if it does, I'll call the police.'

'You'll do that?' Dave said. 'Call the police if he continues?'

'Yes, yes, absolutely.'

'I don't know. I think we should check Debs is okay,' Dave said.

'Leave it, Dave. Some things are best not getting caught up in.'

'Why on earth is she with him?' Jane said. 'There is absolutely nothing appealing about that man whatsoever.'

Trevor stepped outside onto the decking, but Walter and his wife were already out of sight.

'Money,' Tim said to Jane. 'There can be no other reason. She's with him for the money.'

CHAPTER ONE

Wednesday 1st September

10:17 a.m.

As he checked the ongoing and fresh Storm Log reports of each reported crime in the various districts that his department covered, Detective Inspector Robbie Chilcott stared wistfully at his computer screen. He'd been on duty at the Bristol Central Major Crime Investigation Team since 7 a.m. He was starting to suffer the light-headed effects from a caffeine overdose resulting from excruciating inactivity and general malaise. It wasn't unusual for his department to have barren periods when serious crime abated for a day or two, but this had been a ball-achingly dull couple of weeks. There wasn't much stirring in this particular world of murder detectives.

The detectives of the CMCIT had plenty to do. The

department was carrying three investigations in preparation for Crown Court trials, including two separate gang stabbings and the coroner's investigation into the death of Barry Kershaw; an investigation that made a significant impact on the department, and on a personal note, took Chilcott to the edge and back. The Independent Office for Police Complaints were also still involved, sniffing around like a pesky dog and causing the team, especially Chilcott, a not-inconsequential degree of grief. They were particularly interested in Chilcott's methods, something that made him stand out from his peers. He didn't do things to be deliberately maverick, but unfortunately for him, it often just turned out that way. He was unique in how he saw crime, but probably more problematic for him was the distinctive way he tackled it. To some, he was a legend. To others, including his direct line supervisor, Detective Chief Inspector Julie Foster, he was never more than one wrong decision away from bringing down the entire department.

It wasn't that Chilcott was bored as such – this still beats the hell out of general response work or dealing with the repetitive types of jobs his counterparts in district CID had to manage. And it wasn't that he hoped for more murders, perish the thought, but he needed *something* to keep him focussed, driven and away from the hounds of the IOPC.

A *tap*, *tap*, *tap* on the door broke his lethargic stupor.

Detective Inspector Jasjit Chowdhury was standing in the open doorway.

'Hey, Jaz,' Chilcott mumbled. 'How are you doing, mate?'

Jaz Chowdhury approached Chilcott, waving a sheet of

A4 paper held out in front of him. 'Not sure how you're fixed?' he said.

Chilcott waved a heavy hand over the top of his sparse desk. 'Snowed under, as you can see.'

'I've been made aware of a job that might interest you?'

Chilcott frowned and looked back at the ongoing call logs. Had he missed something?

'If you're not free, then I can run it by—'

Chilcott leaned over and snatched the sheet of paper from Chowdhury's loose grasp. 'Let me see that.'

He read the typed report for a few seconds, his frown deepening with each paragraph.

Chowdhury stood back and silently watched his counter-part taking onboard the information.

'What's this crap?' Chilcott said, wafting the sheet of paper through the air like it was meaningless twaddle.

'Looks like a job for the CMCIT,' Chowdhury said.

'Really?' Chilcott asked incredulously and handed the now crumpled report back to his colleague.

'Looks like a complete crock of shite to me. I know I want something to keep me occupied, but I'm not that desperate.'

Chowdhury looked down at the report with bemusement.

'How can you say that, it's a high risk missing person?'

'So?'

'So, it's something that needs proper investigation.'

'By the suits on district. This isn't a major crime issue. Never was, never will be.'

Chowdhury shrugged. 'DCI Foster seems to think it is.'

Chilcott paused and stared disapprovingly at Chowdhury.

'Let me see that again.'

He hinged forwards and snatched the report back, dropping it onto his desk beneath his gaze. He rested his head in his hands as he read the document once more, but this time, with a keener eye.

Finished, he slid the paper back to the side of his desk but didn't pass comment.

'Well?' Chowdhury said after ten seconds of silence.

'I'll make some enquiries.'

'So, I can leave that with you?'

'That's what I said, didn't I?'

Chowdhury bowed with sarcastic reverence and backed respectfully out of the room.

Chilcott waited until he was certain Chowdhury had gone and then stared out through the window at the three-quarters-filled staff car park below. It was the tail-end of the holiday season for officers with young families. He didn't begrudge them their time off; they were a tight unit, and holidays were necessary for the soul. If only he'd followed the same sage advice those years ago, perhaps he'd have a better relationship with his own daughters… and still have a wife. The fact was, he now lived alone, and work was both his poison and his crutch. The months of self-isolation following Jaz Chowdhury's surprise promotion to the CMCIT had hit Chilcott hard. Living in a grubby caravan beneath the flight path of landing aircraft had dented his ego and confidence. But now, six months on since DCI Foster broke the news that *"Fresco"* had killed again, he was getting closer to his old self, and that pinch of investigative desire was keeping him awake at night.

He sighed deeply and searched the papers for a contact number.

'Sergeant Pottersley, Portishead Police Station,' the zealous reply came.

'Hello, Sergeant. This is Detective Inspector Robbie Chilcott, Central Major Crime Investigation Team.'

'Oh, hello, sir.'

'Is it convenient for you to speak right now?'

'Yes – yes, absolutely. Ah, how can I help you, sir?'

'I've just been handed your report on the high-risk missing person from Portishead Marina.'

'Yes, that's right. Debbie Baxter.'

'Yeah…' Chilcott's voice tailed away. 'What can you tell me about the job, and what raises the threshold for CMCIT to investigate this over a district department?'

'I did receive approval from your DCI—'

'Yes, yes, but it's now in my lap, and I want to know why?'

'Well, it's an odd one, really.'

'I can see that.' Chilcott's tone was less than cordial.

'The report has been made by a third party, not the victim's husband—'

'Victim?'

'Um… the MISPER, sir.'

'Go on. What does he have to say about this missing person?'

'That's the interesting part; he's a real odd-ball. Very defensive and states his wife is visiting her sister in north Wales.'

'Has that been confirmed?'

'No… we-uh… we haven't found any details about a sister in north Wales, or anywhere come to that.'

Chilcott rolled his eyes. 'Okay. Was he asked for an address?'

'Um, no… I don't think so. We have run all other relevant checks on both the subject and her husband, Walter Baxter, but neither come up on the radar.'

'It says here that she's been missing for eleven days,' Chilcott said.

'Yes, sir.'

'Well, why don't we have more information than this?'

'It was only reported to police four days ago… on day seven.'

'Yes, I got my O-Level in mathematics, Sergeant.'

'Sorry, I didn't mean to—'

'So, back to my original question – why does this warrant my team looking into this?'

The sergeant hesitated, and Chilcott heard him clearing his throat away from the mouthpiece.

Chilcott raised both eyebrows with impatient reticence.

'I've got a hunch,' the sergeant finally offered.

'You've got a hunch?'

'Yes, I can't prove anything, but—'

'But?'

'The husband is hiding something.'

Chilcott didn't answer.

'The husband is hiding something; he has to be.'

Chilcott huffed loudly into the mouthpiece and turned with glazed eyes out of the window.

The sergeant didn't say anything immediately. Perhaps

he was sussing on the fact that he was wasting Chilcott's time.

'I'd really like you to investigate this, sir,' he finally plucked up the courage to say.

'Would you?'

'If anyone can get through the tough exterior skin of this bloke, it's you, sir.'

Chilcott half-smiled. A little flattery went down well from time to time. He puffed out air through his lips, making them flutter with a sound like a wet fart.

'Okay, I'll entertain your imagination. Tell me about him.'

'I know this is going to sound odd—'

You have no idea?

'But he looks like a serial killer.'

Chilcott closed his eyes.

'Did you just say, *"He looks like a serial killer?"*'

'I did, sir. And you'd know what I meant if you saw him.'

'How long have you been in the job, Sergeant?'

'Me? Sixteen years.'

'And what do you recall about your training days, right back to when your policing career began?'

'Never to judge someone on their appearance alone?'

'Never judge someone on their appearance alone, that's right. And what have you just done?'

'It's not—'

'Come on… what have you just told me, and what have you just done?'

'But you have to see him.'

'I'll be the judge of that.'

The sergeant didn't answer.

'Where is he now, this… husband?'

'On his boat.'

'At Portishead Marina?'

'Yes.'

'Does he live on his boat?'

'Yes, I think he does.'

'Is it a *big* boat?'

'It's a sailing yacht, sir.'

'Is it a *big* sailing yacht?'

'Fairly big – I don't know anything about sailing, so I—'

'And neither do I, Sergeant. So why isn't a CID detective investigating this instead of a homicide detective?'

'You will have to ask the DCI, sir. I can't answer that.'

Chilcott nodded and cast his gaze once again out of the window into the car park.

'I will,' he uttered wearily. 'Don't worry. I will.'

CHAPTER TWO

10:42 a.m.

'This job you've got me on, Julie,' Chilcott said, waltzing straight into the DCI's office.

'Do come in,' DCI Julie Foster said sarcastically. 'I'm not busy with anything.'

Chilcott tossed the case paper onto her desk.

'It's bullshit.'

Foster peered up at him with the disdain his disruptive and insubordinate entrance deserved.

'You don't like it?' she asked.

'Crock of shite, if you ask me.'

'I don't believe a thirty-one-year-old female missing for eleven days is a *crock of shite*, as you so eloquently put it.'

'I get that, but why us? Are we not snowed under enough with the shortage of staff and the backlog of cases? We should only be dealing with the serious stuff.'

Foster removed the reading glasses from the tip of her

nose, folded them slowly and placed them carefully onto the desk in front of her.

'Sit down,' she said.

Chilcott rolled his eyes but did as she told him.

'Since you've been back with us, you've barely taken a day off, Robbie. What with the Fresco murders—'

'Neither of us has.'

The DCI waved his comment aside.

'That may well be the case, but I'm in charge of this department. You aren't, and your welfare is on my shoulders. This is a nice little job you can get your teeth into and have a change of scenery at the same time.'

'I don't want a change of scenery.'

The DCI stood up and pushed the door closed.

'Rob, I've watched how the Fresco killings affected you. It's gone deep. I get that, and I understand the Herculean effort you put into that case.'

He glanced at her and then looked away. Operation Fresco was a case that had plagued and tormented Chilcott as his only unsolved murder. It cost him his marriage, his home and his self-respect. But then *"Fresco"*, as the department had nicknamed the killer, murdered again, and Chilcott grasped his chance for redemption. He got justice but nearly cost Chilcott his life.

'This job is a perfect way for you to put all that stress behind you. A nice, gentle case by the sea. How could you possibly want to turn that down?'

Chilcott pinched his lips tightly between his fingers and caught her eye again.

'What do I know about boats?'

'You might not know anything about boats, but you sure as hell know how to close out a murder enquiry.'

'Who mentioned murder? This is just a missing person case, isn't it?'

The DCI smiled thinly and gave Chilcott a knowing once over.

'You know Jaz and I can handle the department. We were coping just fine before you returned from exile.'

'It's a detective constable job, not a case for a DI who should be here directing serious investigations. I can't remember the last time I got my hands dirty on a poxy MISPER case. I had eleven years of that crap on district.'

The DCI returned to her seat and unfolded her spectacles, placing them back into position on the tip of her nose.

'Fine, I'll give the gig to Jaz then. I'm sure he could use a break too.'

'Hold on,' Chilcott said with an outstretched arm. 'If I take it, I don't want it to be seen as charity or some kind of *light-duty*.'

'It's not, and it won't.'

'What resources will I have?'

'You can have one DC to do the *dirty work*, as you call it. I'll leave you alone to manage and progress the case as you see fit, and you can report back to me as and when you have any results.'

'But I'm still based here?'

'Look,' Foster said, turning her chair to face him. 'This isn't a way of trying to get rid of you if that's what you're thinking? We've only just got you back! There's an office at Portishead HQ. You can use that. It's an old admin office, fully kitted out with everything you'll need. I use it when I'm there. You can use that, or you can deploy from here. It's your choice.'

'I want Fleur Phillips then.'

'No can do. Fleur is tied up with the Operation Fresco case. The coroner has put a tight deadline on that file, and I can't spare her for this—'

'Go on, say it…'

Foster's face softened, and she gave Chilcott a wry squint of the eye. 'This case, I was going to say.'

Chilcott groaned.

'Okay, I'll take Richie Allen.'

'He's yours.'

'Just like that?'

'Just like that.'

Chilcott looked around the boss's room and wiped a finger beneath his nose.

'Do you want to break the news to DC Allen, or shall I?' Foster asked.

'I'll tell him,' Chilcott said, taking back the case paper from Foster's desk.

'Keep me appraised.'

'I'll have this sorted by this time tomorrow; you'll see.'

He made for the door but paused at the exit.

'Hey,' he said, turning with a slight smile. 'Thanks for thinking of me.'

Detective Constable Richie Allen was a well-liked member of the team. Chilcott had only known him for the six months since his return to the department, and DC Allen had less than one year's major crime investigation experience, but he was dogged in his style and was a keen thief-taker. Still only thirty-seven and single, Chilcott had taken an instant liking to Allen, who in turn, seemed to know a great deal about Chilcott's achievements and some of his less than illustrious antics.

'Allen,' Chilcott said, passing DC Allen's desk and continuing towards his office. 'A word, please?'

DC Allen looked up over the top of his work station and rose gingerly from his chair. He followed Chilcott and timidly tapped his knuckle on the door to his DI's office.

'Come in, Richie. Take a seat.'

DC Allen stepped guardedly into the office and lowered himself onto one of the soft blue chairs, his bottom only just perched on the end.

'How are your crimes looking, son?' Chilcott asked.

'Um, I'm pretty much on top of them, boss. I'm sorry if any are dragging. I'll ensure I—'

'Give me numbers. How many cases are you juggling?'

'Five ongoing investigations, sir, not including the Powlett fraud.'

'I'm taking you off the Powlett fraud.'

'Why… what have I done?'

'You haven't done anything wrong. I need a detective to work on a case with me, and I chose you.'

'Oh… thank you, sir.'

'Don't worry about your existing workload; we'll be back to normal in no time. Just tie up any loose ends you had planned for the rest of this week.'

'Okay, boss, that's no problem. Uh, when do we start?'

'As soon as you're ready.'

'I can be ready by the end of play today,' DC Allen beamed enthusiastically. 'Thanks for having faith in me, sir.'

Chilcott looked blankly for a second at his young, keen colleague.

'I'm going to be honest – I wanted Fleur Phillips, but she's unavailable. This is a good opportunity, son. Do as I say and not as I do, and we'll get along famously.'

CHAPTER THREE

Thursday 2nd September

08:44 a.m.

Portishead Marina on the north-western fringe of Bristol was a recently modernised and improved marina. Unusually, the water was landlocked by large barriers similar in appearance to double canal lock gates. The vista was an impressive sight with luxury high-rise apartments encasing row upon row of pleasure craft from one side of the marina to the other. The place felt like it was dripping with money.

'What's first, boss? Are we going to speak to the MISPER's husband?' DC Allen asked as they strode along the frontage of restaurants and cafés.

'No, we're not. We already know he's suggesting his wife is with her sister. I think before we chat to him, we should speak to the marina manager; introduce ourselves and get a lay of the land, or water, as the case may be.'

He stopped beside an empty outside table and looked inside the large plate glass window of the nice-looking café.

'But first, we're going to have a brew. Let's just sit back and people watch for a while.'

DC Allen looked puzzled.

Chilcott peered up at the breaking clouds in the sky and positioned a metal chair to make the most of the warmth on his face.

'This'll do lovely,' he said, crossing his outstretched feet before him.

DC Allen followed suit and sat down on the opposite side. He looked around for a moment. 'Not many people to watch, boss.'

'Just trust me.'

A waitress joined them outside and sprayed the metal table top with a heady sanitizer-fuelled spray.

'Are you eating with us today, gentlemen?' she asked.

'Just drinks, thanks,' Chilcott said.

'Would you like the wine list, sir?'

Chilcott scratched the top of his head and smiled at the girl. 'I would… but we'll just have coffees, for now, thanks.'

They gave their orders, and Chilcott sat back against his seat and took in the surroundings. There was no denying it; this was a picturesque and entirely relaxing location. DCI Foster had indeed done him a favour.

'Do you know anything about boats, Richie?'

'Me? No, nothing, boss. Other than they make me feel sick when I'm on one.'

Chilcott smiled. He knew that feeling only too well.

'This is how we learn. We observe. We blend in. We watch.'

'And drink,' DC Allen quipped.

'There's always time for coffee. Rule one of the detective's handbook.'

Coffee done, they headed for the marina manager's office situated at the sea-bound mouth of the marina. More like an elevated viewing platform than an office, the operation was similar to a scaled-down air traffic control tower. Introductions at the door over, the manager, Simon Dupont-Avery, took them up to the control room, boasting an impressive bank of closed-circuit TV monitors and communications equipment.

Chilcott nodded satisfaction as he looked around the small glass-walled room.

'What a nice job to have.'

'It's a lovely job,' Mr Dupont-Avery replied. 'Do you gentlemen sail?'

'No… I wouldn't know the front from the back,' Chilcott quipped, giving DC Allen a little wink.

'The bow from the stern,' Dupont-Avery corrected in a teacher-like tone.

Chilcott waved a dismissive hand back at him. 'See, that's exactly what I was saying.'

'I saw you earlier at Le Parisien, having coffee. Is this your first time here at the marina?'

So much for blending in.

Chilcott nodded and looked around the office again at the modern technological equipment.

'Yeah, it's our first time, in a work capacity anyhow. This must be one of the most crime-free places in Bristol?'

'I'd like to think so. We certainly try to keep it that way.'

'Do you keep records of who is staying on the marina at any one time?' DC Allen asked.

'Yes, of course, you can't just turn up. Demand for berths is high since we updated the marina facilities. People come from far and wide to moor their boats with us.'

'And what about daily movements?' Chilcott asked.

'The Bristol Channel is challenging, even for the most experienced of sailors. The tidal range is the second highest in the world, somewhere between twelve and fourteen metres. Subsequently, that means many of these vessels are limited to when they can get out to the open water. For safety's sake, we log requests to leave and return to the marina, as we have to manually open and close the marina gates to allow egress and access, but we don't do anything else with those records. That would be like big brother watching, and we wouldn't want that.'

'Perish the thought,' Chilcott muttered as he leaned in closer to a bank of small, coloured HD TV monitors.

'How long do you keep the mooring records for?' DC Allen asked.

Chilcott looked up from the screens and gave his colleague an approving nod.

Dupont-Avery moved towards the window with a confident swagger.

'For as long as you like. We have records dating back to 2011, but again I stress, purely for archive purposes.'

'We only need this year. Got that, have you?' Chilcott asked.

'Yes, of course.'

Chilcott beamed a smile.

'I'm sorry. You still haven't said why you are here. You said you were…' Dupont-Avery curled his lip and peered towards Chilcott. '…murder detectives.'

Chilcott didn't answer and asked a question of his own instead.

'Got a good grasp of things here, though, haven't you? You know, who comes, who goes?'

'Well, I wouldn't say—'

'You noticed us.'

Chilcott stared at the man with a no-nonsense determination of someone who wasn't about to be placated with managerial gibberish.

Dupont-Avery shook his head.

'I'm sorry… I…?'

'You noticed us over there at the coffee shop.' Chilcott pointed over to the corner of the building line to the side entrance of the café.

'You can't see the tables from here, so how did you notice us? Was it the cameras?'

'I first noticed you when you walked towards the gangway beneath us.'

He pointed down to the walkway at the top of the lock gates.

'What made us stand out?'

Dupont-Avery chuckled. 'Well, neither of you are dressed for the ocean.'

'That's good,' Chilcott said. 'It's good to be vigilant, especially in this day and age.'

Dupont-Avery hesitated. '…You… still haven't said why you are here?'

Chilcott tossed DC Allen a theatrical look of surprise. 'Haven't we?'

'No. You haven't.'

Chilcott opened the pages of his daybook and thumbed through, even though he knew the name he was searching for.

'Debbie Baxter, she's one of your locals, is she?' Chilcott smiled.

'Yes, Debbie and her husband have been with us for about a year now.'

'So…?' Chilcott said, inching towards the glass-walled observation point. 'Which is their boat?' He immediately turned and watched Dupont-Avery. There was no searching of a computer database or handy desk-top manifest, and he came alongside Chilcott.

'It's at the end of row seven, at bay ten.' Dupont-Avery pointed out into the marina. '*Death Do Us Part,*' he said with a whimsical intonation.

'Death Do Us Part? Is that the name of the boat?'

'Yes.'

'What sort of a name is that?'

'Granted, it's an unusual name for a boat, but we see all sorts here. We only stipulate that there is no profanity or innuendo in a vessel's naming. We have families living on the water and in the apartments, as well as thousands of visitors each year. It wouldn't do to have such words displayed, and we must uphold a certain quality of life here.'

'Which one is it?' Chilcott said, leaning his head closer to the glass. 'They all look the same to me.'

'Oh, it's a beauty. A two thousand and twenty, Amel

Sixty. It's the only one here; in fact, it is possibly only one of several in the UK at this present moment in time.'

Chilcott showed his ignorance of the subject with a shrug.

'It's a beautiful craft, wonderfully made,' Dupont-Avery continued.

'Amel Sixty – sixty feet long, by any chance?'

'Yes, that's correct.'

Chilcott grasped DC Allen's shoulder with his firm grip. 'See, Richie. I said I'd get this sailing malarkey in no time at all.'

Dupont-Avery blinked slowly.

'So, let's say, you know, for argument's sake, I wanted to splash out some of my pension in a few years' time for one of those bad boys – what would it set me back?'

Dupont-Avery's lips twitched, and he attempted not to break into an impertinent smile.

'I'd suggest you'd need a little more than a police pension, Detective. Though one has to admit, one wouldn't know what that was.'

'Try one.'

'Well…' Dupont-Avery said, staring fancifully towards the far away yacht at the end of jetty seven. 'I'd suggest *that* Amel Sixty would most certainly be in the region of seven figures.'

'A million quid?'

Dupont-Avery faced Chilcott with a superior; *you can't afford this lifestyle* kind of look. 'That's correct.'

'Their boat cost them a million quid?' Chilcott's eyebrows were nearly touching his fading hairline.

'Yes, it's now possibly one of the most expensive yachts

we have here.'

'Holy shit,' Chilcott breathed and looked out of the window once again. 'Can you take us down there? I'd love to see what a million quid's worth of boat looks like. Wouldn't you, Richie?'

DC Allen was watching his supervisor with the kind of awe reserved for kids meeting their football heroes. 'Um, yes… of course I would.'

'They are down there, right?' Chilcott asked Dupont-Avery. 'Mr and Mrs Baxter?'

'Well, I haven't seen Debbie for a while now.'

Chilcott pursed his lips and held them protruding as he turned to his colleague. 'What's that?' he asked, seeking clarification.

'I've seen a lot of Walter, but not of Debbie.'

'Since?'

Dupont-Avery adjusted his rimless glasses higher up his nose.

'Since the twenty-first of August.'

'The twenty-first of August?' Chilcott repeated to DC Allen, who jotted the date in his daybook.

'What happened on the twenty-first of August?'

'*Death Do Us Part* moored here for the first time.'

Chilcott scowled. 'I thought you said they'd been here for over a year?'

'I did, but *Death Do Us Part* is a new yacht to the Baxter family and has only been here since the twenty-first of August. They departed the marina on August the fourteenth with their previous yacht, *AWoL*, and returned in *Death Do Us Part.*'

'Absent without leave?' DC Allen asked.

'Another Way of Life.'

Chilcott was staring out of the window once again.

'And was Mrs Baxter here when *Death Do Us Part* arrived on the twenty-first?' he asked.

Another quick touch of the specs and Dupont-Avery shrugged. 'I assume so.'

'Assume so?'

'I don't recall seeing her as they passed through the lock, and I know I haven't seen her around the marina since.'

Chilcott turned to him. 'But you saw her leave on *AWoL* when they left?'

'Yes, absolutely, I was controlling the lock gates. I do believe Mrs Baxter waved to me as they departed.'

Chilcott and DC Allen shared a silent moment.

Chilcott stepped slowly towards the marina manager. 'I'm not expecting you to know this,' he said, secretly hoping to be wrong, 'but, do you know where they picked their new boat up from?'

'Yes, I do.'

Chilcott's eyes widened in anticipation of the answer.

'They were sailing to Cornwall or south Devon depending on their progress and then collecting their new yacht from Salcombe, south Devon, before making the return journey back here.'

Chilcott ran a hand down over his face.

'So, just to be clear, you last saw Debbie on the day she left here but did not see her return, and you haven't seen her since.'

'That's correct.' Dupont-Avery's expression grew quizzical. 'But she's at her sister's, is she not?'

Chilcott sniffed the air. 'You tell me.'

CHAPTER FOUR

They decided that as they were there, they might as well try to speak to some of the owners of the neighbouring boats. Dupont-Avery took it upon himself to escort the detectives through the keypad security gates, down onto the main pontoon. They strode along the wide section of floating walkway until they came to a smaller jetty running off at ninety degrees: Row Seven.

Motor yachts and sailing boats were secured to fastenings on either side of the narrow walkway that would have looked like a two-sided wide-tooth comb if viewed from above.

'The Baxters' yacht is on the end of this row,' Dupont-Avery announced. 'And a number of these other boats are also permanent residents with us.'

'Does one of these boats belong to a Mr David Reynolds?' DC Allen asked.

Dupont-Avery walked them to the rear of a tall and wide motor-cruiser on the left-hand side of the jetty, roughly half way along the row of vessels.

'This is Dave's Sunseeker, but he won't be here today. He generally visits for the weekends only. It's a nice cruiser, this; very well-appointed inside.'

'Do you go inside many of these boats?' Chilcott asked.

'Sometimes, if I'm invited aboard. It's a small perk of my job to see these beautiful vessels upfront and personal, so to speak.'

Chilcott nodded. 'We'll need to catch up with him at some point; he's the person who made initial contact with the police.'

'I see,' Dupont-Avery said, seeming to make a mental note of that particular detail.

'What else can you tell us?' Chilcott asked.

'Uh, this part of the marina is a particularly sociable community.' He waved over to a couple seated on the rear deck of another motorised cruiser. 'I could introduce you to some of them if that would help?'

'Great. Lead the way.'

They stopped at the back of a large Princess yacht named, *She T'appens*. The occupiers had somehow managed to get that name through the Dupont-Avery prohibition net.

'Hello, Jane. Hello, Trevor,' Dupont-Avery said.

'Hey, Simon,' Trevor called back. 'Trusting one of the minions with the controls, are you?'

'I'm going back shortly. I just wanted to introduce you to these two gentlemen from the police.'

Chilcott noticed the couple peek at each other.

'Good morning,' he called out. 'I was wondering if we could trouble you for a brief moment?'

He saw tension in their faces that wasn't there moments before.

'It's okay; there's nothing to worry about. You may be able to help us with some enquiries we're conducting.'

'We weren't expecting visitors today,' Jane fussed, standing up from her lounger.

'The officers are here regarding Debbie,' Dupont-Avery said. 'Have either of you seen her recently?'

They looked at each other and mumbled something privately before simultaneously agreeing they hadn't.

'Have you spoken to Walter yet? He was around here earlier,' Trevor said.

'We're working our way along the jetty. We'll speak to Walter next. My name is Detective Inspector Chilcott, and this is my colleague, Detective Constable Allen. We'd appreciate any time you can give us.'

'Yes, of course, we'd be happy to help in any way we can. Would you prefer to speak inside?' Jane asked.

That's interesting, Chilcott mused and cast a sideways glance over at Baxter's yacht.

'That might be a good idea.'

'Okay, hang on a moment. I'll just have a quick tidy up,' Jane said, making towards the inner doors.

'Please don't go to any trouble on our—' But Jane had already stepped inside and closed the doors.

'We're very sorry to trouble you, and I'm really sorry if we've interrupted your celebrations,' Chilcott said, noticing a glass of something fizzy in Trevor's hand.

Trevor laughed. 'Oh, we aren't celebrating anything special, as such.'

Chilcott looked at his watch. It had only just turned 11 a.m.

Jane returned to the outer deck. 'Okay, we can all go inside now.'

'We appreciate your time. It'll just be a few questions about your neighbours if that's okay?'

'Oh God, not the serial killer?' Trevor said in a playful voice of jeopardy.

Jane jabbed her husband in the midriff with her elbow and gave him a stern look.

Chilcott watched their interaction with growing interest.

'Quite possibly,' he said. 'Perhaps we should talk inside. I've never been on anything this luxurious before.'

'Yes, please do,' Trevor said, leaning forwards to assist Chilcott and then DC Allen onto the rear of the yacht. Dupont-Avery remained on the jetty.

'Trevor Hicks,' he said, giving each of the detectives a vigorous handshake. 'And this is my lovely wife, Jane.'

Chilcott and Allen extended their greetings in return.

'Can I fetch either of you gentlemen a drink?' Trevor asked.

'Ah, no, but, thanks all the same.' Chilcott was practically salivating at the thought of sinking a glass or two of champagne. 'We really won't keep you long, but thanks again.'

'Come inside, gentlemen. Welcome aboard *She T'appens*.'

'Yes, I couldn't help but notice the name,' Chilcott grinned.

Trevor chuckled. 'We couldn't resist it. I'm not sure Simon has the foggiest idea what it really means; if he did, we'd probably have to change it.'

The inside of the yacht was luxury itself; cream and

white leather seating, chrome furnishings and a sparkling drinks cabinet bursting with bottles of alcohol.

'Very nice,' Chilcott commented as he looked around. 'Very nice indeed. What a lovely way to live!'

'Thank you,' Trevor replied. 'It's not a bad life, I suppose. What's the point in having money in the bank? You might as well use it while you can.'

Chilcott turned to Jane. 'You stopped your husband just now when he said something about *the serial killer*; why was that?'

'Oh, he was just being silly. He doesn't know when to stop sometimes.'

Chilcott looked at Trevor, who bowed subservience to his wife's better judgement.

'Who were you referring to? Was it someone here on the marina?'

Trevor tracked his eyes towards his wife. 'It was nothing,' he said.

'Walter Baxter, by any chance?' Chilcott asked and saw recognition in both of their faces. He was bang on the money.

'What do you know about him – Walter Baxter, I mean?'

Trevor rubbed the back of his head and sneaked a glance at Jane once again before answering.

'Interesting bloke, I suppose, but not our "type", though. Don't get me wrong, Debs is more our kind of people, but Walter is just a little bit too... how can I put it politely... well, he's just too pent up.'

'Okay,' Chilcott said. 'I guess we're all different.'

'Some more so than others,' Jane quickly put in.

They clearly felt the same way about Walter Baxter.

'How would you say you all get along?' DC Allen asked.

'All right. Nothing special. Again, we have no issues with Debs, but I know he disagrees with our lifestyle.'

'Which is?'

Trevor smiled and poured himself another glass of champagne.

'Life is for living. We are here for such a short length of time. If you can't enjoy the moment, then…' he shrugged, '…then what's the point?'

'And presumably, that's not Walter Baxter's outlook on life?' Chilcott said.

'Anything but,' Jane cut in over her husband. 'Deb likes a drink and a damn good laugh, just like we do, but he would never let himself go – if you know what I mean?'

Trevor whispered something quietly in his wife's ear, and she nodded.

'So, when did you last see Deb?' Chilcott asked.

They both looked at each other and quietly compared notes.

'We think it was when we had a little party on the boat. They both came for a short while.'

'When was that?'

'It was uh, Friday the thirteenth. I know that because we were wondering what would go wrong?'

'And what did go wrong?'

'Um… nothing,' Trevor said, scratching the side of his nose.

'How were they,' Chilcott asked, 'the Baxters – at the party?'

'Deb was loving it,' Jane said. 'She was having a drink and chatting to everyone.'

'Who else was there?'

'We had *Gekko* and his wife. *The Captain* and *Stainer*—'

'Use their proper names,' Jane scalded her husband. 'The officers don't know who you're talking about.'

'Oh yeah. Sorry, it's a habit.'

'No problem – you were saying?'

'I have to try and remember their proper names now,' Trevor laughed. 'Okay, Tim and Rosemary Collins, Dave Reynolds, Ben and Sarah Staines, us, and of course the Baxters.'

'Did you hold the party in here?'

'Yeah, we throw a lot of parties, but not everyone comes all the time. We generally like to have a bash on Fridays, but we also sometimes hold them on Saturdays.'

'And Mondays, Tuesdays,' Jane interrupted.

Trevor sipped from his glass. 'Well, it's nice to be sociable.'

'Do the others live on their boats too?' DC Allen asked.

'No, we're the only people who live here permanently,' Jane said. 'Apart from Walter and Debbie. Tim and Rosemary stay on the marina for maybe half of the month, so they'd be classed as semi-resident. Ben and Sarah come down each Thursday and leave on the Sunday or Monday, and Dave tends to spend the weekends on his boat because he's working elsewhere during the week.'

'So, you are all quite different in your approach to this boating life?' Chilcott asked.

'Definitely,' Trevor replied. 'That's what makes this community so great. We all share a common bond, but our background lives are very different from one another.'

'And what were your backgrounds – you've obviously done well for yourselves?'

'I'm a doctor, or rather, a retired doctor,' Trevor said. 'I worked for the military.'

'Good for you. I don't blame you enjoying life now.'

Trevor raised his glass in reply.

'What about Walter and Debbie?' DC Allen asked. 'How would you describe them?'

'Oh, Walter is absolutely anal about his boats. But then, he's a snotty-yachty,' Trevor said.

'A what?'

'Ignore him,' Jane said. 'Trevor doesn't understand anyone who actually sails their boat. He thinks they view us motorised sailors as unworthy or dirty polluters, or something.'

'They do,' Trevor implored. 'Don't try to tell me they don't look down on us like a bunch of hicks.'

'Um, darling… we *are* the Hicks, dear.'

They both laughed and clinked glasses.

'So, back to this party,' Chilcott said, attempting to get everyone back on track. 'What time did Walter and Debbie leave?'

'Hmm,' Jane murmured with a finger to her lips. 'Were they the first to leave?' she questioned aloud.

'Uh, yes. I believe they were,' Trevor responded.

'Did you notice anything about them?'

Jane gave her husband a flared stare. Chilcott read it like Braille.

'Go on. Was there something you saw?'

'It was nothing,' Trevor said, playing it down.

'Nothing?'

'Walter was in a foul mood,' Jane blurted out.

'Was he?'

Chilcott turned to Richie and nodded for him to take notes.

'Any particular reason for him to be in such a foul mood?'

'He doesn't like Debs drinking,' Trevor answered quickly.

'Why not?'

Trevor glanced the way of his wife. 'Beats me.'

Chilcott stroked his jaw as he carefully studied the couple. They were at odds with each other for some unknown reason.

'Right, I need a top-up,' Trevor said. 'Are you sure I can't convince you gents to join me?'

Chilcott raised a declining hand.

Trevor stepped down into the galley area and removed a large bottle of champagne from the fridge, and as he did so, Chilcott turned to Jane.

'Why do you think Walter was in a bad mood, Jane?'

'It's quite obvious to me; Debs is a very attractive young lady.'

She looked over her shoulder in Trevor's direction and spoke louder so that he realised her following comments were directed at him.

'And all the men have eyes for her.'

DC Allen scribbled eagerly into his daybook.

'You said, *young lady?*'

'Yes, she's at least half his age.'

Trevor walked back behind his wife's line of sight and gave the officers a look of nodding approval from behind her back before opening the champagne bottle with a loud pop.

'I hope you don't intend taking this yacht out later?' Chilcott said.

'Gosh, no, don't worry, officer, everyone's safe from me today.'

'I honestly have no idea why she is with that man,' Jane mumbled beneath her breath.

Chilcott raised a brow. 'Could it be because of his wealth?'

'Not all women are with their partners for the money, Detective.'

'You don't need to tell me that,' Chilcott said. 'Otherwise, we cops would all be single.'

Trevor chuckled. Jane didn't.

'How were they the day after the party?' DC Allen asked.

'We didn't see them,' Jane said. 'They were gone very early. They had a departure time with the high tide, and we didn't get up until quite late.'

'So, you didn't see them at all on the Saturday?'

'No. Only on Friday night.'

'That's great,' Chilcott said. 'We appreciate your time.' He scanned the inside of the boat again. 'If you don't mind me asking, what would a boat like this set you back?'

'We don't mind at all,' Trevor said proudly. 'This one is actually mortgaged.'

'You can mortgage a boat?'

'Yes, it's similar to a house mortgage. Few of the larger boats here will be purchased outright. We paid half up front and the rest is on a repayment basis over fifteen years.'

'I see,' Chilcott said and placed his business card down on the seat. 'I'll leave you my number. If you think of anything we've not covered, or you remember something from that party, please call me at any time.'

They both smiled.

'It was a pleasure to meet you and see inside your beautiful boat.'

'Anytime,' Trevor said, folding an arm over the back of his wife's shoulder. 'We hope you find Debs, and we pray she's okay.'

Chilcott gave a thin smile. He'd heard enough in the last five minutes to know that was becoming less of a likelihood.

CHAPTER FIVE

As they continued towards the end of jetty seven, Chilcott felt aware that the Hicks were still watching them.

'Did you get all that down?' he asked DC Allen.

'Yes, of course, boss.'

'What did you make of them?'

'I liked them. I wish I had a bit of that unruffled attitude to life.'

'Smoke and mirrors, Richie. Smoke and mirrors.'

DC Allen gave his boss a sideways glance.

'There's something they're holding back, son. I don't know what it is, but there's more to come – I can sense it.'

They reached the farthest point of the outer mooring, and Chilcott fixed his eyes on the large, gleaming sailing yacht at the end; the name emblazoned in a fancy font type; **Death Do Us Part**.

'Have you seen him this morning?' DC Allen asked Dupont-Avery, who was still waiting on the jetty for them.

'Yes, he had breakfast at Le Parisien.'

'You are very observant,' Chilcott commented, still looking at the stern of Baxter's large white yacht.

'It's my job to be observant. People's safety relies upon it.'

Chilcott didn't answer and murmured, 'Uh–huh.'

Death Do Us Part was long and sleek with glistening chrome rails that caught the sunlight and reflected it into Chilcott's face. A large, tan-coloured platform at the rear of the yacht stepped up towards a canopied wheelhouse with a seating area large enough for up to ten people. The decking continued around the side rails and joined a large sun deck at the bow. The inside cabin, which was below the level of the main deck, was hidden by a glass door just wide enough for one person to negotiate at a time.

'Don't suppose they have a doorbell?' Chilcott said, trying to peer into the vessel from the jetty.

'Walter,' Dupont-Avery called out. 'Walter, this is Simon. Are you inside? I have someone here who wants to talk to you.'

Chilcott cocked his head and listened for sounds of movement, and then the narrow glass door of the cabin opened outwards, and a slim, bespectacled, grey-haired man came into view. He ambled slowly up the steps from within the cabin and was drying his hands on a kitchen towel.

'Hello, Walter. Sorry to bother you like this. These gentlemen would like a word with you if that's okay?'

Baxter walked towards them and peered first at DC Allen and then at Chilcott through his thick black, semi-rimmed glasses. Dull grey eyes gave away nothing of his thoughts.

'Good morning,' Chilcott said, edging forwards with an

outstretched arm over the gap between the jetty and the back of the yacht.

Baxter looked down at Chilcott's hand for a second but did not attempt to shake it. The kitchen towel continued to work vigorously through his palms and fingers.

'Sorry if this is a bad time,' Chilcott said.

'A bad time for what?' Baxter countered.

'We are here on a…' Chilcott paused, ready to assess Baxter's reaction, 'welfare visit.'

Baxter didn't flinch and continued rubbing the kitchen towel.

'Can we see your wife, please?'

'She's not here.'

'Where is she, sir?' DC Allen asked.

Baxter looked down at the kitchen towel, and it stopped moving. He slowly folded it with a certain precision, making a straight edge with each meticulous fold.

'She's with her sister.' He placed the towel down onto a circular chrome table in the centre of the seating area behind the wheel.

'Which is where?' Chilcott asked.

Baxter looked at Chilcott and held his gaze for longer than was necessary. 'Pen-y-Cae,' he finally said.

'Penny where?'

'Pen-y-Cae. Near Wrexham, north Wales.'

'The full address please?' DC Allen asked, poised with a pen to write the details into his daybook.

Baxter turned to the younger officer. 'What's this about?' he asked.

'May we come on board so that we can have a proper chat with you in private, please?' Chilcott said.

'No,' Baxter replied, returning his attention to Chilcott. 'You may not.'

Chilcott forced a smile.

'Forgive me. We haven't properly introduced ourselves. This is Detective Constable Richie Allen, and I am Detective Inspector Robbie Chilcott of the Central Major Crime Investigation Team here in Bristol.'

His voice tightened. 'We can have this conversation here, or perhaps you'd prefer to have it at the police station?'

'Is there a problem here?' Dupont-Avery asked anxiously.

'I don't know.' Chilcott scowled at Baxter. 'Is there a problem here?'

Baxter picked up the kitchen towel, unfolded it, and once again began wiping it between his hands.

'We are here on a simple welfare matter, Mr Baxter,' Chilcott said. 'But that can just as easily change. I'm sure you understand.'

The towel stopped moving between Baxter's hands. 'You wanted to know where my wife was, and I told you.'

'Give me the full address, and we'll leave you alone.' Chilcott's voice trailed away, 'for now.'

Baxter stood tall with a self-assured aloofness before turning around and making his way back inside the cabin, closing the glass doors behind him as he dropped down inside and out of sight.

Sixty long seconds went by, and DC Allen leaned into Chilcott. 'What do we do now, boss?'

'He's got another half-minute, and then I'm going in there, whether he likes it or not.'

'I… I don't think you can do that,' Dupont-Avery said,

overhearing their quiet conversation. 'This yacht is private property, just like anyone's home.'

Chilcott gave Dupont-Avery a knowing smile and then called out loudly, 'Mr Baxter, you have twenty more seconds to get that address out to me. After which time, I will use the powers afforded to me by the Police and Criminal Evidence Act to board this vessel and take you into police custody. Where you will stay until I am satisfied you have nothing to do with your wife's apparent disappearance.'

The glass doors opened, and Chilcott and Allen stood in readiness for Baxter to reappear, but he didn't.

'I'll take that as an invite,' Chilcott said beneath his breath. He looked down at the metre-wide gap of the sea sloshing between the jetty walls and the back of Baxter's yacht. 'How do I get on this thing?'

Dupont-Avery leaned forwards and pulled an integrated gangplank down from Baxter's yacht to meet the edge of the jetty.

'Be careful, boss. We don't know if he's tooled up.'

DC Allen hustled in behind Chilcott, and they both stood at the opening to the cabin and looked cautiously inside. Baxter was seated just below them on a white and brown leather three-sided bench. A fresh mug of some sort of herbal tea was steaming on the table in front of him.

Chilcott shot a keen eye around the inside of the cabin. It was beautifully designed and spotless, like new. It made the inside of the Hicks' boat look tired and dated. A folded piece of paper lay on the table's edge in front of Baxter.

'There,' he said. 'Take the address and leave me alone. You are not welcome here.'

Chilcott climbed down the steep steps until he was in the

cabin with Baxter. He lifted the paper and opened it up. There was a name; Alison Williams and a Welsh-sounding postal address.

'Telephone number?' he asked.

Baxter slanted his head and locked eyes with Chilcott.

'You wanted the full address. You now have the full address. You are now also standing within private property. So, unless you intend arresting me on some unfounded and spurious allegation, I would respectfully request that you and your colleague leave my yacht immediately.'

Chilcott bit down and smiled. He waved the addressed piece of paper in the air between himself and Baxter before stuffing it in his trouser pocket.

'Come on,' he said to DC Allen, who watched them from the hatch entrance. 'There's only so much of this posh bullshit I can take.'

As he turned to ascend the steps back onto the deck, Chilcott stopped and faced Baxter. 'One last thing before we go, Mr Baxter. When did you last see your wife?'

Baxter slowly lifted his mug of tea, took a measured and deliberate sip before answering.

'Debbie went to visit her sister on the morning that we arrived at Salcombe Marina.'

'Which was?'

'Monday the sixteenth of August,' Baxter answered without so much as a hesitation.

'Heard from her since, have you?'

Baxter lifted his mug of tea, took another steady sip and stared blankly ahead into space as if he hadn't heard the question.

'Does she have a car?'

Baxter slowly lowered his mug, still avoiding eye contact with Chilcott. 'No, she does not own a car.'

'Then how did she get to north Wales?'

Baxter stared steadfastly at Chilcott. 'She used her initiative.'

Chilcott smirked and gave the cabin a last once over with a keen eye.

'I think we'll meet again, Mr Baxter. I think we'll meet again.'

Back at the marina manager's office, Chilcott stared, unmoving out of the viewing window towards Baxter's yacht.

'I want to know the moment he tries to leave,' he said without looking at Dupont-Avery. 'And trust me, he will.'

'I'm not sure I can—'

Chilcott quickly spun around. 'You can and you will. And if you don't, you'll be obstructing a police investigation. You've got this lock gate – use it. You can prevent him from leaving or keep him trapped inside until we get here. Either way, he is not to leave this marina, do we understand each other?'

Dupont-Avery flapped his arms and spluttered his reply.

Chilcott slid his business card onto the flat glass surface on the bank of electronic equipment.

'I think Mr Baxter will be making plans to leave fairly soon. Please call me the moment that happens.'

As he left the office, DC Allen caught up with Chilcott. 'What do we do now, boss?'

'I don't know about you, but I'm ready for a spot of lunch.'

Chilcott tucked into a club sandwich at the same table they'd occupied earlier in the day. He had already phoned the office and requested an urgent send-to at the sister's address near Wrexham. Local officers in that area would make the appropriate enquiries about Debbie's welfare and feed it back directly. Chilcott estimated that the task would take an hour or two to complete, depending on what else might be ongoing in the Wrexham area. So, in the meantime, sustenance was always a good second option.

'What did you make of him?' he asked DC Allen, who refrained from eating due to some sort of health drive he was pursuing.

'Total weirdo, boss. His appearance, that hand-wringing stuff, he was just... well... odd.'

'He's got OCD, I would suggest. He's probably scrubbing the decks where we stood as we speak. I know it's a new boat, but that cabin was absolutely gleaming.'

'Do you think there's more to this?' DC Allen asked.

Chilcott took a large bite from his sandwich and asked, 'Do you?'

DC Allen scratched above his eye as he thought about his answer. 'Well, we haven't got any evidence of anything happening—'

'No, we don't. But we also don't have Debbie Baxter.'

'But what if she isn't at the sister's address?'

'I'm not expecting her to be there.'

DC Allen's eyes widened. 'And, then what?'

Chilcott wiped crumbs from his mouth with the back of his hand. 'Well, then I suggest we get that smart-arse in for questioning.'

'On what grounds?'

Chilcott guffawed and then tucked back into his lunch until he had cleared the lot, all the while, looking at his junior colleague.

'Till death do us part, Richie. Till death do us part.'

CHAPTER SIX

2:19 p.m.

With no word or update from the enquiries in north Wales, they had returned to the office in Bristol, and Chilcott had taken it upon himself to call Dave Reynolds.

'Hello, is that Mr Reynolds?'

'Yes, who is this?' came a confident reply.

'My name is Detective Inspector Chilcott. I work at the Bristol Central Major Crime Investigation Team. I've been looking into your report about Debbie Baxter.'

Reynolds was silent for a second or two.

'Mr Reynolds?'

'Yes, um… sorry. You've caught me a bit on the hop.'

'Is it a convenient time?'

'I'm driving, but I'm on hands-free,' he said quickly. 'Just give me a moment to pull over somewhere, please.'

Chilcott waited for a minute and listened to the slowing engine tone and the tell-tale clicks from the indicator.

'Hi, sorry about that.'

'No problem. Is it all right for you to talk now?'

'Yes, yes, I'm in a supermarket car park.'

'Good. So, your report to the police – do you just want to run that by me again?'

'Well,' Reynolds said, drawing breath. 'I reported it to the police because I hadn't seen Debs at the marina for a while.'

'Go on.'

'She left with her husband a couple of weeks back to collect a new yacht, and when he returned to the marina, she wasn't with him.'

'And where would you say she was?'

'I… I wouldn't know?'

'But you suspect something bad has happened, which is why you've called the police.'

'I suppose so, yes.'

'Why?'

'Pardon?'

'Why – why would you suspect something bad has happened?'

'Um, because I can't think of any other reason why she wouldn't be there?'

'So, would you say that was unusual behaviour for Debbie Baxter?'

'Absolutely.'

'Have you spoken to her husband about it?'

'No.'

'Why not?'

'Because the last time I saw them together, he threatened me.'

'He threatened you?'

'Yes.'

'You'd better tell me about that then.'

'We were at a party, and Walter was being rough with Debs, so I tried to stop him from hurting her.'

'Okay.'

Suddenly, Chilcott was acutely tuned in to what Dave Reynolds had to say.

'Describe how he was rough with Debbie.'

'He didn't seem to like the fact that she was having a good time.'

'Are we talking about the night before they left to collect their new boat?'

'That's right.'

'Go on; you were about to tell me about this rough behaviour.'

'Well, Walter literally pulled Debbie out of the cabin and dragged her along the jetty towards their boat.'

'And you saw this?'

'Everyone saw it.'

Chilcott frowned. 'Including Trevor and Jane Hicks?'

'Yes, everyone who was there at the party saw what Walter did.'

Chilcott stroked his jaw and pondered the information as it worked around his inquisitive mind.

'And what did Debbie do?' he asked after a moment.

'There wasn't much she could do. Walter may be a lot older, but he's a man and much stronger than Debs, besides there's *something* about him.'

'Hmmm.'

'So that's the reason I didn't ask him about Debbie when he returned to the marina on his own.'

'That's fine. You did the right thing. Would you be willing to provide a statement detailing exactly what Walter Baxter did that night?'

'Yes, I'll do anything I can to help Debs.'

'Good, we've got your number. When are you next in Bristol?'

'I'm planning on coming down over the weekend.'

'To the marina?'

'Yes.'

'Good. I'll ask one of my team to meet you there and grab a quick statement from you if that's okay with you?'

'Absolutely. I hope you throw the book at him for whatever he's done to Debs.'

'And what might that be, Mr Reynolds?'

'I dread to think. He's clearly capable of anything.'

'Okay, thanks for now, Mr Reynolds. We'll be in touch again before the weekend.'

Chilcott ended the call and headed straight for the DCI's office.

Chilcott paced DCI Foster's office deep in contemplation.

'You're troubled,' she said.

'Damn right, I'm troubled.'

Foster looked over to a seated DC Allen, who seemed in a better shape to deal with his emotions.

'How long does it take to conduct a simple bloody send-to?' Chilcott said, striding back and forth along the length of the room.

'I thought you were unconcerned about this case – *a job for the district officers*, you said if I'm not mistaken?'

Chilcott shot his boss an anguished expression. 'Yeah, well…'

'We don't know what else they are dealing with up in Wrexham, Robbie. They might have run out of officers to make the enquiry.'

'Baxter has probably already buggered off. We may never find him again.'

'Or, he may still be there,' Foster said in a reasoning tone.

'You did ask the marina manager to phone you, sir,' DC Allen chipped in, trying his best to assist.

'Pah,' Chilcott grumbled, dismissing the comment.

'What makes you think he's going to leave the marina in any event?' the DCI asked.

Chilcott stopped pacing with a sudden abruptness and faced his superior.

'His wife has been missing for the best part of three weeks, not several days as we first thought. And Baxter has made no apparent attempt to speak to her.'

'How do you know that?'

'I know.'

'Okay,' Foster said. 'Tell me what else you know.'

'They both left Portishead Marina on August the four-teenth on their old boat, *AWoL* and Debbie Baxter hasn't been seen at Portishead Marina since.'

'When did Walter Baxter return?'

'According to the marina manager, Baxter booked back onto his mooring on Saturday the twenty-first of August with his new boat; *Death Do Us Part*.' Chilcott shook his head.

'But Debbie wasn't with him.'

The DCI looked at her desk calendar and slid her finger along the dates.

'Okay, so that's now actually twenty days since anyone last saw her at the marina, including today.' She cupped her chin in her hand. 'Hmmm, that's not good.'

'Just ask yourself why Baxter didn't report her missing?' Chilcott said as he paced the office once again, but this time with even more urgency.

The DCI watched him with ever-narrowing eyes.

'Okay,' she said.

'I haven't got to the best bit yet,' Chilcott said.

The DCI sank back in her seat. 'I'm all ears, Robbie.'

'I've just been told by the original informant that Baxter assaulted his wife at the Hicks' party the night before they left Portishead. Dave Reynolds tried to intervene, and Baxter threatened him with violence.'

'Why isn't that on the original Storm report?'

'Because nobody asked the right questions.'

'Apologies for the interruption, Ma'am,' one of the detectives from the incident room said, tapping at the door.

'Yes, is it something that can wait a moment?'

The detective looked at Chilcott.

'I think you'll want to hear this, Ma'am.'

'Go on.'

'I've just had Wrexham Police on the phone.'

'At last,' Chilcott said.

'They've spoken to the sister, and Debbie wasn't there.'

'Okay, where is she then?' Chilcott asked.

'That was all they said. Sorry, sir.'

Chilcott held his arms out to the side. 'What – are you telling me that was all they said?'

'Yes, sir.'

'Jesus Christ! Having waited all this time for the result, and that's all they say. There was no explanation of when she last saw Debbie, when they last spoke or where else she might be?'

The officer shook her head.

'I've got a good mind to call that bloody officer and send them back to the address. Have we got their name?'

'PC Novaks, sir.'

'In fact,' Chilcott said with a tightening jaw, 'if a job's worth doing, it's better just to do it yourself. Have we got a telephone number and name for the sister; did the officer at least manage to get that for us?'

'Yes, sir.'

'Give it to me. I'll call the sister myself.'

The detective jotted the sister's name and number onto a sheet of paper, and Chilcott whipped it from her grasp.

'Thank you,' he said. 'I'm sorry if I've been abrasive. It's not your fault.'

The detective caught DC Allen's eye and backed out of the room.

'Do you mind if I use your phone, Julie?'

'Be my guest.'

DCI Foster vacated her seat and sat down alongside DC Allen as Chilcott tapped in the number from the torn off slip of paper. He put the phone on loudspeaker, and they all listened as the phone repeatedly rang.

Finally, she answered the call.

'Hello, is that Alison?'

'Who's this?'

'Hello, my name's Detective—'

'I've already told you lot. I don't know where my sister is, okay?'

Chilcott looked across the room at DCI Foster and DC Allen. Foster didn't look impressed.

'I'm sorry, let me explain the reason for my call. I'm a detective inspector from Bristol. My name's Chilcott.'

He waited for a response but only heard the disgruntled sounds of sighing and groaning. He continued nonetheless.

'I know this is probably distressing for you, but let me reassure you that we—'

'The only thing distressing me is you lot not leaving me alone and pestering me about my little sister.'

Another glance towards his colleagues told Chilcott they were equally surprised at the cold tones of Debbie's sister.

'Has anyone explained to you the reason for our enquiries about your sister?'

'I don't care, to be honest.'

'About Debbie?'

'Who else would I be talking about?'

'Can I ask; when was the last time you saw her?'

'I dunno, five or six years ago. Before she decided to throw away a career in search of the *perfect life*.'

'What did she use to do?'

'She was a nurse. I'm a nurse. Our mother was a nurse. She'd be mortified if she were still alive, bless her soul.'

'And your dad?'

'He died soon after she left us.'

'Do you have any other brothers or sisters?'

'No.'

Have you spoken to Debbie recently?'

'No.'

'Could you say when the last time was that you spoke with Debbie?'

A few silent seconds went by.

'I haven't spoken to her since dad's funeral.'

'You've had no contact whatsoever since that time?'

'Practically none.'

'Have you ever met her husband?'

'No, and I don't want to either.'

'Listen, I'm sorry you've had your differences, but your sister is missing. She hasn't been seen for almost three weeks now. Would you have any idea where she might be?'

As he waited for the reply, he saw Foster whispering something to DC Allen.

'No – sorry,' Alison replied.

'And could you think of any reason why Debbie's husband, Walter, would say she was with you for the last two weeks?'

'I haven't a clue. You'd have to ask him. But I can tell you. She hasn't been here.'

Chilcott noticed Foster walking towards him.

'Okay, Alison. Sorry for troubling you. If you should hear anything, would you mind getting in touch, please?'

'I suppose.'

Chilcott thanked her for her time and gave her his mobile phone number.

Foster breathed in slowly and let out a groan. 'Okay, let's start a major enquiry. It sounds suspiciously like our missing person might be occupying Davey Jones' locker from what I've just heard. How many officers do you need?'

'On the face of it, I need a relatively small team; everything's fairly well contained. We've got two or maybe three land locations. There will be CCTV to review, a handful of witnesses to trace and interview. We'll need some high-tech crime support for phones and computers and that sort of thing, and a standard forensic search of the boat.'

'What about other premises or vehicles occupied by Baxter?'

'We won't know those details until we ask him.'

'Okay. Tell me about the witnesses.'

'We're already on top of that as far as Portishead Marina goes. We would obviously have to check the other locations where they may have stopped over on route to Salcombe, but we can coincide that with the CCTV recovery.'

'Hmmm.'

Chilcott stood up from his boss's seat. 'What's on your mind, Julie?'

'Deaths or murders at sea in these circumstances are rare but notoriously difficult to prove. You'll have to be absolutely sure about this, Robbie?'

'I've seen and heard enough already to know this is worth pursuing.'

'I'll take your instinct to the bank every day of the week. You know that.'

'So, shall we get Baxter in, put him in the hot seat and see what gives?'

'Yes, do it. And let's see what our other enquiries throw up in the meantime.'

Chilcott pulled a face.

'What?' Foster questioned.

'He does seem a bit anal about the boat's cleanliness. I mean, I get it; it's a stunning bit of kit.'

'If there's evidence to be found, I'm sure CSI Parsons and his team will find it.'

'Fine,' Chilcott said, gesturing for DC Allen to stand up.

'Get yourselves kitted up and head back down to the marina. I share your concerns, so let's make this visit formal and get Baxter in for questioning. Take a team with you and obtain his mobile phones, computers, cameras, anything that might assist our investigation. We'll also need all of his wife's phone and banking details; basically, the works for a missing person, stroke, murder victim. You know the drill, lads. Oh, and let's seize control of his yacht and ramp up a full forensic investigation.'

Chilcott stared at his boss. 'I've got a seriously bad feeling about this case, Julie. This has all the ingredients of a perfect murder.'

CHAPTER SEVEN

They were back at the marina within the hour, and to Chilcott's utter horror, *Death Do Us Part* was no longer moored beside the jetty.

He stomped headlong up to the marina manager's office and barged through the door.

'I told you to contact me when he planned to leave,' Chilcott boomed.

'You can't come in here like—'

'Where's he gone?' Chilcott shouted over Dupont-Avery's protestations.

'Who?'

'Fucking Walter Baxter, that's who!'

Chilcott pointed down towards the moored yachts on the jetty. 'Where's he gone? The boat's not there.'

'I didn't see—'

'Bullshit – you see everything. I hope you're not deliberately trying to hinder my investigation?'

Dupont-Avery looked towards his colleague, who quickly scuttled away and out of the office.

'He left about half an hour ago,' Dupont-Avery finally conceded.

'Where's he going?'

'I don't know.'

Chilcott thumped his fist against the communications terminal. 'I'm not playing around here. How far can he get in half an hour?'

'I don't know… not far. He would have been under motor power for most of it rather than sail. Please...' he pleaded, holding out protective hands, '… please refrain from attacking my equipment. It's expensive and not easily replaced.'

'Have you got direct contact with him? Can you call his boat?'

'Of course. We use VHF, channel eighty.'

'Raise him. Get him back here right now.'

'I'm not sure I can—'

Chilcott stepped forwards and lifted the VHF handset. 'If you don't, I will.' His eyes burned wide with uncompromising intensity.

The manager fumbled the controller from Chilcott's grasp and transmitted his message.

'Portishead Marina to Death Do Us Part. Do you copy, over?'

They waited, but there was no response.

'Portishead Marina calling Death Do Us Part. Do you receive me, over?'

Still nothing.

'Can he hear us?' Chilcott asked impatiently.

'If the radio set is on and the volume is up, yes, of course he can hear us.'

'Just tell him to return, right now.'

Dupont-Avery shifted uncomfortably on his feet.

'Portishead Marina – this is a request for Death Do Us Part to return to the marina facility immediately. Please acknowledge, over.'

The hiss of VHF static told Chilcott all he needed to know.

'Do you have contact with the coastguard?'

'Yes, of course.'

'Get hold of them. I need to speak to them urgently.'

'Uh… this isn't protocol—'

'Do I have to do this myself?' Chilcott glared.

Dupont-Avery did as requested, reaching the nearest Coastguard station within moments and gave the handset to Chilcott.

'Hello, this is Detective Inspector Chilcott from the Central Major Crime Investigation Team based in Bristol. Who am I talking to, please?'

'This is Station Officer Henry, over.'

'Are you the most senior officer on duty?'

'I am the most senior officer on duty at present, over.'

'A luxury yacht left Portishead Marina approximately thirty-five minutes ago and is headed out into the Bristol Channel.' Chilcott gave Dupont-Avery a slanting look. 'Direction of travel unknown. I need it intercepted and returned to Portishead Marina ASAP, please.'

Chilcott waited but heard only the faint crackle of static airwaves.

'Do you receive, over?' he said anxiously, flexing his fist.

'I'm not sure we can—'

'The male onboard this boat is wanted on suspicion of

murder, and the boat needs to be seized for evidential purposes before it gets too far away.'

Dupont-Avery stumbled backwards into his high stall, his face stricken at Chilcott's sudden announcement.

'We only have three available staff at present, over.'

'Then get someone to back you up.'

'That will take time to organise.'

'Jesus Christ!' Chilcott spat away from the mouthpiece. 'What does it take to get a bloody boat out?'

The coastguard was silent for a few seconds and then said, 'We have helicopter support from St Athan. It's currently training off the Watchet coastline. I could enquire if they could divert and conduct an initial sweep for the vessel, over?'

'Good. How long will that take?'

'Five minutes to request and five minutes flying time to your location, over.'

'Do it.'

'What are we looking for, over?'

Chilcott turned to Dupont-Avery and held the phone receiver out towards him. 'Tell them what they need to know.'

Dupont-Avery stepped gingerly forwards and fed the information to the coastguard officer.

Chilcott's leg ticked up and down with impatient anxiety, and he faced DC Allen with clenched teeth and fire in his eyes.

'And what should we do if we locate the vessel, over?' Chilcott heard the coastguard ask.

Chilcott snatched the radio back from Dupont-Avery.

'Tell us immediately and then turn it around and escort it back to Portishead Marina. Is that understood?'

'Understood, over.'

Chilcott thrust the handset back at Dupont-Avery. 'Thanks for your help,' he said in disdained tone.

CHAPTER EIGHT

Trevor and Jane Hicks were lounging on the rear deck of their Princess cruiser when Chilcott and Allen disturbed them.

'Ahoy there,' Chilcott shouted to gain their attention.

Trevor jumped up from the cream leather seat and waved to the officers.

'Hello again, detectives. How's it going?'

'Not as good as you,' Chilcott replied. 'Any chance we can come aboard and have another chat, please?'

'Of course.'

Trevor extended a narrow platform allowing the officers to walk aboard.

'Do you have news?' Jane asked.

'We've um, we've come to give you a bit of an update.'

'Ooh, okay. Shall we go inside?' Trevor asked.

Chilcott instinctively looked to the large void where Baxter's yacht should have been. But looking over to the other jetties, there were plenty of people milling about and tending to their boats.

'Probably a wise move,' he said.

'Can I get you gentlemen a drink?' Jane asked.

'No, but thanks,' Chilcott answered.

'How about you, would you like anything?' Jane asked DC Allen. 'I've noticed your colleague does a lot of the talking for you both.'

'That's a privilege that comes with rank and experience, Madam,' Chilcott commented dryly.

DC Allen glanced at Chilcott, who returned a single nod of the head.

'Coffee would be great, if that's possible, please?' he asked politely.

'Yes, of course, I'm sure we've got some here somewhere.'

'Oh, please, don't go to any—'

'No, no, it's no trouble,' Jane said, ducking out of sight behind the sunken galley worktop.

'So?' Trevor said. 'Have you found Debs yet? Is she okay?'

'No,' Chilcott said blankly. 'In fact, the investigation has taken a turn, which is why we are here.'

'Oh! That sounds ominous,' Trevor said, taking himself to the half-moon leather seat and offering the officers a seat on a long leather bench opposite him.

'That party; the night you last saw Debbie. You previously said that Walter was moody?'

Jane reappeared from behind the worktop, holding a dusty jar of Nescafé coffee like it was some sort of trophy. 'Found some,' she announced, clearly pleased with herself.

'When we spoke to you before, you didn't mention the

fact that Baxter had physically dragged his wife away from your boat. Why was that?'

Trevor put a hand to his face and looked behind for his wife's support.

'It's okay,' Chilcott said. 'That's why we talk to as many people as we can. Either something's not seen, or perhaps it's just forgotten?' He gave Trevor a knowing stare. 'Or maybe it was something you didn't view as being out of the ordinary because you'd seen it before?'

'I-uh… we-uh…'

'We didn't want to cause any problems for Walter,' Jane said, coming back towards them. 'Yes, he's weird and all that, but we just wanted to keep our heads down. We're not in the habit of getting involved in other people's trials and tribulations.'

'Hmm, an interesting concept,' Chilcott muttered.

'Sorry, what is?' Trevor countered.

'That you wouldn't want to intervene while one of your close friends is being assaulted.'

'I didn't mean it like that,' Jane came back quickly. 'You know?'

Chilcott shrugged. 'No, I don't know.'

'It was bang out of order,' Trevor said. 'But the rest of us were too pissed to get involved or be in the middle of someone else's domestic dispute.'

'So, they were having a domestic argument?'

'Not exactly; Walter is just different. He's not a party boy, while the rest of us are.'

'Including Debbie?'

'Absolutely. She is most definitely held back by Walter, in more ways than one, I'm sure.'

Chilcott nodded his understanding. DC Allen was taking keen notes in his daybook.

'Could you hear any continuation of the domestic after they left your boat?'

'No. We had music playing, and obviously, there was loud talking, plus the alcohol.'

'Yeah, remind me again. What time did you wake up the next day?'

'Us? Around nine, nine-thirty, something like that?'

'And they were already gone?'

'Yeah, their boat was gone. They had to leave with the high tide as we've previously mentioned.'

'Hmmm.'

Chilcott looked at Jane. 'Any chance I could have a coffee as well, please?'

'Yes. Um, yes, of course.'

As Jane made the drink, Chilcott stood up and looked out through a side window into the marina.

'What would the normal routine be for leaving the marina and heading out into the open sea? I mean, you have those two locks to get through for starters.'

'That's right. We radio through to the marina office and wait for a slot to navigate the locks. It's busier later in the day as the craft come and go in both directions, but usually, the morning traffic is just one direction: out.'

'So, let's say it was you leaving on an early tide. What would you have to do to get beyond the marina and into the Bristol Channel?'

'I'd have a shower for starters,' Jane said, bringing Chilcott his drink.

Chilcott thanked Jane and took a sip.

'A shower in here?'

'God no! I'd go to the shower block; there's so much more space, and the facilities are excellent.'

'Where is that?'

'Just beneath the marina office, there are showers and toilets there,' Trevor said.

'Oh, okay.' Chilcott looked at DC Allen, who duly scribbled the details in his book.

'Would there likely have been a queue on the Saturday morning when Walter and Debbie sailed?'

'Highly unlikely. Most people would still be in their beds if they had any sense.'

'So, let's be clear,' Chilcott said. 'On the morning that Walter and Debbie Baxter last left this marina, the sailing window of opportunity was somewhere between 7.15 and 9 a.m. Is that correct?'

'Yes,' Jane answered, joining Trevor on the seat opposite Chilcott and Allen.

'And there's a good chance Debbie would have freshened up in the shower block or at least used the facilities before that time frame?'

'Yes, and Walter, come to that.'

Chilcott bit his inside cheek. 'And what about the procedure of getting the boat from the mooring to the lock gates. Is that an easy process?'

'It depends.'

'On what?'

'Where you are in the block of yachts. If there are ten boats moored alongside one another and you're on the outer side, it'll be easier than if you were on the inside. And it would also depend on if you were stern or bow end into the jetty.'

'Can you remember where Walter's boat was?'

'He was in row ten, the outer position,' Jane said, 'where he is now. His old boat was also longer than most, so they needed easier access to the mooring station.'

'And it was facing the lock gates,' Trevor added, 'making the process easier still.'

'Would it have taken both of them to launch?'

'Probably,' Jane said.

'More than likely with their old boat,' Trevor said. 'But it wouldn't matter so much with their new boat because it can be solo-sailed if needs be. It's one of the main selling points of the Amel range. The sails can be furled and unfurled from the wheelhouse without having to step up onto the deck. That's one reason why they are so expensive; all that technology. But of course, that's in the open water and not much use in the confines of the marina.'

'What part would the marina manager play in a yacht leaving the marina?' Chilcott asked.

'Well, they would allocate a time and control the gates from the observation tower.'

Chilcott lifted his cup and took several long slurps of coffee.

'Do you know if any other boats left the marina on the Saturday Walter and Debbie left in their old boat?'

'Wouldn't know, sorry,' Trevor said. 'We only knew about Walter and Debs because they told us they were sailing at the party.'

'Well, Debs told us,' Jane said, talking over the top of

her husband. 'Walter didn't want to talk about much at all, remember?'

'Well, thanks for the coffee,' Chilcott said, rising to his feet. 'If you think of anything else that might be useful, do let us know. You've got my card?'

'Yes, yes, it's here somewhere,' Jane said, lifting a glossy magazine from the table and looking underneath.

'You've been such a great help, thank you. Would you mind giving us a formal statement at some point – just covering what we've chatted about today? It'll be beneficial to us, and I can get one of my team to drop by when it's convenient?'

'Um, yeah, I guess,' Trevor said, turning to Jane.

'Great. We'll be in touch.'

'Is Walter coming back today?' Jane asked timidly.

Chilcott rubbed his face and looked out beyond the lock gates towards the channel.

'He should be back very soon.'

He looked at Jane for a long moment. 'Why do you ask?'

'I'm not sure I feel safe here anymore?'

'Trust me. You're as safe here as anywhere. This is a beautiful location and a wonderful way of life. Don't be concerned about Walter Baxter. He's got us to worry about now.'

CHAPTER NINE

5:22 p.m.

The pulsating vibration of a large red and white Sikorsky helicopter deafened pretty much everything else around them. Chilcott and DC Allen stood amongst a gathering of people at the mouth of the marina who were pointing and staring up in awe of the enormous rescue aircraft hovering just a couple of hundred feet above sea level. Beneath it, Baxter's yacht was being escorted back to the marina by a coastal patrol vessel.

'That's what I like to see,' Chilcott said to DC Allen over the thrum of rotor blades, 'cooperation between agencies.'

DC Allen was looking up at the looming aircraft, but Chilcott's sights were fixed solely on Baxter's yacht.

The coastguard peeled away and allowed Baxter to bring his yacht in alone for the final couple of hundred metres, watched every inch of the way by Chilcott's keen eye.

They stood on the side of the lock as Baxter slowly edged his yacht into the marina and waited for the outer lock gates to close before making their way down to jetty seven.

A line of four uniformed police officers from the nearby station, DC Allen and Chilcott, with his arms folded, waited beside the empty mooring as Baxter made the final manoeuvres to bring his yacht close in.

'Are you ready for this?' Chilcott asked DC Allen.

'Absolutely, boss.'

'As soon as he's in and secure, go aboard with uniform, and you arrest him on suspicion of murdering his wife.'

'Got it.'

It was for these moments that they had all become police officers. The buzz of energy from the team felt palpable.

Baxter was alone at the wheel, and staff from the marina assisted in tying the yacht to secure cleats on the pontoon.

'We're coming aboard. Stay exactly where you are,' DC Allen called out and was swiftly followed on to the yacht by several uniformed police officers.

Chilcott remained on the pontoon, his attention fixed on Baxter.

'Walter Baxter,' DC Allen said, taking hold of his arm in a classic straight arm restraint. 'I am arresting you on suspicion of murdering your wife, Debbie Baxter, between Saturday the fourteenth and Saturday the twenty-first of August this year. You do not have to say anything, but it may harm your defence if you do not mention when questioned, something that you later rely upon in court. And anything you do say may be given in evidence. Do you understand?'

Baxter stared down at Chilcott but said nothing.

'Tell custody we're one up, and we'll be there as soon as we can,' Chilcott said to the remaining police sergeant standing nearby.

'Yes, sir.'

'Would you be kind enough to ask a couple of your team to stand guard until we return with CSI, please? No one goes on board unless I say so. Understood?'

'No worries, sir,' the sergeant said, gesturing to her officers to join them.

Chilcott waited until he had the officer's undivided attention and hustled in close.

'This will have created quite an impression on the locals,' he told them. 'No one gets close to this boat, is that clear?'

'Yes, sir,' one of the young PCs replied.

'It should only be a couple of hours, and then you'll be on your way.'

'I'm happy to stay as long as it takes, sir.'

'Thanks. I appreciate your help. If anyone asks what this is about, which I'm sure they will, refer them to the website, but don't say anything about the investigation.'

'We understand,' the sergeant said.

Chilcott stepped forwards into Baxter's path.

'Handcuff him to yourself, Richie. Place a coat over the cuffs so no one can see them. Let's give Mr Baxter the dignity he may or may not deserve.'

Baxter sneered at Chilcott. 'You don't have to handcuff me. I'm not about to escape.'

Chilcott smiled. 'You're right; you're not.'

CHAPTER TEN

It was nudging 7.45 p.m. by the time DC Allen returned to the marina. Chilcott had remained and had done his best to appease an increasingly flappy Dupont-Avery. The drama with the helicopter and Coastguard vessel had drawn quite a crowd. Social media had also been busy. Unfortunately, it had also attracted the attention of a local news reporting crew. Chilcott decided the safest action was to shut down jetty seven altogether. Anyone on their boats had to remain inside. Anyone returning to their boats had to be escorted by officers and told to stay until the police cordon was lifted. Most, including Trevor and Jane Hicks, decided to remain and watched the unfolding proceedings with significant interest.

'All right, Richie?' Chilcott said.

'Yes, boss. Baxter is safely tucked up. I kept the first interview time open with the custody skipper, given the time it is now.'

'Good. How are the uniform officers doing at the security gate?'

'It seems the world and his wife has heard about the arrest.'

'Yes, it does, doesn't it? How was he when he was booked in, any significant statements?'

'Not really. He kept telling us we'd made a massive mistake and was making general demands to see his solicitor.'

'Who is it, anyone we know?'

'It's a Leah Holman. I've never come across her before.'

'Me either. I'm not expecting much from him at this stage, to be honest. We've got a hunch he's done something, but until we get some kind of forensic hit or stronger evidence, I'm not expecting him to sing.'

'Any ETA for the CSI team, boss?'

'Should have been here by now. They must be caught up in the traffic. Did you see the TV cameras when you came in?'

'I saw where the outside broadcast van is parked but didn't see where the cameras were positioned.'

'Assume they are recording us at all times. Let's keep this one ship shape and Bristol fashion.' He gave DC Allen an ironic twitch of the brow.

Over Allen's shoulder, Chilcott saw Crime Scene Manager Nathan Parsons and two of his team walking towards them wearing full-body white hooded coveralls.

'That should get the crowd excited,' Chilcott uttered sarcastically. 'Nathan, how the devil are you?' he said.

'Whatcha got?' Parsons asked.

'We have a boat for you today. Something a little different for you to play with.'

'It's all the same to me. Boat, barge, bus; it's all about being methodical. Where has the crime taken place?'

'That's the thing; we don't know. We've got a missing person who we suspect has been murdered, and the body has more likely than not has been dropped over the side out at sea.'

Parsons scratched the side of his face. 'Okay, and you want me to perform a miracle?'

'Basically.'

Parsons looked back at the lines of people watching them from behind the marina railings.

'It's not going to be straightforward. I'll have to look this type of boat up on Google. These things are notorious for hiding numerous little cubby holes.'

'Do whatever is necessary. Baxter isn't going anywhere anytime soon, so what's not completed today can be finished tomorrow.'

'Who else has been inside?'

'Baxter was arrested on deck by Richie, and I went inside the boat earlier today, but no further than the start of the table that you'll see as you drop down into the cabin.'

'Were you forensically aware?'

'As aware as I could be.'

'Okay. We'll start at the stern deck and work our way forwards while we still have limited daylight. Then we'll head inside.'

'Is there any way you can block the onlookers?' Chilcott asked.

Parsons looked around. 'Not really. We can erect a screen on the jetty, but that's not going to do much other than attract more attention.'

'Agreed. How long do you think you'll need?'

'Who knows? This could take a while to examine. We'll take photographs and video first and see if we come across anything that remotely fits a crime scene.'

'Noted.'

'I'm not being funny, but unless we know what we are looking for specifically, we could spend our entire forensic annual budget examining this boat. Just how thorough do you need us to be?'

'I'd suggest a cursory search for starters. See if anything looks out of place—'

'I wouldn't know.'

'I hear you, but do your best. Let's capture a comprehensive photo album of the layout; how things look now; any clothes that are hanging or folded in wardrobes; toiletries on display that might belong to Debbie Baxter – you know the score.'

'You know this will be like a Tardis, albeit a posh one. People live on these things.'

'I know. But I'm led to believe this is a brand-new boat, so if you come across any scuffs or marks that could be significant.'

Parsons nodded. 'Right, well, we'd best be getting on with it before we lose this daylight.'

'Thanks, Nate. We'll head back to custody and prepare ourselves for an interview.'

CHAPTER ELEVEN

Sergeant "Steely" Steele was behind the charge desk at the custody suite. A no-nonsense custody skipper of nearly fifteen years, he had seen pretty much every kind of human being come and go through his doors.

'All right, Robbie,' he said, seeing his old friend enter the custody suite. 'Are you here for the chap from the boat?'

'That's correct. How's he been?'

Sergeant Steele gave Chilcott a knowing look. 'Is he going to be here with us for long? He's already upset my detention officer.'

'Who knows?' Chilcott uttered, looking off into space. 'Got anything to update me with?'

'Apart from having all of us prosecuted for wrongful detention? No, not much.'

'One of those is he?'

Steele rolled his eyes. 'He knows the chief, apparently.'

'Great,' Chilcott groaned. 'He is one of *those*. Any update from his brief?'

'Yeah, that's an interesting one too,' Steele observed. 'She's into probate rather than criminal law.'

'You're kidding? Doesn't he know the amount of shit he's in?'

'It seems not.'

'Any idea when she'll be available?'

'I'm available now,' a female voice came from behind Chilcott and DC Allen. It was Leah Holman, Walter Baxter's solicitor.

'Ah, Miss Holman, we were just—'

'So I heard. Detective Inspector Chilcott, I assume?'

Chilcott held out his hand to greet her. 'That's right, pleased to meet you, and this is—'

'Hi, I'm Detective Constable Richie Allen,' he said eagerly, bustling past Chilcott to greet Miss Holman with two outstretched hands.

Chilcott gave his colleague a calculated gaze, and if he wasn't mistaken, his young detective had a noticeable glint in his eye.

'Shall we go and have a little chat?' Chilcott suggested, breaking the extended eye contact between them.

Miss Holman brushed hair away from her face. 'Yes, I think we should.'

As they walked through to an empty interview room, Chilcott gave DC Allen a long and measured stare.

'Is that right, what the custody sergeant said?' Chilcott asked as they took their positions around the interview table. 'You are a probate lawyer?'

'I am indeed, however, I practised criminal law for nearly ten years in Oxford before deciding on a turn in the legal road. So, you can be rest assured, I've seen enough custody units in my time to know what I am doing.'

'I wasn't for a moment suggesting otherwise.'

'But you wanted my client to appreciate the gravity of his position, and I can assure you, he is in no doubt as to that.'

'Good.'

'Speaking of which, do you have any evidence for me to put to my client prior to the interview?'

'Forensic officers are currently searching Mr Baxter's yacht. It may take a while; it's a rather specialist piece of equipment to search.'

Miss Holman returned a featureless expression.

'When do you anticipate, you will complete said search?'

'I don't expect us to be in a position to ask your client anything about forensics tonight, so more likely than not, questions around those topics will be at some point tomorrow.'

'Are we holding off interviewing my client until then?'

'No, absolutely not. I want to ask your client a few relevant questions that aren't forensically driven.'

'Such as?'

A cynical smile crossed Chilcott's lips. 'How about giving him a chance to tell us where his wife is for starters?'

Miss Holman scratched her forehead. 'I'll speak to my client now, but I can't promise he will give up any information at this time.' She glanced at DC Allen, and her face softened, just a little. 'Until we see evidence relating to this allegation, I will be suggesting my client makes no comment to any of your questions.'

'Fair dos,' Chilcott said.

'Fine. Shall I let the custody sergeant know when my client is ready?'

'No need. We'll be here, ready and waiting.'

Miss Holman gave Chilcott a *professional* smile and then left the room.

'You all right, son?' Chilcott asked DC Allen once Miss Holman was out of earshot.

'Me? Yeah, of course. Why?'

'You're looking a bit flushed in the cheeks, son, that's all.' Chilcott stood up, winked and walked out into the hallway.

Walter Baxter entered the interview room with the calm assurance of a man in complete control. He shot Chilcott a confident gaze and sat down opposite him, next to his brief.

'I got you a coffee,' DC Allen said, nudging a cardboard MaxPax brew towards Baxter.

'I got one for you too,' he smiled and handed the second drink to Leah Holman.

'I don't drink coffee. It's a poison of today's society,' Baxter said, pushing the paper cup away at arm's length. 'I only drink responsibly-sourced tisanes.'

'I'm afraid I don't know what they are. I could get you a tea instead?'

Baxter recoiled with a look of disgust.

'Thank you. Thank you so much,' Miss Holman whispered to DC Allen.

'My pleasure,' DC Allen beamed.

Chilcott glared at his subordinate.

'When you're quite ready, perhaps we can begin?'

DC Allen sat back in his chair, but not before sending a sideways glance to Miss Holman.

'This interview is being video recorded for evidential purposes,' Chilcott began. 'You are under arrest on suspicion of murdering your wife, Debbie Baxter, between Saturday the fourteenth and Saturday the twenty-first of August this year. You do not have to say anything, but it may harm your defence if you do not mention, when questioned, something that you later rely upon in court. And anything you do say may be given in evidence. Do you understand what I just said to you?'

'You've already told me that,' a relaxed Walter Baxter replied.

Miss Holman leaned over towards her client and quietly spoke in his ear.

'We are following procedure, Mr Baxter. You are legally represented by Miss Holman here. However, we still have to go through the legalities of this interview to ensure that you are fully aware of your legal rights and the potential implications of the interview process upon you.'

Baxter huffed and faced away as if disinterested in anything Chilcott had to say to him.

'Keeping you from something, are we?' Chilcott asked.

Miss Holman shot Chilcott a disapproving glare.

'Where was I? Oh yes… Have you had sufficient time to consult with your legal representative prior to this interview?'

'No comment.'

Chilcott smirked, and the tips of his ears lifted.

'I'm not sure you've got the hang of this interviewing lark yet, Mr Baxter. You're not implicating yourself in any way by confirming you've had enough time to chat with your solicitor.'

A nod from Miss Holman encouraged Baxter to agree.

'Right then. You've heard what you've been arrested for. Tell me everything you know about your wife's disappearance.'

'No comment.'

'That's it,' Chilcott said, sliding forwards on his forearms. 'You're getting the hang of this now.'

'I'm sorry, are you going to treat me like a fool throughout this interview, if so—'

'What?' Chilcott spoke over him. 'What are you going to do?'

Miss Holman closed the cover of her notebook and unfolded her legs.

'My client may benefit from additional time of speaking with me in private.'

Chilcott signalled nonchalantly with a hand. 'Up to you, Mr Baxter. DC Allen and I aren't going anywhere.'

'No. No – I'd rather just get this over and done with, thank you.'

'I can tell you're an intelligent man, Mr Baxter, and I'm sure you can grasp how this works. The longer you prevaricate, the longer you're in here, simple as that.'

Chilcott leaned back, and the chair groaned under his weight. He studied his subject's face and interlocked his fingers on the desk as he waited for his moment to begin.

'Where were you off to, Mr Baxter, before we brought you back to the marina?'

'Before you humiliated me in front of my friends, you mean.'

Chilcott peered down at the notes in his daybook and put a hand to his face. 'What friends might they be, Mr Baxter?'

Baxter's face creased, and he straightened his back.

'Well?' Chilcott prompted after twenty seconds or more of silence.

'I was about to conduct sea trials on my new yacht if you must know.'

'I must.' He squinted at Baxter.

'You weren't trying to leave the area then?'

'No. I have no reason to leave.'

'Hmmm.'

'I'm sorry. What does that mean?'

Chilcott tapped a forefinger against his pouting lips. 'Well, your wife is missing. Nobody has seen her in almost three weeks. We cops are sniffing around the marina, and then you head off into the sunset.'

'I have not murdered my wife.'

'Okay. Tell us where she is then.'

'I've told you already. I don't know?'

Chilcott noticed Baxter rubbing the back of his head as he spoke. 'I thought she was with her sister, but you say she isn't.'

'That's right, she isn't.' Chilcott slid his arms forwards on the table again. 'But we are going to find her; I can assure you of that, Mr Baxter.'

'Well, when you do, make sure you bloody-well tell her what an utter drag this is.'

'I tell you what. Let's go back to basics. Just run us through your journey from Portishead Marina on Saturday the fourteenth of August to your final destination at

Salcombe Marina and vice-versa, but fill in the gaps in between, would you?'

Baxter gave Miss Holman a questioning look.

'It's okay,' she said. 'If you want to answer the question, you can tell the officers everything you told me, but you've had my advice regarding the necessity to answer any questions at this present time.'

Baxter rubbed behind his neck as he thought about his options.

'We left Portishead at seven twenty-five in the morning on a falling tide. We sailed the entire day and moored overnight at St Ives. The next morning, we left St Ives on a falling tide at eight-fifteen and timed our approach into Salcombe on the rising tide. There, Debbie left before I was up the next morning, and then I organised the hand-over of *AWol* and the collection of the Amel Sixty. I left Salcombe on Wednesday and made the return journey back to Portishead, arriving on Saturday the twenty-first.'

'Well, there's a lot of "yachty" detail in there; falling tides; rising tides, but very little about where you stayed over, or perhaps, where you ate or drank?'

Baxter blinked. 'You wanted details, so I gave you details. The tides gave us extra speed. It would have been a near-impossible journey had we not been precise with the timings of the tides.'

'Okay, I get that.'

'We stayed on the yacht the entire time.'

'You didn't go ashore at St Ives? That seems something of a missed opportunity, given what a beautiful place it is.'

'It is; however, we moored at sea and didn't step ashore.'

Chilcott narrowed his gaze. *That's convenient.*

'What about Salcombe?'

'We had to moor in a designated spot due to the hand-over of the yachts the next day.'

Chilcott tapped his fingers against the table. 'And did you go ashore that night?'

'No.'

'And you would say that Debbie left early the next morning before you woke up?'

'She did.'

'Why?'

Baxter shrugged. 'I don't understand?'

'Why would she leave early next morning when the whole point of you both being there was to pick up your new boat?'

'You'd need to ask her.'

'Did something happen between you prior to the morning when she left?'

'No.'

'No arguments? No issues? Maybe something going on in her sister's life that needed her immediate involvement?'

'No.'

Chilcott sighed profoundly and gestured over to DC Allen to take over the questioning.

'Mr Baxter,' DC Allen said. 'Can you tell us a little about yourself? Perhaps something about your background?'

Baxter closed his eyes and groaned softly. 'Like what?'

'You clearly lead a lavish lifestyle.'

'Do I?'

'That certainly looks like an expensive hobby.'

'It's not a hobby. It's my home.'

'Still costly, no matter how you look at it. How much did your yacht cost you?'

'I paid the going rate for a yacht of that class, not that I believe that is any of your business.'

'I think you'll find that it is, Mr Baxter,' Chilcott cut in. 'Until we can rule you out of our investigation, pretty much every topic is on the table.'

The look that followed between them would melt ice.

DC Allen coughed to prompt Baxter to continue.

'It was one point two million Euros,' Baxter finally conceded.

'Mortgaged?' DC Allen asked.

'No,' Baxter replied indignantly.

'How could you afford that?'

'It's called money.'

'And insurance?' Chilcott said.

Baxter hesitated, and then a look of realisation crossed his face. 'You think this is a life insurance fraud.'

'Do I?' Chilcott said.

'That's what you're heading towards. Well, yes, we do have life policy cover. Doesn't everyone?'

'I don't,' Chilcott said.

'Most sensible people do, and Debbie and I took out a policy after our marriage.'

DC Allen was ready with his pen. 'Which was when?'

'March the second, 2016.'

'Have you contacted them yet about your wife's missing status?'

'No, I haven't.'

'You know we can check that out, Mr Baxter?'

'Be my guest. Check what you like.'

'We will, thank you. I think we're coming towards the end, for now, Mr Baxter. But I just wanted to ask you something that's troubling me – what were you and your wife arguing about at the party on the night before you sailed out of Portishead?'

'Arguing? We weren't arguing about anything.'

'Oh?'

'What are you talking about?'

'We've got several eyewitnesses, who know you, who all say that you were physically dragging your wife away from the party on the Hicks' boat.'

'Nonsense.'

Chilcott scratched behind his ear. 'Okay.'

Baxter looked with confusion between the two officers and then at his solicitor.

Chilcott held up a finger as he pondered his next question.

'What about threatening Dave Reynolds then? I take it that didn't happen either?'

'He's a…'

'Go on.'

'He fancies my wife. It's blatantly clear to everyone.'

'And you took exception to that.'

'No, we had an early start the next morning, and it was quite clear that some at the party were encouraging my wife to get drunk. That would have spoiled our plans for leaving at the optimum time to catch the falling tide, and so I had to interject.'

'By physically dragging your wife away against her will.'

'If that's what it took?'

'So, you're admitting to an assault?'

'What? No!'

'Mr Baxter, this isn't the stone age. You can't go around forcing people to do things against their will with the use of physical violence.'

'I wasn't violent. I didn't lay a finger upon her. I was pulling her away by her clothing.'

Chilcott sank his head and let out an exasperated puff of the cheeks.

'I think I've heard enough for the night. Get some rest. We'll speak to you again tomorrow.'

'What, I'm not getting out of this God-forsaken place tonight?'

'Nope. You're staying here, and I think I might pop back to the marina for a quick pint on the quay. It's been a long day.' Chilcott gave DC Allen a nod and left him in the room to tie off the interview.

Chilcott was alone in the office, just a reading lamp illuminating half of his desk. He'd let DC Allen go home over an hour ago, and the remainder of the office was dark and abandoned for the night. His mobile phone disturbed him from a temporary malaise.

'Chilcott,' he said, trying his best to sound as alert as possible.

'Robbie, it's Nathan Parsons.'

'Nate, sorry mate, I wasn't expecting…' He searched the computer screen for the time. It was 10:43 p.m. He rubbed deep into his eye sockets with the knuckles of his fingers. 'Are you still down at the marina?'

'Afraid so.'

'Call it a day, mate. It's not going anywhere, and you are back there tomorrow.'

'No, it's not that. We've found something that I thought you should know about tonight.'

Chilcott sat upright. 'Go on.'

'There's a large storage unit beneath the bed at the stern of the boat. When we removed the sheets and bedding, we discovered a small round viewing window that looks down onto the propeller shaft. I guess it's designed for maintenance purposes or something.'

'Uh-ha,' Chilcott said, turning to a fresh page in his daybook. 'Go on.'

'Well, the yacht has blue down-lighting beneath the hull, so the water is quite clear underneath, and it is quite obvious there is a piece of jewellery, possibly a bracelet or necklace, or something shining in the water that's entangled around the propeller shaft.'

Chilcott's stare widened.

'Can we retrieve it?'

'Not tonight. It would be impossible. We'd need to send a dive team down to untangle whatever it is and then attempt to recover it in as complete a state as possible.'

'Yep, sorry mate, I keep forgetting what time it is.'

'Do you think she got mangled in the propellers?' Parsons asked.

Chilcott played the possibility over in his mind.

'Who knows? It's a good shout. If she has, then presumably we'll also find traces of bodily tissue or clothing in the same location?'

'Possibly.'

'I wonder what it would take to lift the boat from the water?' Chilcott thought aloud.

'No idea, but my team and I have photographed the exhibit from the inside of the yacht. We were going to call it a night as we can't do any more without a dive team, but I need your consent for the policy book.'

'Yes, yes, of course. I'll be back at the marina at 7 a.m. I'll see you there at 9, if that's enough rest for you all?'

'Yep, sure,' Parsons groaned and then hesitated for a beat. 'Robbie…' he said. 'This has all the makings of a big one.'

Chilcott glazed over.

'Yep… it's certainly beginning to look that way.'

CHAPTER TWELVE

Thursday 2nd September

6:45 a.m.

Chilcott was pacing up and down the fringe of the marina. The warmth from the rising sun beat down pleasantly upon his face. This was going to be a hot one. Distracted, he watched as swallows skimmed the glassy surface of the water, picking off small insects. If it weren't for his impatience, this would be a perfect morning. A key-code barrier secured the walkway to the pontoon, and there was no sign of anyone in the marina manager's office to let him through. He could see Baxter's boat in the distance casting a perfect white silhouette on the water. At least that was still there. He slapped his forehead with recognition; there was a way he could get onto the pontoon. He whipped out his daybook and skimmed the pages until he found the telephone number he was looking for.

The phone rang off before being answered, but Chilcott was in a determined mood and tried again. And again. And again, until finally, he got a response, of sorts.

'Hello,' came the faint and disinterested voice of Jane Hicks.

'Mrs Hicks, this is DI Robbie Chilcott.'

'What time is it?' she asked, sounding as if she was wearing a pillow over her face.

'Early, I'm sorry for the intrusion.'

'Don't you lot ever sleep?' she said wearily.

Chilcott eased the phone away from his ear. It was a good observation.

'Only on Sundays,' he joked. 'Look, I need to gain access to the pontoon. Could you or your husband come and let me in, please?'

'Wha… what time is it?'

'Just before seven.'

'In the morning?'

'I certainly hope so, Mrs Hicks.' He listened with a mischievous smile and imagined the comedic scene of Mrs Hicks making futile attempts to rouse her husband from a comatose sleep.

'I tell you what. You stay where you are, but give me the code so that I can let myself onto the pontoon. I'll forget it almost immediately; I promise – ask my ex-wife if you need reassurance.'

'Ah, I shouldn't do this, but—'

'But I *am* the police.'

'Six, four, three, one.'

'Thank you. Can you just stay on the line until I'm through?' He didn't hear a response but punched the code, and the door latch opened with a click.

'Thank you, Mrs Hicks, you're a star.'

Going by the silence, she was already back asleep.

Chilcott bounded along the walkway until he reached the end berth and Walter Baxter's yacht. He crouched and stared down into the green, cloudy water and prayed the item of jewellery was still attached to the propellers. His thoughts wandered, and he imagined mackerel and crabs attracted by the shiny object and taking small nips at it.

'Damn shame,' a male voice from behind a startled Chilcott.

'Good morning, sir,' Chilcott replied, trying not to appear surprised by the unexpected comment. 'What is... what's a *damn shame*?'

'Well, Debs getting involved with the likes of him.' The man pointed directly at *Death Do Us Part*.

Chilcott straightened his legs and wished he hadn't squatted down for quite so long as his knees creaked with fifty-odd years of wear and tear. The older gentleman standing behind him appeared in no hurry to go about his business.

'Know them, do you?' Chilcott asked.

'Of course.'

The man pointed to the opposite row of gently bobbing yachts; his was the next but one, back from where they stood.

'There's my yacht, there. We all know one another here, though granted, some better than others if you know what I mean?' He gave Chilcott a knowing lift of the brow.

'So, who might you be then, sir?'

'I do apologise. I'm Tim Collins.'

'Ah yes, I've spoken to you on the phone. I'm Detective Inspector Chilcott.'

'I know who you are.'

'You were at the party the night before Baxter and his wife left to collect their new boat.'

'That's right. I was there with my wife, Rosemary.'

Chilcott looked beyond Collins' shoulder. They were alone.

'Have you got a spare ten minutes, Mr Collins? I do appreciate it's early.'

'No, that's absolutely fine. Would you like to come aboard my boat? My wife has just put on a pot of coffee.'

'That's very decent of you, thank you.'

Mr Collins welcomed Chilcott aboard and introduced him to Rosemary as they entered the compact cabin area.

'Can I just say,' Chilcott said, taking a quick gander around the inside of the yacht, 'I do apologise if my forensic team disturbed your sleep last night?'

'Not at all,' Mr Collins replied. 'We found it all quite fascinating. As entertaining as an episode of Bergerac!'

They took a seat, and Mrs Collins handed Chilcott a very welcome mug of coffee.

'So, what is your take on Debbie Baxter's disappearance?' he asked them.

They both looked a little perplexed, and then Mr Collins replied, 'Well, he's killed her, hasn't he?'

'Has he? I think we're still trying to ascertain that particular detail?'

Mr Collins placed his cup of coffee down onto the table. 'I'm sorry, but I thought Walter had murdered Debs?'

Chilcott cocked his head.

Mr Collins turned to his wife. 'Isn't that what Jane told you?'

'Yes, that's what Jane said.'

Chilcott relaxed his shoulders. 'I see. You've heard that from Jane Hicks, not because you know that for a fact?'

'That's right,' Mrs Collins replied.

'I think she may have got a little ahead of herself,' Chilcott reassured them. 'There is still an awful long way to go before we can say with any certainty where Debbie Baxter is.'

'But Walter has been arrested?' Mrs Collins questioned.

'Yes, he has. That is standard procedure, given the circumstances.'

'What has he said?' Mr Collins asked.

Chilcott smiled. 'Not a lot yet, but I'll be speaking to him later this morning. In any event, I can't divulge the intricate details of an ongoing police investigation. I'm sure you'll understand?'

Chilcott watched his hosts with interest. They appeared to be his kind of people: down to earth, honest, inquisitive. And their boat was understated, compared to the others he'd been on at the marina. It was almost caravan-like.

'Tell me,' he said. 'That party; the night you last saw Debbie Baxter. Did anything untoward happen?'

'No,' Mr Collins said. 'We had a fabulous night. Rosemary certainly did. She got herself a little bit too tipsy.'

Chilcott faced Mrs Collins, who smiled back at him innocently and dropped her head enough to show Chilcott she was feeling slightly embarrassed about her behaviour that night.

'That's all right,' he said. 'It's not an offence to enjoy yourselves.'

Mr Collins scratched behind his ear and appeared to drift away for a moment.

Chilcott waited for him to speak again, confident that something was troubling him.

'Thinking about it,' Mr Collins said. 'Debs and Walter were the last to come to the party.' He looked to his wife for confirmation, but she just shrugged a non-committal shoulder.

Chilcott grasped the moment of cognisance. 'And what did they do once they arrived?'

'Well, Trevor was being his usual entertaining self and doing his best to wind up Walter, and Debs sat beside me for the majority of the time they were there.'

'What did you talk about with Debs?'

'Oh, you know; small-talk. We chatted about them setting off to collect the new boat the next day. Uh, we spoke about the unusual name for the new boat…' Mr Collins paused and scratched the back of his head again.

'Unusual?' Chilcott repeated.

'Well, yeah, it's a negative name, isn't it; *Death Do Us Part*. I even asked Debs if it was tempting fate somewhat?' He stopped talking and looked down and away for a few seconds.

'And I suppose it did.'

'What do you know about them as a couple?' Chilcott asked.

'Well, Debs was a real beauty, both inside and out. I really enjoyed talking with her.'

Mrs Collins glanced at her husband but didn't comment herself.

'Mrs Collins? And did you have much to do with Debs or Walter?'

'No, not really. Walter is a very private man, aloof in fact.'

'What about Debbie?'

She scratched beneath her nose and talked behind her hand. 'She was pleasant, I suppose.'

'Did you talk to her about anything that night?'

Mrs Collins shook her head. 'No. Debbie was only talking to the men.'

She kept her eyes on Chilcott, who returned a single nod of understanding.

Chilcott opened his daybook and took a moment to look through the notes taken from his conversation with the Hicks'.

'I understand there were three other people at the party as well? A Dave Reynolds, and a Ben and Sarah Staines, is that correct?'

'Yes, that's right,' Mr Collins said.

'What can you tell me about them?'

'They are more friends of Trevor and Jane than us. We know them fairly well, but I'd say they were more their kind of people.'

'Party people?'

'Yes,' Mrs Collins said.

'Do they always party with the Hicks'?'

'Um, not always,' Mr Collins said.

'But generally, if she's there,' Mrs Collins added.

'Debbie?'

Mrs Collins nodded from behind her mug.

'How long would you say you've known them, Walter and Debbie, that is?'

'We've known them since they arrived at the marina, so as long as anyone else here.'

'And what would you say is the reason an attractive, young woman is with an older—' Chilcott stopped himself and wafted his hand as he attempted to grasp the most appropriate words, '…more complex, possibly even, unsuited man?'

'Obvious, isn't it?' Mrs Collins said.

That was the response he was expecting her to say, and Chilcott had formed a similar opinion himself.

'I wouldn't necessarily agree with what you're insinuating,' Mr Collins said to his wife. 'Debs is a lovely girl.'

Chilcott watched Mrs Collins roll her eyes and stare into a space that was anywhere other than near her husband.

'And let me ask that question again, but this time from his perspective?'

Chilcott noticed Mr Collins' lips twitch as he considered the prospect, but he was more interested in seeing the reaction from Mrs Collins.

'I don't think they have a *normal*, couples' relationship,' she turned back to Chilcott. 'I just can't imagine it.'

'Okay. Go on.'

'Well, even when they were together, they weren't together. The only physical contact I saw between them was when he was dragging her away like he did that night.'

'Yes, I heard about that. Did you see anything more? Did he use any other kind of physical force?'

'No, but he does try to control her,' Mr Collins added.

'Perhaps that's because she needs controlling.' His wife glared at him.

'Oh, come on – you just don't take to her because she's popular with the men. You can hardly say that she needs controlling.'

Chilcott watched silently, taking in their interaction with interest.

'Talking of men,' he said, 'how does she get along with Ben Staines and Dave Reynolds?'

'Dave has a thing for her,' Rosemary Collins quickly answered.

'In what way?'

'It's never a public show of affection. You'd never really see them together at the parties.' She paused as she recalled. 'If anything, they actively keep apart from one other.'

Chilcott made a note in his book.

'Would they speak at all?' he asked.

'Yeah, of course. I saw Dave talking to Debs that night,' Mr Collins interjected before his wife could answer. 'Nothing is going on between them. They are roughly the same age and probably have more in common than the old farts like us. That's all it is.'

'Well, if I could see it, then so could Walter,' Rosemary countered. 'It could account for the way he treated her.'

Chilcott bobbed his head. 'It's a sound proposition and one that I'll take on board. Thank you.'

Chilcott heard voices outside on the jetty. He looked out and saw Crime Scene Manager Nathan Parsons and his CSI colleagues. They were early. That's what he liked about his CSI team.

'Well,' he said, standing. 'No rest for the wicked. Thank you so much for the coffee and the chat. It has been most enlightening.'

'Oh, is there more entertainment?' Mrs Collins asked.

'We're just completing our search of the yacht and should be out of your way by mid-morning. Do let me know if you think of anything else that might assist our investigation. It has been a pleasure to meet you both.'

As they said their goodbyes, Chilcott stepped up onto the pontoon and joined his colleagues at a determined pace.

CHAPTER THIRTEEN

By 9.30 a.m., the pontoon was a mass of activity with a specialist PolSA (Police Search Advisor) team taking control of the search of the yacht. They parked their large incident vehicle nearby, the sight of two fully-kitted underwater search divers setting up on the jetty drew a considerable number of onlookers from both boat owners and visitors alike. DC Allen and Chilcott stood a safe distance back, so as not to disturb the search team, but which also fulfilled another objective: to keep Simon Dupont-Avery from getting himself too involved.

The operation was simple: locate, retrieve and secure the jewellery object wrapped around the propeller shaft. Once complete, finalise any forensic recovery from inside the craft before heading back to Patchway custody suite where Walter Baxter would be asked to account for the findings.

As the divers vanished beneath the water's surface in a shallow grouping of bubbles, Chilcott looked behind and noticed both the Hicks and Collins paying close attention to proceedings from the decks of their respective boats. He couldn't stop them looking on, and to be honest, he didn't blame them. This investigation was proving to be anything but "a cut and dried" case.

'What do you suppose it is?' DC Allen asked Chilcott as they looked on. 'A neck chain, a bracelet?'

'Guess we'll find out soon enough.'

'And what if we confirm it is some of her jewellery?'

Chilcott watched bubbles breaking on the surface as the divers moved towards the stern of the yacht. 'Well,' he said, 'then I'd suggest Baxter has a lot to answer for, wouldn't you?'

'Still doesn't prove he's killed her, though, does it, boss?'

Chilcott gazed back at his astute colleague.

'No, it doesn't. But you give me a better explanation of how a piece of her bling comes to be eight feet underwater and tangled around the boat's propeller shaft?'

DC Allen shrugged.

'Exactly.'

Chilcott studied the lead officer communicating with his divers through a comms system and could hear that they were attempting to untangle a thin chain of some description from the vessel's propeller shaft.

"*Diver one to panel. Five bells.*"

Chilcott approached the dive attendant. 'What does that mean, mate?'

'Diver one is coming up.'

'Has he got something?'

'He's completed the task.'

Chilcott waved DC Allen over to join him.

'Have they got it?' DC Allen asked, leaning over the edge of the jetty and peering down into the water.

'We're about to find out.'

The wet-suited and masked heads of both divers broke through the murk and appeared on the surface beside the vessel's hull. The attendant assisted them towards the side of the jetty.

Chilcott watched closely as they extracted themselves from the water and sat on the edge of the jetty slats, removing their breathing apparatus in a routine and well-drilled fashion. One of the divers then handed the team leader a small rubber pouch.

Chilcott stepped closer.

'Can I see that, please?'

The lead PolSA lifted the object from the diver's pouch and transferred it to a clear forensic exhibit bag, giving the item a moment's consideration and then handed it to Chilcott. It was a decorative gold wrist chain with several small pendants, some of which appeared to be coloured stones of some description.

'Can you ask your guys to knock up a statement exhibiting this chain, please?'

'As soon as we're free from here, I can get them done and emailed over to you,' the lead PolSA replied.

'Excellent.'

'Is there anything else you want my team to do while we're here?'

'Can I just ask, was there any sign of damage beneath the hull or material fragments caught up with the chain?'

The lead PolSA went over to his divers and came back almost right away.

'Nothing else evident from visual examination,' he said. 'If there were anything, my guys would have seen it.'

'In that case, that'll be everything. Thanks for turning out. You've been a huge help.'

'That's what we get paid for.'

Chilcott gave a thumbs up to the dive team and turned with DC Allen to walk away.

'Where are we going, boss?'

'We're taking this pretty little chain, and we're going to ask Walter Baxter all about it.'

CHAPTER FOURTEEN

Baxter was seated in the interview room, Miss Holman alongside him. She'd already seen the chain exhibit and given ample opportunity to speak to Baxter about its presence beneath his yacht. Now it was the turn of the cops to ask the questions.

'Mr Baxter,' DC Allen said, taking the lead in this interview. 'I'm sure your legal representative has explained to you the reason for this interview.'

'Yes, my solicitor has informed me.'

Chilcott assessed Baxter's demeanour as DC Allen spoke; he was a cool customer, considering. He then noticed how DC Allen kept looking at Leah Holman and could feel palpable energy between them. Chilcott glanced down at her wedding ring finger, there was no band, and he already knew Richie was single. No wonder he'd been so keen to take the lead through this interview.

'You lot planted it there,' Baxter spat bitterly with a contorted and angry face.

'Planted what, Mr Baxter?'

'The chain. There's no way it could have got there any other way.'

DC Allen held up the small, clear forensic bag so that Baxter could see it. 'This chain?'

'You know I mean that chain because you lot put it there.'

Chilcott was growing restless. If there was one thing he hated, it was questioning his integrity.

'Who does this chain belong to, Mr Baxter?' DC Allen continued.

'You already know that. Stop playing mind games with me.'

'I'm not playing any type of game, Mr Baxter. I'm merely attempting to identify the owner of this—'

'Just ask me what you need to know and get me out of here,' Baxter spoke over him.

Miss Holman leaned in towards her client and gave him some private words of advice.

'Please, carry on, officer,' she said, glancing back at DC Allen and brushing hair back over an ear with a hooked finger.

'Thank you, Miss Holman. Sorry, Mr Baxter, you were about to say who this chain belongs to?'

'My wife.'

'Your wife?'

Baxter glared at DC Allen. 'That's what I said.'

'How frequently would your wife wear this particular item of jewellery?'

Baxter looked at his solicitor, and she nodded for him to provide the answer.

'Every day.'

DC Allen allowed a few seconds of silence to underline the significance of that statement.

'Every day,' he finally repeated. 'In that case, please explain how this has come to be wrapped around the propeller shaft of your yacht?'

'No.'

'No?' DC Allen questioned. 'Well, I can think of at least one scenario. Can you?'

Baxter didn't reply.

'It took a specialist team of divers over fifteen minutes to recover this. I take it you don't own any diving equipment?'

'Of course, I don't. I'm seventy-two years of age, for Christ's sake. What would I need with diving equipment?'

'Then can you tell us how it would have ended up wrapped around the propellers of your boat?'

'You already know what I think, and I'm not admitting to anything I haven't done.'

'How old is your wife again?' Chilcott said.

'Sorry?'

'Your wife. You just told us you are seventy-two. How old is your wife again?'

Baxter scowled at Chilcott and looked to his legal representative, who bobbed a shoulder and continued to jot down Chilcott's question, verbatim.

'I don't see what that has to do with anything.'

'It's a simple question, Mr Baxter,' Chilcott said.

'I know it's a simple question. I'm saying I don't see the relevance?'

'She's much younger than you, though, isn't she?'

'Thirty-one. She's thirty-one. Okay?'

Now it was Chilcott's turn to allow a silent moment to

emphasise the point. DC Allen was doing a fine job of letting his number two enter into the games.

'You've done all right for yourself then, haven't you? I've seen the photos of her, and I have to say, she's a very attractive woman.'

Baxter looked away.

'Don't you like that, the fact other men find your wife attractive?'

'I don't believe I said anything to give you that impression?'

'You didn't need to, Mr Baxter. Your body language told me all I needed to know.'

Baxter thrust himself back into his seat.

'Get jealous, do we?' Chilcott continued. 'With other men looking at your *young* wife?'

'I don't believe my client has said anything that remotely suggests your accusation, officer. You are putting words into my client's mouth.'

'It was just an observation, Miss Holman.'

Chilcott licked his lips and slowly leaned forwards, closing the space between himself and Baxter.

'There's what… forty-one years difference between you two? I'm curious… how does a relationship like that work? Are you still, you know, able to *satisfy* a beautiful young woman like that?'

Miss Holman lowered her pen with a loud slap and looked uncompromisingly at Chilcott for a long second.

'I'm sorry, I don't see the relevance in this line of questioning?' she said.

'Don't you? I think it's a very pertinent and valid line of questioning.'

'I'm sorry, I must disagree. You are creating a motive to suit a fanciful crime, of which there is absolutely no evidence suggesting my client is guilty of committing. You have simply failed to confirm that a crime has been committed in the first place, and you are clutching at straws to make *something* stick.'

Chilcott pondered the face of Baxter's solicitor. She was correct; he was clutching at straws, but that hadn't stopped him from getting to the truth in the past.

'Uh, Miss Holman,' Chilcott said, directing his questions away from Baxter. 'You're what, late thirties yourself? Perhaps you could comment; would you find Mr Baxter sexually attractive?'

Miss Holman recoiled.

'I beg your pardon?'

She jumped up to her feet. 'This is outrageous. This interview is over. I suggest that unless you provide my client and me with any form of evidence against him, I will be seeking the authorisation from your superior officer for Mr Baxter's immediate release from custody.'

Cheeks flushed; she held Chilcott's gaze and encouraged Baxter to join her as she stomped out of the room.

Once they were clearly out of range, Chilcott sniffed loudly. 'That went well.'

'I–I don't…' DC Allen tried to speak.

Chilcott stood up from his seat and patted DC Allen on the shoulder before making his way for the door.

'I like her spirit,' he said. 'She's a keeper. You could do a lot worse than her, son.'

CHAPTER FIFTEEN

Superintendent James Hendy found Chilcott and DC Allen in a back room of the custody suite and disturbed them from reviewing their interview notes.

'Chilcott – a word.'

Chilcott looked up from his papers at Superintendent Hendy. In Chilcott's opinion, he was far too young to be an officer of rank, moreover, of a rank superior to his own.

'Please…' Chilcott answered contemptuously.

'I beg your pardon?'

'Please – you missed that polite little qualifier when you asked me for a word.'

'What?' Superintendent Hendy bristled. 'Just come here.'

Chilcott put his hand on DC Allen's forearm and pushed himself up from his chair. 'Keep on looking, Richie. I'm sure the answer's there somewhere.'

Superintendent Hendy stepped away from the table towards the corner of the room so that DC Allen was less likely to hear their conversation. Reluctantly, Chilcott joined him.

'This Baxter case,' Hendy said. 'What is the current state of play?'

'He's in the bin, and we're still working on him.'

'Yes, so I've heard. You have also embarrassed a professional visitor to this custody unit.'

'I didn't mean to—'

'I don't care what you meant to do, Chilcott. However, there is now a formal complaint about your conduct during the interview.'

Chilcott shrugged. 'Goes with the territory. Perhaps you'd like to give it a go for yourself someday, or did you miss that particular lesson at Hendon?'

'Don't push me, Chilcott. Nothing would give me more pleasure than to see you gone from here.'

Chilcott narrowed his stare but managed to keep his mouth firmly shut. Superintendent James Hendy was among *the new breed* of cop. He was educated to degree standard but possessed the operational nous of a gnat. He was one of three senior officers who decided Chilcott's fate after his little mishap with DI Jaz Chowdhury, who, of course, was another of the new breed. Hendy had made his feelings transparent at the hearing; he wanted Chilcott out. It didn't matter that he was one of the most revered and successful detectives ever to grace the streets of Bristol. Hendy saw Chilcott as a threat and Chowdhury as an ally. This was their first encounter since that disciplinary hearing, and it was clear to Chilcott that time hadn't necessarily been such a good healer.

'Now, to this prisoner; why is he still here?'

'Because we're still playing cops and robbers.'

Hendy raised a finger and pointed it directly at Chilcott's face. 'Don't try me.'

'We're still working on the evidence, boss,' DC Allen called from across the room.

Hendy acknowledged Allen with an outstretched arm and pointed index finger but kept his eyes firmly on Chilcott.

'You've got three hours, Detective Inspector Chilcott. You either get some evidence to interrogate that suspect lawfully or release him from this custody unit without further delay. Do we understand ourselves?'

'We understand me, but I can't say with any certainty that we understand you… *sir*'

Hendy chomped down, stared ferociously at Chilcott and mumbled something incoherently before storming out of the room.

'Why doesn't he like you, boss?' DC Allen asked Chilcott after he returned to the desk.

'I don't know, son. I can't please everyone all the time.'

'But that sounded personal.'

'Come on,' Chilcott said, changing the subject. 'We're up against it now.'

'Where are we going?'

'To see the forensic team. We've got to find some bloody evidence against Baxter, or he's getting out of here.'

Crime Scene Manager, Nathan Parsons, folded his arms in a passive-aggressive stand of defiance.

'I can't magic up evidence that isn't there, Robbie.

There's just no obvious crime scene inside that boat. We've swabbed areas of the cabin where her DNA would likely be, but the suspect claims she left before he picked up this boat, so it would be no surprise if we didn't get a hit.'

'And that would only strengthen his claims. But there must be something? What about the chain?'

'Impossible to examine, due to water contamination. Other than being found in an unusual place, it once again proves nothing.'

'Jesus! He's going to walk. You know that?'

'I don't know what else I can do, Robbie? Barring CCTV of him dumping her over the side and sailing back on his own, we're stuffed.'

'What did you just say?'

'We're stuffed.'

'No... sailing back on his own.'

'I was just saying, CCTV would show she wasn't there with—'

'You beauty, that's it!'

Chilcott scooped up his daybook and hurried out of the door.

Chilcott disturbed DC Allen from cooking a microwaved ready-meal and was immediately intercepted by DC Philips, holding phone provider results.

'Listen to this, sir,' she said. 'We found Debbie's phone details from a search of Walter Baxter's phone records.'

'Yes, I knew that.'

'Bear with me, sir. We ran a check with her phone provider, and these are the results.' She lifted a thick report containing three-months' worth of phone data, including incoming and outgoing calls, text messages and phone lists.

Chilcott could see highlighted several lines on the first page in yellow marker pen.

'Good. Go on.'

'There are many calls and text messages to someone called, "Davie". It seems Debbie was reaching out to "Davie" for help.'

'Help, what sort of help?'

Chilcott looked down at the report. 'May I?' he said, taking it from DC Phillips' hand.

'You will see a number of text entries where Debbie is saying to "Davie" how lonely and sad she is feeling. Some even describe how she feels unsafe or scared.'

'In this report?'

'Yes, sir.'

Chilcott flipped through the first half dozen pages. There were numerous highlighted entries.

'Hold on a moment,' he said, leaving the report on the table and stepping into his office.

He returned almost right away with his daybook, which he hurriedly whipped through. Stopping at a page, he compared his daybook to the telecoms data. 'Bingo!'

Phillips and Allen waited eagerly for the explanation.

'She was contacting Dave Reynolds. That is who is shown as "Davie" on these reports. Contact Dave Reynolds and get his permission to run a telecoms report against him. If he refuses, threaten to arrest him for obstructing a police investigation. That should concentrate his mind.'

'Yes, sir.'

'Good work, Fleur. I'll have a look through these pages and see if anything else pops out.'

'But that's not all, sir.'

'Oh?'

'Debbie's phone was last used on Saturday the fourteenth of August at around three fifteen in the afternoon. That means they were probably somewhere between Portishead Marina and St Ives. I'd suggest over halfway.'

'How does that compare to phone mast triangulation?'

'It's about right, sir. The final land triangulation was from a mast near Widemouth Bay.'

'So, we think the phone has probably gone down in the ocean?'

'Yes, sir.'

'Makes sense. Okay, we need to get onto St Ives marina and coastguard. Speak to someone there who can tell us how many people booked in for the night and ask them to secure CCTV. Make that a priority.'

'Yes, sir.'

As DCs Phillips and Allen went off to make their various enquiries, Chilcott spent the next thirty minutes digesting the telecoms report. There were well over one hundred contacts between Debbie Baxter and Dave Reynolds in the three months leading up until her outgoing communications ended. It was clear from the last text message from "Davie" that he anticipated seeing her again, and *"…soon XXXX"*.

CHAPTER SIXTEEN

Chilcott stared at Baxter across the table for a long and uncomfortable silence. He'd arranged with custody to have an impromptu interview of Baxter based on the recent information gathered from the phone records. It wasn't a game-changer, but at last, it was something tangible to put to Baxter.

'I thought the reason for this additional interview was to ask my client questions, officer,' Leah Holman said.

Chilcott slowly bobbed his head, not once taking his eyes away from Baxter's.

'This is becoming oppressive now. I respectfully request that you ask my client valid questions pertinent to the allegation put against him or allow my client to leave this interview,' Miss Holman said.

'We already know that it takes only one person to sail your new yacht,' Chilcott finally said.

'Is that a question, or a statement, officer?' Miss Holman asked.

This time, Chilcott ignored the solicitor's input and

continued speaking. 'You leave Portishead with your wife in your old boat that takes both of you to sail, yet you return in your new boat that can sail single-handedly, and you are alone.'

Baxter turned to his brief.

'You seem a little confused?' Chilcott observed. 'Let me just repeat that for you, but this time I'll make it a bit simpler.'

Baxter snapped back at Chilcott's impertinence with a snarling glower.

'It takes two of you to sail out, but only one of you to return.'

Chilcott sat back in his seat and brushed speckles of dust away from the front lapel of his suit jacket. He used the silence to reinforce his next question.

'Isn't that the whole point of owning an Amel Sixty; you can do everything yourself with those fancy controls? No need to have a crewmate?'

Baxter hooked a finger beneath the collar of his shirt and tugged it away from his neck several times. He was either letting the cool air in or allowing hot air to escape. Either way, he didn't answer.

'And upon your return,' Chilcott continued, 'you are alone, and your wife has... *vanished*. To me, that's a compelling detail, especially when we factor in that your wife's phone hasn't been used since the day you both left Portishead Marina. When not only did all forms of communication from your wife's phone end, but so did the mast signal identifying the location of that phone.'

Chilcott steeped his fingers and rested his chin on top. 'You know about phone triangulation, I trust? People like us, the police, can track the location of a phone within a twenty-kilometre radius by identifying which phone mast is sending or receiving digital signals to that phone.'

He paused for a few seconds. 'Tell me, Walter… how does that look to you?'

Baxter rubbed his face with repetitive, anxious strokes, and then he answered.

'She dropped her phone in the sea,' he said from behind the cover of his hand.

'There's nothing I can do about that. It's her own, clumsy fault.'

'You've never mentioned this before. Why is that?'

'It has never come up before.'

'Where were you when she lost her phone?'

'I was at the wheel, steering the yacht.'

'And what was Debbie doing?'

'She was stowing the jib because the wind was increasing. It must have gone over the side then.'

'What was she doing with her phone out while stowing the jib?'

'I don't know. You'll have to ask her.'

Chilcott cut Baxter a penetrating stare. 'I wish I could.'

Baxter reacted with a roll of the eyes.

'How do we know Debbie didn't follow the phone into the water?'

'I don't think my client needs to answer that question, officer. Once again, you are creating hypothetical theories without a single shred of evidence to back them up.'

Chilcott raked his head towards Miss Holman. 'But there is evidence, compelling evidence. It's a known fact that your client returned to Portishead Marina alone. It's a known fact that he could sail the new boat single-handedly. It's a known fact that his wife's phone was last used and last located between Portishead and St Ives whilst at sea. It is also known that your client's wife had over one hundred phone communications with Dave Reynolds in the three months leading up to and including the day we suspect she vanished without a trace.'

He turned back to Baxter, his deadpan expression concealing a minor coup.

'Did you know that too, Walter, about your wife's *interest* in Dave Reynolds?'

Baxter's mouth tightened, and he lifted himself higher in his seat.

'How would you describe their relationship, Walter, because I know how that looks to us?'

Chilcott noticed Baxter's fists ball on top of the table.

'You see, that provides more significance to the threats you made towards Mr Reynolds on the night of the party.'

Miss Holman leaned sideways towards her client and quietly encouraged him not to answer.

Chilcott allowed himself a smile and removed the telecoms report from his file.

'This is a report from EE – your wife's phone provider. It contains details of every call and text since June; to and from your wife's mobile phone.'

He cocked his head. 'Intrigued?'

'Well…' Chilcott thumbed through the pages. 'It makes for interesting reading.'

He cleared his throat and put on a slightly feminine tone to his voice as he read one of the entries.

'*I don't know how much longer I can take the mood swings. It's just tearing me apart.*'

He looked at Baxter for a long moment, and in the same voice, he continued, '*Can I see you this Thursday? I can come to you in Bristol. I'll tell Walter that I'm seeing Bethany.*'

Chilcott creased his brow and let a few painfully quiet seconds pass.

'I've got to admit, that must sting?'

But there was still no response from a now hunched Baxter, shielding his dropped face behind his arms that were gripping the top of his head.

This time, Chilcott put on a deeply masculine voice.

'*I miss you already. Please, please take care of yourself. I cannot wait to see you again soon. Kiss, kiss, kiss, kiss.*'

'That last one is from Dave Reynolds to your wife's phone when it was last used. Was that the straw that broke the camel's back?'

Baxter lifted his head. His eyes were wide and reddened. 'I didn't kill my wife,' he seethed through gritted teeth.

'Thing is,' Chilcott sighed, 'there's a huge body-sized gap in your account, Mr Baxter. A gap that could be easily filled by you finally telling us the truth.'

Baxter slammed his hands down loudly on the table, pushing himself up. 'I am telling you the bloody truth. I didn't kill my wife.'

Miss Holman attempted to steady her client, but he stood up and continued shouting at Chilcott.

'I don't care what you say to me or what you think I've done with my wife. I haven't killed her, and I don't know where she is?'

'Well, you don't seem overly concerned that your wife is *missing*, Mr Baxter... if you don't mind me observing?'

'What do you want me to do? How should I be reacting?'

Chilcott and DC Allen shared a look.

'Unless you have any fresh evidence other than pure speculation to put to my client, I think we are simply going over old ground,' Miss Holman said.

Chilcott huffed loudly and slid forward on his elbows.

'You're not going anywhere. I'm applying for an extension of custody time, and I'm going to find evidence to prove you killed your wife.'

He stood up from the desk and walked out of the room, leaving DC Allen to conclude the interview.

DCI Foster had been watching the interview from the images beamed to the satellite room nearby. She joined Chilcott, and they found an empty interview room to speak privately.

'What are you thinking, Robbie?'

'I don't like it one bit.'

'Nor I, but that's not going to take us any further. What do you think we should do with him?'

'It's the perfect murder: no witnesses, no real evidence, no body, and billions of gallons of tidal water between us and the prospect of finding his wife.'

'So, you still think we are looking at murder?'

Chilcott rocked backwards. 'Come on. It has to be. You've seen him in there. He's a nailed-on wife killer.'

DCI Foster walked over to one of the stainless-steel seats and sat down.

'You don't think so?' Chilcott asked, sitting opposite her.

'You've said it already, Robbie. We have no corpse, and we have no evidence to prove a crime has even taken place.'

'That's never stopped us in the past.'

'And look at the hot water that's gotten us into. Overzealous suspicions don't do the department any favours, Robbie. How many more times do you need to be put under the microscope to realise that?'

'Oh, come on. We have to keep Baxter in. We've got reasonable grounds to suspect a crime has been committed. That's all we need.'

'All we need to question him, which we've now done.'

'No. Now we have a motive.'

'I'm with his brief on this one, I'm afraid, Rob. Text messages between his wife and Dave Reynolds don't prove Baxter killed his wife. They don't even prove anything was going on between them.'

Chilcott looked at his supervisor with astonishment. 'I can't believe you're saying this?'

'Release him, Rob. We've gone as far as we can take it for now. Save the remainder of the custody clock, and if we find more evidence, or if he slips up, we can get him right back in.'

'What if he buggers off on his yacht? He could be long gone before we know anything about it.'

'He could have done that already, but he didn't.'

'Only because we forced him to return, thanks to a sodding great helicopter and a high-powered Coastguard interceptor.'

'We don't know that with any certainty. He said he was doing sea trials.'

Chilcott clamped his jaw. 'You're going soft.'

'Release him under ongoing investigation.'

'What if we obtain surveillance authority to watch his movements? That might lead to further evidence?'

'It might, but it's unlikely. If he has murdered Debbie Baxter, she is submerged somewhere in the Bristol Channel or somewhere off the west coast of Cornwall. Unless a favourable tide brings her ashore somewhere, we're never going to recover the body.'

'But it could? It's happened before.'

DCI Foster shook her head. 'I said it from the start, Rob. These cases, well, they're almost impossible to prove. I've made up my mind, release him under investigation. Continue the telecoms and financial checks, and if something else arises, we can bring him back in for questioning.'

'I'm not comfortable with this, Julie.'

'You don't have to be. It's my decision. And that's final.'

Chilcott had refused to take Baxter back to his boat and had left it for two of the detectives to fulfil this task.

They dropped him on the far side of the marina, the opposite side to the gated pontoon. That was one thing Chilcott had influenced.

Baxter didn't look back at the police car as he strode purposefully ahead. He guessed they had let him out where they did on purpose so that they could watch him back to his yacht. But he had other intentions.

He was in luck; the lights were still on in Le Parisien, and there were still ten minutes until closing time. The cops had seized his mobile phone, his laptop and, in turn, scuppered any means of communicating digitally with the outside world. But Le Parisien was one of the few places left in this modern era that still had a customer payphone.

He double-checked his watch; 10.51 p.m. He quickly traversed the zig-zag walkway across the lock gates and headed directly for the café.

He wasn't concerned about being seen. They'd have to see him sooner or later, and it might as well be straight out of the blocks. Besides, they'd be seeing plenty of him tomorrow.

The owner was the first to clock him, but she didn't stop him from coming inside. He knew that tongues would have been wagging and opinions of his guilt already decided, but he didn't get this far in life by being a wallflower. He walked through the narrow corridor that leads to the ladies and gents' toilets without breaking stride. He looked around first and then fed a two-pound coin into the retro-eighties phone meter. That was enough. This was only going to take moments.

He didn't need a phonebook, his photographic memory was all he needed to recall eleven simple numbers, and he punched them in as he scanned the corridor for signs of CCTV cameras.

'It's me,' he said quietly as the call was answered. 'I'm back out.'

He listened to the reply.

'No, I'm still under investigation.'

He waited as the recipient gave him instructions.

'Don't worry. I will. Listen… one of the police. I just don't trust him.'

He bit his lip as further instructions were given. Sensing someone was coming, he curled in closer to the wall and pressed the phone tightly to his ear as a female customer walked beyond him to use the facilities.

'I'll call you again once I know we're in the clear,' he said.

He nodded as he listened to the reply and then sighed despondently.

'Yeah… bye.'

CHAPTER SEVENTEEN

Saturday 4th September

09:46 a.m.

Dave Reynolds was jet-washing the sides of his cruiser when Walter Baxter walked purposefully past him towards his yacht. They clamped eyes, but uttered no words, and Baxter barely broke stride despite the coil of water hoses in his path.

Reynolds watched and waited until Baxter was out of view back inside *Death Do Us Part* and then quickly ducked inside his cabin and made hastily for his phone.

'Walter's out,' he softly spoke so that Baxter wouldn't hear him through the thin skin of the vessel. 'He just walked past me. He's back on his yacht now.'

Moments later, Trevor Hicks emerged from inside his

cabin and stood on the rear entertainment deck of his boat. He saw Reynolds reappear outside and nodded over to him.

Reynolds scuttled up the jetty and jumped aboard Trevor's boat.

'I wasn't expecting him to be released so soon,' Reynolds uttered in a clandestine tone. 'I thought he'd be heading for prison.'

'Me too,' Trevor replied in an equally secretive tone. 'When did he come out?'

'Must have been late last night because I didn't see him return.'

'Me either.'

'What do we do; do we speak to him, ignore him?'

Trevor scratched his head.

'I guess we act normally. I mean, we've got nothing to be concerned about, right?'

Trevor looked over Reynolds' shoulder towards his boat. He saw the bright yellow coil of jet washer hose, several full and zipped duffle bags, black bin liners tied and stacked neatly to the side and an assortment of recycling boxes ready to dispose of.

'Looks like you're going somewhere?' he said.

'I've cancelled my mooring arrangements. I'm not sticking around here any longer.'

Reynolds shot a glance towards Baxter's yacht. 'Especially not now.'

'Not because of what happened?'

Reynolds shrugged. 'There's plenty of other good marinas in the south, and maybe it was time for a change anyhow. I've been coming here for nearly six years.'

Trevor couldn't tell if Reynolds was trying to justify his decision or convince himself of the same.

'When are you going?'

'I'm catching the tail-end of this high tide. I've got the last slot.' He looked at his watch. He didn't have much time.

'Were you going tell us? I mean, were you going to say goodbye?'

'Of course.'

Reynolds looked over once again at *Death Do Us Part*.

'But I wasn't expecting him to be back so soon. I can't stand the thought of what he might have done to Debs. She didn't deserve any of it.'

Trevor looked over to the end of the moorings and saw Baxter staring back at them through the open drapes of his cabin. He quickly turned his back so that Baxter couldn't see his lips, and he quietly spoke. 'He's watching us now, Dave. Don't turn around. We can't let him win. You leaving, well, what message does that send out?'

Reynolds rubbed his forehead. 'It's not *just* because of him. I've got business elsewhere as well as here in Bristol. I can run the operation from anywhere as long as I have a phone and WiFi.'

Trevor dropped his head, crestfallen. 'It's the end of our group, isn't it?'

'Baxter ended the group, not me. And maybe it's time that we all took stock of the situation here and moved on.'

'I like it here. I'm not moving anywhere, especially as a result of him.'

'How do you know it will stop with Deb? Who's to guarantee any of us are safe from him? Can you promise Jane's safety?'

'Oh, come on. That's a bit dramatic, isn't it?'

'Is it? Do you know that for sure? Are you willing to bet a life on it? I'm not.'

Trevor glossed away the suggestion. 'Look, Jane's not here at the moment, but I'm sure she would have wanted to say a proper goodbye. We'll miss you, buddy.'

'Yeah, I'll miss you both too.'

They embraced with a firm hug and fist-bumped one another on the back.

As Reynolds stepped off Trevor's cruiser, he looked along to the end of the jetty. Baxter was standing on his rear deck, watching his every step.

CHAPTER EIGHTEEN

The whiteboard contained a crude sketch of the marina with the position of Baxter's boat drawn in red. The witnesses, such as they were, identified as W1, W2 and W3, and the relative positions of their boats in comparison to Baxter's yacht. There were various scribbled notes of dates, times and names, and a blown-up, pixelated A4-sized print of Debbie Baxter copied from a photo frame inside the main bedroom of the yacht. But no matter how long he stared at the details, none of what he was viewing could prove a murder, let alone Walter Baxter as a wife killer. Chilcott balled his fist and lowered his chin squarely upon it. His leg ticked up and down as he analysed the information on the board. He considered the salubriousness of the marina and the apparent wealth of its clientele. He thought about the party crowd and the initial reluctance of the witnesses to speak out about Baxter's behaviour towards his wife. But he was troubled mainly by the general lack of anything except supposition. His frown was nearly touching his nose. In all his service, he'd never dealt with a murder like this.

He took a moment staring at the names of each individual in turn; Walter Baxter; Debbie Baxter; Trevor and Jane Hicks; Rosemary and Tim Collins; Dave Reynolds and Sarah and Ben Staines. All these people had contact with Debbie the night before she was last seen. Still, so far, none were coming forward with anything remotely evidential, other than how Baxter forced his wife away with him from the party boat. His eyes settled on Dave Reynolds' name. One thing was for sure; his interest in the disappearance of Debbie went well beyond a concerned friend or bystander.

DC Allen came over and disturbed Chilcott's musings.

'Boss, I've just got off the phone to the coastguard. They're on point with the search for Debbie Baxter's body. All RNLI and Coastguard stations from Portishead to Salcombe are on standby for reports of bodies in the sea.'

'Thanks, Richie,' Chilcott answered from behind his fist.

DC Allen followed Chilcott's fixed gaze to the board.

'What are you thinking, boss?'

Chilcott remained transfixed to the notes and huffed his answer through his nose.

'Boss?'

Chilcott broke away and looked at his detective. 'What if he didn't kill her?'

'Come again?'

'What if Baxter didn't kill his wife?'

'How do you mean, he's—'

'Where's our evidence?'

'The chain around the prop shaft?'

'I'm glad you've mentioned that – it's a red herring.'

145

'Sorry, boss?'

'Think about it. We have assumed that Debbie Baxter went missing on the way to Salcombe, on or around the time we lost all trace of her phone. They hadn't yet taken possession of *Death Do Us Part.*'

'Yeah…?'

'We've been concentrating on the wrong boat, Richie. We need to track down *AWoL*, and Nathan Parsons and his team need to give it a forensic going over.'

'Of course,' DC Allen said. 'But… what about the chain? That doesn't make sense if Debbie was murdered on *AWoL.*'

'Exactly.'

'So how did it get there?'

Chilcott turned back to the board and folded his arms.

'It's just as well we're detectives and can find that out, son.'

'So, what do we do next?'

'You're going to get on the phone and locate *AWoL*. And when you've done that, we'll send Parsons and his team to examine it.'

'I'm on it, boss.'

'Good – make it your priority because we're headed back to the marina as soon as you're free. I want Baxter to know that we're not going away. I want us to make an overt display of speaking to all of the other witnesses so that we're right in Baxter's face. This is a tight-knit group. They share the same passion. They live a life on these boats like a team or a tribe. They've even got nicknames, for Christ's sake.'

'A bit like us?'

'Exactly! We're inclusive, and so are they.'

'So, you think they know more?'

Chilcott stroked his chin, and his eyes rested again on Dave Reynolds' name.

'That is what we need to find out. I want to know all about them, every single one of them. I want to know where they came from, where they work or used to work, how much their boats cost them or how much they've borrowed. I want to know how long they have known Baxter and his wife and how they first came to meet. I want to know what they really think of Baxter and his wife, and then, maybe, we'll have something to work with.'

'What about Baxter?'

'We leave him alone. We let him see just how hard we're working on the others. We know they'll talk amongst themselves; they're a close community.'

'And what about Dave Reynolds?'

'Yes, Dave Reynolds. He is someone I'm looking forward to speaking with.'

Chilcott smiled for the first time that morning. 'Let's shake the nest and see who gets stung.'

'But what if Baxter goes? If he sails away?'

'I've been thinking long and hard about that very thing. He's still under investigation and can leave Portishead, but he can't hide. I've already spoken to the coastguard and border agencies. He's on their radar.'

'Even so, boss, that doesn't mean he can't vanish.'

'What would be the actions of an innocent man, Richie?'

'I–uh… well, I guess you'd want to clear your name?'

'That's right, and you could only do that if you stuck around.'

'So, if he leaves, that's an indication of his guilt.'

'It could be? On the flip side, if he stays, it doesn't necessarily mean he's innocent. Come on, son, these enquiries won't do themselves.'

'Yes, boss, I'm on it now.'

As DC Allen headed away with a motivated stride, Chilcott turned back to the board and Dave Reynolds' name.

'What else do you know, Mr Reynolds?'

CHAPTER NINETEEN

They arrived at Portishead Marina just shy of lunchtime. DC Allen had located *AWoL* to be in a dry dock at a Salcombe sailing boat brokers. Unfortunately, it was still going through a deep cleaning process before re-ownership; however, Nathan Parsons and team were en route to examine what was left. This time, Chilcott was with three other detectives in a show of force and a display of determination. They had a solid game plan; who would speak to whom, what they would ask and how overtly they would go about it. The midday sun was beating down on the glassy-calm waters, and the marina was alive with the joyous weekend activity of sailors and visitors alike. Yet the tall mast of Baxter's yacht cast an ominous shadow over all others on jetty seven.

As the detectives went about their enquiries, Chilcott revisited the marina control centre.

'Thanks for allowing us onto your marina again,' Chilcott said to Simon Dupont-Avery. 'I do appreciate your support and cooperation during this investigation. I know it's not a good look for your patrons and visitors to have such a police presence.'

'That's fine,' Dupont-Avery replied. 'I need to know if we have bad apples in the barrel.'

'That's a good analogy,' Chilcott commented as he looked down towards jetty seven. 'I might use that myself. Has Baxter submitted any further requests to leave the marina?'

'Not yet, but time is running out for him if he plans to catch today's tide.'

'What's the window of opportunity?'.

'Tidal clearance is between 18.10 and 21.50.'

'And what about tomorrow?'

'You can roughly add an hour each day, give or take ten minutes.'

'Have you seen him today?'

'Yes. He used the laundry room early this morning and was waiting in the café.'

'What time was that?'

'I was in a six this morning because we had early departures, so, I would estimate, I saw Walter at around six-thirty, perhaps six-forty this morning.'

'Is that normal to use the laundry at that time, do you know?'

'There's certainly nothing abnormal about it.'

'How frequently would your customers normally use the laundry facilities?'

'How long is a piece of string, Detective?'

Chilcott bobbed his head.

'Just how long is all this going to continue?' Dupont-Avery asked. 'I mean, the police activity on the jetty?'

Chilcott walked back over to the window. 'How long is the proverbial piece of string, Mr Dupont-Avery?'

'I'm serious. I know you need to do your jobs, but this is bringing undue negative attention to our small community. It's not just those on the water. It's the homeowners over-looking the marina as well. All the police and news reporter activity, well, it's creating a bad taste.'

'I appreciate it's not what you're used to, and believe me, we'd like this to be over as quickly as you, but it's rarely that straightforward.'

'Couldn't you keep him away, give him some sort of curfew not to return?'

'No. This is his home, and as such, he's entitled to live here.'

'There must be something you can do? This whole situa-tion is causing considerable unrest.'

'If I had my way, Baxter would be enjoying the delights of a twelve by eight cell as we speak, but it's not up to me and my wants. That's why we are asking all these questions of you and your customers. We are building a picture, a jigsaw if you like. And at the moment, there are a lot of missing pieces. As soon as we can slot them into place, we can move things along and be out of your hair.'

The marina manager's phone rang, and Dupont-Avery answered.

Chilcott looked down at his watch and then back at Dupont-Avery, whose body language had stiffened. His eyes tracked to Chilcott's; they were wide as if he was being told a shocking secret. He looked at the bank of digital equip-ment and tapped several buttons.

'I've booked you in for 18.15. Be prepared and ready for

departure before that time, please. And for your information, we won't be accepting any returns beyond 21.45, so if you intend returning to your berth tonight, you'll need to be back through the gates by then.'

He ended the call and lowered the phone, glancing sideways at Chilcott.

'That was Walter Baxter. He's requesting to leave at six-fifteen this evening. I didn't know what to do, so I—'

'That's fine,' Chilcott said. 'Honestly, that's fine. We should know what he's planning than not to know at all.'

DC Fleur Phillips met Chilcott at the pontoon security gates.

'Whatcha got, Fleur?'

'I've spoken to Trevor and Jane Hicks and have all of their details, but they tell me Dave Reynolds has gone.'

'Sailing or gone, gone?'

'He's gone. Left this morning, by all accounts.'

'Why, did they say?'

'Apparently, he feels unsafe with Baxter being back on the marina.'

Chilcott pulled a face. 'Okay. But we have no indication Baxter has shown any physical violence towards anyone else, other than the verbals towards Reynolds at the party.'

'No, sir.'

Chilcott scratched his forehead. 'All right. Do we know where he went?'

'They believe he's possibly on his way to another marina somewhere in the south. He didn't specify where exactly.'

Chilcott sighed and looked over at the vacated space on jetty seven.

'No dramas, we've got his mobile number.'

'We do.' Philips tapped the cover of her daybook. 'And an email address.'

'Good. Can I leave you to make contact with him when we get back to the office, please, Fleur?'

'Of course, sir.'

'How are the others getting on?'

'I think we're pretty much done.'

'Good. Good. Can you just come with me for a second, please?'

Chilcott and Phillips walked along the pontoon to jetty seven. They stopped beside the empty void left by Dave Reynolds' absent boat, and Chilcott stared down into the waters as grey mullet skimmed the surface for food particles. Detectives Allen and Chiba joined them, and they stood behind Chilcott for a silent minute.

Chilcott turned slowly, looking all around him, taking in the sights and scenery of every detail contained within his line of sight. He stopped turning when he reached the end of jetty seven. Baxter was standing on the stern of his yacht, arms folded, and he was staring right back at Chilcott.

'Good,' Chilcott murmured. 'That should do it. Come on, team, let's get back to the office.'

CHAPTER TWENTY

5:55 p.m.

Chilcott had spoken to Dave Reynolds by phone, who said he intended to find a mooring at an alternative marina, leave his boat there and spend the rest of the summer concentrating on his business ventures. At the time of the call, he was at sea off the North Devon coastline near to the Lundy Races, which, he said, was quite tricky to navigate, and so he wasn't able to chat for long. He freely admitted to having numerous contacts with Debbie Baxter but maintained that their friendship was purely platonic, and his interest in her was entirely based on her safety. Chilcott didn't know if he believed that or not, and without seeing Dave Reynolds face-to-face and reading his body language, he couldn't exactly challenge it either. The conversation was left with Reynolds promising to update Chilcott with details of the marina he chose to occupy. He also managed to establish a few details about Reynolds' boat, just in case he failed to deliver on his promise. If Reynolds decided to play silly buggers, Chilcott could feed the boat name to the coast-guard and much like a DVLA check on a vehicle number plate; they could track and locate *Liquid Asset* as and when required.

Portishead Marina was still busy, despite the lateness of the day. However, unlike earlier, there was a menacing ripple on the water's surface due to deepening skies and an increasingly brisk westerly breeze. And also, unlike earlier, instead of basking in the sunshine, the resident sailors were attaching blue canopies to the exposed areas of their boats, clearly preparing for an oncoming storm.

Chilcott was alone. The rest of the team had either completed for the day or were back at the office, top and tailing their tasks before heading off to make the most of whatever was left of their weekends. None of them knew of his plan, apart from the one person who needed to know; DCI Foster. But then again, she didn't know everything.

He reached the end of jetty seven and called out, 'Mr Baxter. Mr Baxter, are you there?'

Walter Baxter appeared from within the closed cabin. His facial expression was long and unfriendly, and there was no cordial greeting on his part.

'Hello, Mr Baxter. I'm glad I've caught you. Would it be okay to come aboard, please?'

'Won't you just leave me alone? Your constant presence here is becoming tedious.'

'I just need a few moments of your time.'

'Should I be talking to you without my solicitor?'

Chilcott looked furtively over his shoulder back along the jetty. 'This isn't an official visit.'

Baxter didn't reply.

'I probably shouldn't be doing this,' Chilcott said, 'but this conversation isn't going on record, and it won't affect your case. You have my word on that.'

Baxter's eyes narrowed, but Chilcott suspected his interest in what he had to say would be piqued enough to allow him on board.

'What guarantees do I have that whatever you want to talk about won't affect my case?'

Chilcott smiled on the inside. It appeared he had a good measure of Baxter.

'As I said, you have my word. This is just you and me. I'm not making an official record of anything we say.'

Baxter began walking towards the cabin door.

'Wait,' Chilcott said. 'You can see I'm on my own. When have you seen me on my own before this?'

Baxter stopped and turned around. He looked Chilcott over and then back along the jetty as he considered his options.

'I'm just about to catch the tide. If you want to speak to me, you'll have to come along.'

'Oh,' Chilcott laughed. 'I'm not a sailor.'

'Then I'm not talking.'

The balance had suddenly turned to Baxter's advantage. Chilcott looked up at the darkening skies. An ominous-looking summer storm was brewing with half of the sky now an angry blue-grey colour. He wasn't joking when he said he wasn't a sailor. Two return journeys on Brittany

Ferries with his ex-wife had proven each time that he didn't have the constitution for the open water.

'I'm not waiting. I have to go,' Baxter said. 'I'm not prepared to miss another sea trial for you.'

Chilcott glanced upwards once again and shook his head as he stepped aboard.

Chilcott took a seat behind the wheelhouse as they glided gently away from jetty seven towards the exit of the marina. Baxter didn't talk, and Chilcott didn't ask him anything. As they waited for the outer lock gates to open, Chilcott looked up at the marina manager's viewing tower and saw Dupont-Avery standing at the window peering back down at him, a confused expression troubling his face.

'Do I need a buoyancy aid or something?' Chilcott finally asked Baxter as they headed out beyond the confines of the marina.

'Depends.'

'Depends on what?'

Baxter slowly turned to face Chilcott. 'If you want to live?'

He pointed a finger towards the sky. 'That's a fierce storm.'

'You don't have to tell me that. I've changed my mind. Can I get off, please?'

'No, you cannot.'

Chilcott began to sweat beneath his suit. 'Look, I'm not a sailor. I don't do boats.'

'Well,' Baxter murmured, 'today, it seems like you are.'

Chilcott stood and looked back at a small crowd of

onlookers gathered at the mouth of the marina. Dupont-Avery was still visible in the viewing tower.

No other boats were leaving the marina. However, a handful was waiting near the lock gates to return. Chilcott saw one sailor attempting to get Baxter's attention by waving his arms above his head, shouting out something incoherently and gesturing wildly with his arm in the direction of the marina.

This was rapidly turning out to be one of Chilcott's less thought-out decisions.

'Hold on to something, or sit down,' Baxter directed. 'This is going to get lively.'

'Can I just quickly use your toilet, please?'

'No, you cannot.'

'I'm desperate. If I don't go now, I'll…'

Baxter's face tightened. 'Be quick.'

'Where do I go?'

'Step through the galley. The head is the second door on the right.'

'Thanks. I appreciate it.'

With Baxter busy at the wheel, Chilcott climbed down into the luxurious cabin of the yacht and found the toilet cubicle, which was better appointed than most hotel suites. But he had no intention of using the facilities.

Several minutes later, he reappeared on deck.

'You took your time,' Baxter commented. 'I do hope you haven't made a mess down there.'

'No, nothing like that − I was busting to go, that's all. I'm very impressed with the inside of your boat. It's beautiful.'

'It's a yacht, not a boat. Take a seat.'

As Chilcott did as instructed, spray splashed his face

from the bow of the yacht, now dipping and surging through the roughening seas. Baxter had unfurled another sail, and they were now pitching at an uncomfortably steep angle.

'Seriously, do you have a spare lifejacket?' Chilcott asked as he held on tightly to a chrome railing behind his seat.

'Under the cover you're sitting on,' Baxter said without looking around.

Chilcott lifted the lid on a storage unit beneath him and picked out a bright red buoyancy aid, which he pulled down over his head in record time and pulled tightly around his waist.

'Where are we going?' he asked, bracing himself once again.

'Sea trials. I haven't taken her out in conditions like this before, so this will be a good test.'

'A test of what?'

'Whether she stays together or not?'

'Oh Jesus! Are you sure it's safe?'

Baxter continued spinning the large spoke wheel between his hands but didn't respond.

Chilcott looked back in the direction of the now distant marina. *Jesus Christ, what have I done?*

Without warning, Baxter pitched the yacht aggressively, and Chilcott was suddenly staring through horrified eyes down at the rushing water just inches from the lowest edge of the yacht. He gripped the chrome rail with both hands, clinging on with all his might to prevent himself from falling towards the sea. Baxter had already braced himself and was fighting with the wheel.

'Shit,' Chilcott yelled. 'You could have told me you were going to do that.'

Chilcott could see a menacing smile on Baxter's face.

'You wanted to talk to me about something?' he said calmly as he manoeuvred the yacht through another drastic change of direction with a thunderous swing of the boom.

Unfortunately for Chilcott, he was experiencing a full display of Baxter's controlling and coercive behaviour that the others had so unanimously described.

'I'm not sure now is the right time,' Chilcott said. 'Can I just concentrate on holding on?'

As he stared, wide-eyed at the splashing waters inches from his feet, Chilcott felt the increased need to swallow as saliva built in his throat. *Oh no!*

It was the same urge he'd experienced on the cross-channel ferry when he'd spent most of the trip with his head in a stinking, dirty bowl of a toilet cubicle.

Don't think about it. Don't think about it. Don't think about it.

But the more he told himself not to think about the nauseating sensation; the higher his stomach rose towards his throat.

Baxter looked at him with sadistic eyes.

'You're looking a little green, Detective,' he said and thrust the yacht once again into another violent manoeuvre.

Chilcott could feel an instant sweat. 'Oh, God,' he said and made straight for the cabin door as tears streamed from his eyes.

'Stop,' Baxter shouted. 'Not in there. If you're going to be sick, do it over the side. But you're cleaning up any mess.'

Chilcott peered desperately at Baxter, and the mere mention of *that* word was enough to open the flood gates.

He pressed a hand against his mouth and staggered to the side of the boat.

'Not that side, you fool. The other. You never vomit into the wind.'

Chilcott stumbled as quickly as possible to the other side of the yacht, which Baxter had now pitched in Chilcott's favour, narrowing the distance between himself and the ocean. Blindly reaching out, he grabbed the steel wire of the external rails like it was a lifeline. The salty wash and spray from the bow completely covering him with each dipping slice through the angry swell. His suit was utterly sodden. He lay flat on the deck and extended his head over the side, and in that exact moment, he lost all bodily control.

He didn't attempt to move. What was the point? He was cold and shivering like he had the flu. In fact, given a choice between feeling this bad and death, he'd take the latter option every day of the week. Why the hell had he agreed to this – what on earth was he thinking?

He had no idea how long he lay in that position, but finally, he became aware that the yacht was no longer swaying and was in much calmer water. He retracted his head from over the lip of the yacht and drew himself up to his knees. Wiping his mouth and face with the drenched arm of his suit jacket, he looked towards the wheel; Baxter wasn't there. He turned, and Baxter was standing over him, a metal bar clutched between his hands.

Suddenly, all feeling of his sea-sickness vanished. He attempted to spin onto his side, but Baxter had him trapped between his legs.

'Hand me this when I ask for it,' Baxter said sourly. 'We're going to find a place out of the easterly wind until you feel better.'

Chilcott wavered and then took the long metal bar from Baxter's grasp and drew himself to his knees. Baxter looked down upon him, entirely unaffected by the weather conditions.

Up ahead, Chilcott saw a small island rising in the middle of the Bristol Channel.

'Where are we going?' he asked, wiping his mouth once again.

'The sheltered side of Denny Island. It'll be calmer there.'

Chilcott re-took his seat and gathered his composure as Baxter took the vessel close into the small rocky outcrop. Sure enough, the waters settled.

Baxter started walking towards the bow. 'Follow me,' he directed.

Gingerly, Chilcott stood to his feet. His body was still suffering the sensation of being in a washing machine.

'Hand me the Buoycatcher,' Baxter demanded.

'The–the what?'

'The metal pole in your hand,' Baxter said impatiently.

Chilcott handed it over, and Baxter threaded a rope through the end of a metal eye, like threading a super-sized needle before leaning out over the side and hooking a floating buoy with one smooth and easy action. He tied the rope off, and the yacht slowly swung around until it was nose-on to the tide. Baxter turned with a cold and puckered glower and gave Chilcott a once over before walking purposefully beyond him to examine the side of the yacht where Chilcott had been ill.

'You're cleaning all of that off when we get back,' he said with a pointed finger.

'Yeah, I'm… look, I'm really sorry. I did try to say I wasn't—'

'What did you want to talk to me about?' Baxter was now standing directly in front of Chilcott with his arms folded, his body swaying gently with the sideways rocking of the yacht.

Talking was the last thing on Chilcott's mind. 'I, uh… I wanted to ask you about your wife.'

'I thought you said I didn't need my solicitor.'

Chilcott covered his mouth again. '*Urgh*,' he groaned as another unpleasant surge came up from his stomach.

'Wait here,' Baxter commanded. 'If you're sick again, make sure you clear the side of the yacht.'

He walked away and ducked down into his cabin. He was gone for several minutes and then returned with a small plastic bottle of water.

'Take these,' he said, handing Chilcott two tablets.

Chilcott peered down at the small, round tablets. 'What are they?'

'Motion sickness tablets. They'll take the urge away.'

Chilcott looked down into the palm of his hand at the beige-coloured tablets.

'Can I see the box?' he asked.

'Don't you trust me?'

'I don't understand why you'd have motion sickness tablets if you don't get ill from sailing?'

'They were for Debbie. She sometimes felt ill.'

Baxter backed away and sat down on the white leather seat opposite Chilcott and simply stared at him with a curious expression.

'How do we get back?' Chilcott asked.

'The same way we came. But it'll be rougher going back; we're heading into the storm.'

Chilcott looked up at the cobalt blue skies and down again at the small pills in his hand before stuffing them into his mouth and swigging them down with several large gulps of water.

'You wait here,' Baxter said.

'Where are you going?'

'Those will take half an hour to work. I'm going to have a cup of tea and a biscuit.'

Baxter gave Chilcott a withering look and then vanished into the cabin.

CHAPTER TWENTY-ONE

Chilcott was back at his desk with his head in his hands when the DCI came into his office to say goodnight.

'Still here, I see. I thought I saw your light on,' Foster said.

'Yeah, I know,' Chilcott groaned without raising his head from his hands.

'Well, I'm heading off now, and you should go home too. Oh, how did it go with Baxter?'

Chilcott lifted his head slowly from his hands and turned to his boss.

Foster recoiled upon seeing Chilcott's pained expression.

'My god! Are you all right?'

'He took me out on his yacht.'

'In that storm?'

Chilcott bobbed his head.

'Look at the state of you. What's happened to your suit?'

'It wasn't my finest hour.'

Foster blanched as she examined him closer.

'And then when we got back to the marina, I spent over half an hour cleaning the side of his boat.'

'Oh no… you didn't?'

'I did. It was awful. I wanted to die.'

'Oh, poor you. But was it worth it, what did he say?'

'He didn't.'

'He didn't answer any of your questions?'

'I didn't ask him any questions – I was too busy chucking my guts up over the side of the boat.'

'Oh, Robbie…'

'It's okay.'

'What do you mean, *it's okay*? You didn't ask him anything.'

'Painful as it was, that time with Baxter has told me a lot about him.'

Chilcott returned his head into his hands.

'Well? Are you going to share this newfound insight with me?'

'He's a control freak.'

Chilcott looked up at the DCI. 'He took me out on that boat knowing I'd be ill or die in those crazy conditions.'

'Sounds like he's also a good judge of character.'

Chilcott glared at Foster's attempt at sarcastic humour.

'He waited until he had complete influence over the environment, knowing I was in no fit state to function, let alone ask him any questions.'

Foster pondered Chilcott's information for a moment.

'Well, then, that ties in with the witness accounts of Baxter dragging his wife away from the party. Controlling, coercive, bullying call it what you will.'

'Exactly.'

The DCI took her coat off and sat down near Chilcott.

'That still doesn't prove he killed her, though.'

Chilcott leaned back in his chair, clutched his hands behind his head, and gave Foster a pondering stare. 'No, it doesn't. In fact, he had a couple of opportunities to see me off if he wanted to. I was completely at his mercy.' Chilcott shrugged as his mind took him back. 'And to be honest, there were times I'd have taken death over how bad I was feeling.'

Foster's brow creased with concern.

'But instead, he helped me. He manipulated the situation so that he was in complete control. He's a game player. And it has to be noted; he is also a very competent sailor.'

'Hmmm. I'm not sure that detail helps his case in any way.'

'I agree. He gave me some tablets; said they were Debbie's. He said she also suffered from seasickness. If she felt anything like the way I did, she'd be easy prey. A quick flick of the heels, and she'd be over the side in no time at all.'

'Hmmm,' Foster groaned.

'Which means his opportunities to catch her in a vulnerable situation would have been limited to the weather conditions.'

'What was the weather like when they sailed out of Portishead?'

'I checked the historical shipping forecast when I got back tonight. Lundy, which is the area for the whole of the southwest coast, said it was a south-westerly five, veering westerly six. Plymouth, which covers the Cornish tip to Portland, was giving a westerly six to seven, possibly eight later.'

'What does that mean?'

Chilcott glanced blankly at his boss. 'They were sailing from a strong breeze at Portishead into an increasing gale with moderate to rough seas.'

'And just for comparison, what was the shipping condition for Lundy when you were out earlier tonight?'

Chilcott scratched the side of his head, and his mind took him right back to that cold and miserable experience on Baxter's yacht.

'It was a westerly six to seven with increasingly rough seas.'

'So pretty comparable?'

'Yeah, except Baxter was gracious enough to sail behind a great sodding rock which sheltered us until the tablets kicked in. I'm still trying to work out if he actually felt compassion for me, or he just wanted me to stop spewing over his new boat.'

'I'll go for the latter.'

'Yep. That's what I was thinking too.'

They sat in silence for a minute.

'Poisoning is another option.'

'Poisoning?' DCI Foster repeated.

'It came to me while I was aboard. He might have slipped her something early into the journey and then ditched her over the side once things got rough. It would make the job easier and would also be something of added insurance for him. And knowing we'd probably never find the body, our forensic abilities to test for poisoning would be redundant.'

'She'd float back to the surface eventually, once the stomach gasses got to work.'

'Unless he slit her from her gullet to her naval? I've read somewhere that along with being weighed down, it's the only way to stop a body floating due to the build-up of stomach gasses.'

'That's a pleasant prospect.'

'But we'd also have a crime scene with a significant amount of blood, and to my knowledge, we don't have that.'

'Jeez, why does this case have to be so difficult?'

'We'll get there eventually. We always do.'

'You always do, Rob. You always get there.'

'Well… I'm not about to let some smart-arsed control freak get the better of me.'

The corners of Foster's mouth twitched into a smile. 'Listen to yourself.'

'What?'

'Perhaps there's not so much difference between the two of you?'

'But who would you rather have on your team?'

Foster chuckled. 'Just show me I'm right to have faith in you.'

Chilcott tittered and dipped his head.

'I've got a confession to make,' he said after a beat.

Foster's smile eased, and she cocked her head. Typically when Chilcott had something he wanted to own up to, it meant she was in for additional paperwork. And Chilcott wasn't about to prove her theory wrong.

'I put a tracker on Baxter's yacht.'

'You did what?' Foster said, leaping to her feet.

'Well, not a tracker exactly… I plugged a mobile phone into a charger.'

'We didn't have RIPA authority to do that. What the hell were you thinking?'

'I know. I know,' Chilcott said with his hands defensively shielding his face. 'But needs must, and we haven't got time to go through the rigmarole of seeking authorisation for the Regulations of Investigatory Powers blah, blah, blah.'

'Blah, blah, fucking blah? It's the law, Robbie. It's there to protect us. All of us, including you. Get it back, right now.'

'No can do. That would just raise his suspicions.'

'Jesus, Rob! Can't you do anything without bending the rules? You're like a sodding Uri-bloody-Geller in uniform.'

She cradled her head in her hands and groaned at the thought of the potential fallout his unorthodox actions might bring.

'I don't wear a uniform.'

Foster glared at him.

'I've done similar before,' he said, justifying his actions. 'I just haven't told you.'

'Stop,' she glowered. Her rigid index finger was pointing squarely between his eyes. 'Not another word.'

'Suit yourself.'

The DCI flopped back down and covered her head with her arms as if protecting herself from a barrage of Chilcott's misdemeanours.

Picking up on his boss's evident disquiet, Chilcott hummed a jaunty tune and gently tapped his fingertips on the desktop as he waited for her to speak again.

'Enough already,' she barked at him. 'Just sit there in silence, will you. I've got to work out how I explain this one away when Baxter finds that sodding phone.'

'Easy,' Chilcott said indifferently. 'It needed juice, so I plugged it in.'

The razor-sharp stare he received back from Foster told him she wasn't interested in his suggestions on the matter.

'Okay,' she sighed eventually. 'Is there anything you want to tell me before I head off that isn't going to send me to an early grave?'

He bit his top lip and considered his thoughts.

'Don't just sit there. Tell me what's on your mind. I know you too well, Robbie.'

'Okay... do you think it possible that Baxter didn't kill his wife and his account in interview is truthful, or at least partially truthful?'

'It's possible. Why?'

Chilcott wrinkled his nose but didn't answer.

'Robbie?'

'Debbie Baxter can't just vanish into thin air or deep water as the case might be.'

'Are you thinking someone else is involved?'

His eyes met hers for a second before he answered. 'I dunno.'

Foster rose to her feet again. 'Okay. I need to get home.'

'Need? That's not like you. Something you want to share?'

Foster scalded Chilcott with a stern glare.

'I'm going home, and I suggest you do the same. Get out of those stinking clothes and wash. Let's have a briefing with the team first thing on Monday morning. I want to start seeing some real progress with this case, one way or the other.'

'I'll let the troops know.'

'Do me a favour, Robbie,' she said, tying a belt tightly around her jacket, 'no more underhand tactics.'

Chilcott broke into a toothy grin. 'You have to admit though…?'

'No more,' Foster ordered. 'See you Monday. Have a good rest of the weekend.'

Chilcott tapped the skin of his brow with a two-finger salute, and Foster was gone.

As he systematically closed down his computer terminal and readied his desk for Monday morning, he found himself not wanting to leave. And for the next few minutes, he was lost in his thoughts, his mind poring over several scenarios, but none of them giving him the answers he craved.

CHAPTER TWENTY-TWO

Sunday the fifth of September was a much-needed rest day for the Major Crime Investigation Team officers. Although crime never stopped, occasionally, it paid for the investigating officers to take their foot off the gas and recuperate, and this was one such day. Chilcott was standing with a coffee in the centre of the compact and, quite frankly, bland rear garden of his recently acquired two-bed, semi-detached house on the fringes of Longwell Green. It was a step up from the run-down old caravan that had been his place of refuge during his self-imposed exile from the department. Still, at least that environment had provided him with a feeling of freedom, something that already seemed a distant memory. Now, he felt boxed in, restricted, looked upon. He had no choice in the matter, of course. His dilapidated but homely caravan was now nothing more than burnt cinders and a large black scorch mark in the Lulsgate countryside, thanks to the architect of his previous murder case.

As he peered pitifully at the narrow proximity of his boundary fence, he felt more a prisoner in his new habitat than ever before. Had he made a mistake buying this place? Probably, but he'd outstayed his welcome at Julie Foster's gaff, and his presence there had only brought trouble to her door. And so, he'd been forced into a corner, and that was a place Chilcott never liked to be.

He took his mug of coffee and sat down at the cheap patio set he'd picked up from a local garden centre the previous week at an end of summer seasonal sale, or at least, that's how they had sold it. From the flimsy construction, he doubted it had ever been the suggested price of ninety-nine quid, but as he'd paid just half of that, he wasn't overly bothered if it only lasted the few remaining weeks of half-decent sunshine.

He sucked in the morning air and tilted back his head, eyes closed to the low-slung sun and did his level best to empty his mind of work problems. But that was just futile and wishful thinking. His brain had raged all night. He hated the feeling of being bested by anyone. That niggling pneumatic doubt of being made a fool had drilled away at him constantly since his seaward excursion with Walter Baxter yesterday. There was just *something* about this case that didn't ring true. The trouble was, he couldn't decide what?

He stood up from his cheap seat and did several laps of his 'estate' checking his watch in as many times. It was 7.50 a.m. He returned inside and poured another long black coffee from his cafetière, this time buttering two cold rounds of toast that had been waiting in the pop-up slots of his toaster for the last fifteen minutes.

As he bit into the chewy bread, his mind turned back to the scene at the marina, a starker contrast to his own life he couldn't imagine. He blinked as an image flashed into his mind of Baxter's looming face over his prone and vulnerable body while he "repainted" the side of Baxter's yacht.

Had he ever been in a more perilous situation? Probably not even when trapped between the gun sights of a rogue SAS veteran and several crack police marksmen. No, even then, he was still in control of his destiny, to a degree. But Baxter hadn't pitched him over the side, no matter how easy that would have been at the time. Instead, he had gone out of his way to help Chilcott. Were those the actions of a man capable of murdering his wife? As he pondered the question, he nibbled away at the rubbery slice of toast, which he then helped down with a large guzzle of lukewarm coffee before slamming his mug down firmly on the white, marble-effect worktop. *Something's missing?*

He arrived back at the marina by nine. Maybe it would have been easier to have operated from the nearby police headquarters, but he didn't go in for all that corporate-pill bollocks. The corridors of power could be overwhelming with the stench of political correctness and overt subservience to the powers that be. He was sure DI Jaz Chowdhury fitted right in, but it certainly wasn't his scene. And as he looked around at the gently bobbing boats, he realised something; he liked it here. He may not have shared their love of boats, but he got why they did it. He understood the benefits of being in such a calm and beautiful setting.

Instead of seeking out the witnesses, he took himself into Le Parisien coffee shop and sat down beside the large panoramic window facing out into the marina. As he pondered his thoughts with a bacon butty and lashings of brown sauce, what stood out most to Chilcott was the fact that he didn't understand this community as much as he needed to. On the face of it, they had nothing in common with him. They had money for starters, lots of it apparently, and they enjoyed the luxuries of life. But as he watched the early to-ing and fro-ing of the yachting fraternity, he began to recognise something they did share with him; they all appeared comfortable in their skins. They may have been living in or playing on super-expensive boats, but the lifestyle itself was no different to his old existence in his grotty little caravan. Confined spaces, functional facilities; it's just theirs came with a premium price tag. He was basically looking at a glorified caravan park on water. But unlike his choice to live in a remote location miles from the next person, these people were bunking shoulder to shoulder with their closest neighbours. As a result, it would be nearly impossible to keep secrets, particularly given the apparent way gossip spread so freely within this habitat.

A young waitress of about nineteen years came to take Chilcott's plate away.

'Everything all right, sir?'

'Yes, lovely, thank you.'

'Can I get you another coffee?'

'Uh…' Chilcott peered at his watch, forgetting this was a rest day, and he didn't have anywhere else to be.

'Why not,' he smiled, but as the waitress turned, he touched her arm. 'In fact, do you have any beers?'

'Absolutely, we have San Miguel and Stella Artois on tap

and Corona or Budweiser in bottles, unless you fancy cider or a craft beer from the local mini-brewery?'

'A bottle of Bud will be great, thanks.'

The waitress returned soon after with a tray and placed a tall empty glass and a full bottle of beer on Chilcott's table.

'You can pay on exit, sir,' she said.

Chilcott thanked the young waitress, wiped the bottle's lip between his fingers, and placed it to his lips. *This is more like it.*

He had paid for a full day of parking, plenty enough time to allow a couple of these bad boys to slide down and still have time to sober up before driving home. He angled his seat, hooked his feet up on the chair opposite and then noticed far away movement on jetty seven. It was Trevor Hicks, and he appeared to be pulling a long-handled trailer containing several black plastic sacks.

Chilcott leaned forwards and watched, paying close attention to Trevor, who was now on the main pontoon and coming his way. As he got closer, Chilcott raised a table menu and held it up in front of his face as he peered surreptitiously over the top.

Trevor came through the pontoon security gate and continued to a block of recycling containers at the corner of Chilcott's line of sight. He was disposing of his tins, plastic and glass empties, and there were a lot of them. *Had they had another party last night?*

'Excuse me,' Chilcott said, grabbing the attention of the waitress. 'Have you worked here long?'

The waitress recoiled as if Chilcott was slipping her a creepy line or something.

'It's okay; I'm not trying to crack on to you. I wondered if you knew that man over there?' he said, pointing out through the window towards Trevor Hicks, who was coming to the bottom of his first recycling bag.

'Yes, that's Trev. He's one of our regular customers.'

'Do you know many of the boating residents?'

'Some of them, the ones who come in here a lot, anyway. Do you have a boat here, sir?'

'Ah… no, but I'm thinking of buying one. Is there anything I should know or take into consideration before staying at this marina?'

'Not really… everyone is really nice.'

Chilcott noticed a tightening of her face on the word *everyone*.

'Are you sure? You don't seem overly convinced?'

The waitress brushed her doubts aside and took a half-step backwards.

'No, it's lovely… really. You'll love it here.'

'But…?'

She looked at Chilcott for a measured second and then back towards her colleague at the till.

'Something happened on one of the boats here recently.'

'Something?'

Mirroring was a great way to extract more information without coming across too forcefully.

'I don't think I should talk about it,' the waitress fussed, hugging the metal tray close to her chest like it was a shield of protection.

'Does it involve the lady who has gone missing?'

The waitress looked at Chilcott like he had duped her. 'Yes,' she said timidly.

'It's okay,' Chilcott reassured her. 'Someone else told me already. It seems like secrets don't last very long here.'

'Well,' the waitress said, leaning forwards and wiping a ring of condensation from Chilcott's table where his cold beer had been resting. 'You'd be surprised what we hear.'

'I bet,' Chilcott said, taking a swig from the bottle. 'So, what's your take on the missing lady?'

'Debs?'

'Oh, do you know her?'

'Of course. She comes in here all the time.'

'Alone or with her partner?'

The waitress stepped back, and her eyelids drooped as she continued to suss him out.

'Either way.'

Chilcott looked over towards Trevor Hicks, who was manoeuvring the empty trolley around to face the other way.

'Does she have a lot of friends here?'

The waitress fixed her gaze on Chilcott, who took the signal and sipped from his bottle again.

'Are you a reporter or something?'

Chilcott raised his palms in a *don't shoot* pose.

'God no – seriously, I'm not a reporter. I'm just interested in knowing how friendly my neighbours are going to be?'

'Well, if you want friendly, that's who you need to befriend.' She gestured towards Trevor Hicks, who was manoeuvring the trolley back through the gated entrance to the pontoon.

'We call them, *The Party Boat*,' she said. 'I wouldn't be surprised if those bottles were from last night alone,' she giggled.

'They had a party here last night?' Chilcott asked with a surprised tone. He didn't see or hear any signs of a party when he had been on the jetty last night.

The waitress chuckled to herself and smiled broadly. 'Every weekend is party weekend. It's a lot of fun, and they are great hosts.'

'Have you been to the parties yourself?'

'Sure.'

'Sounds great fun. I'll have to make myself acquainted with...?'

'Trevor Hicks. You should,' the waitress beamed and moved on to wipe another tabletop. 'Once you get in with Trevor and Jane, you're friends for life.'

Chilcott acknowledged the comment with a tip of the neck and swig of his bottle and watched with interest as Trevor Hicks walked back towards his boat.

CHAPTER TWENTY-THREE

DCI Foster stood before her team and opened the briefing. DC Allen then came forwards and gave a summary of the information and evidence gathered to date. Enquiries with St Ives and Salcombe marinas came back inconclusive, both of which having bookings under the name of Walter Baxter, but no apparent mention of his wife and limited opportunities for CCTV to confirm her presence one way or the other. The retrieved records did, however, confirm that Baxter arrived at Salcombe Marina late into the night of Sunday the fifteenth of August, where he alone conducted the transaction of the yachts later the next day. Detectives spoke to the owner of the boatyard taking ownership of *AWoL*, who categorically confirmed that Baxter had been alone during the exchange of properties. But this came as no surprise to the detectives as Baxter had previously said his wife had gone to her sister's prior to this and before he woke up that morning. Unfortunately, the entire inside of *AWoL* had been steam cleaned before the officers' arrival. That said, Nathan Parsons and his team did conduct a cursory examination of the vessel, and nothing was revealed about its integrity suggestive of any previous foul play.

Chilcott's attention was stoked when Detective Constable Penny Chiba came forward with more information about the victim. DC Chiba was the financial wizard of the team and the SPOC – Single Point of Contact, with the financial investigation unit. What she didn't know about accountancy wasn't worth knowing.

'I have conducted background analysis on our victim and can confirm that she and Walter Baxter have been married for five years. However, all this time, we have assumed she used the married surname, but this isn't the case. She is still legally known by her maiden name, Debbie Williams.'

'Why didn't Baxter correct us in the interview?' Chilcott asked.

'I can't answer that, sir, but get this – Debbie Williams drew up a prenuptial agreement that Walter Baxter had to agree with before their marriage, in which she stipulated the keeping of her surname and the act of intimate relations between them would be at her behest only.'

Looking around the room, it was clear many of the female officers were giving Miss Williams considerable kudos for her foresight. The men, on the other hand, found this information provocatively amusing.

'They share a bank account for bills and expenses; however, it is clear that this account is sourced entirely from Baxter's pocket via one of his other personal accounts. There is no record of Debbie Williams contributing to this, but she does have her own personal account with Lloyds Bank, which Baxter has no lawful access to.'

The more Chilcott heard DC Chiba speak about their dysfunctional relationship, the more intrigued he was becoming in Debbie Williams.

They already knew the witnesses at the marina had only known the couple since when they first arrived at the mooring, and so any detailed knowledge they may have of them was likely to be limited. It appeared one significant secret had already escaped them; Debbie had a different surname, but why?

Regardless, the witnesses did share one common opinion; that Walter and Debbie were an "odd-couple" and that Debbie did appear on the whole happy, especially when being lavished in Baxter's fortune. She drove a modern Porsche 911 Carrera 4S with a private plate and apparently spent days away at a time from the marina on shopping expeditions, returning with bags from the trendiest of outlets. The financial investigation unit had made some basic enquiries on behalf of Chilcott and identified that Baxter also had property investments in Chelsea, Manchester and Marbella. All owned outright with no outstanding debt, and collectively these properties were worth millions. On the face of it, this appeared to be a classic *Sugar-Daddy* set-up. But Chilcott knew better than anyone never to put too much stock in face value.

'Have we done any PNC checks on Debbie Williams' name?' the DCI asked DC Chiba, who looked anxiously towards Chilcott, clearly exposing her answer.

'I wouldn't imagine so,' Chilcott said, rising to his feet and joining his colleague at the front of the audience of detectives. 'This is clearly recently discovered,' he said, looking sideways at DC Chiba, who quickly nodded confirmation. 'We'll get that done.'

'Right. Make sure that's a priority after briefing,' DCI Foster ordered. She gave Chilcott a lingering look, and he knew exactly what that meant.

Chilcott walked to the whiteboard containing the jotted keynotes of the investigation to date. He used the butt end of a marker pen and tapped it against a name written in large capital letters.

'We've been distracted and too focussed on Walter Baxter,' he said. 'We've taken our eye off the bigger picture, and I'll take full responsibility for that. But that changes as of now. Richie, you stay on Baxter. Let's keep the pressure upon him. Fleur,' he said, turning to DC Phillips, 'I want you to focus entirely on Debbie Williams. I want to know everything about her by the end of play today. Complete those intel and PNC checks and find out from the number plate recognition team where and when her Porsche was pinged in the month leading up to her disappearance.'

'Sir,' DC Phillips responded as she made a note of the tasks in her daybook.

'How much money is sitting in Debbie Williams' bank account, do we know?' the DCI asked.

Chilcott looked again to Detective Penny Chiba, who took her place back on the front row of detectives. 'Pen, can you answer that one?' he asked.

'Over eighty thousand, Ma'am,' DC Chiba answered without having to look at her records.

'In her personal bank account?'

'Yes, Ma'am.'

'What about the joint account with Baxter?' Chilcott

asked. 'How is that looking?'

DC Chiba flashed her eyelids. 'That's even healthier, sir… it was around three hundred and twenty-seven thousand at the last check.'

'I wonder what Debbie Williams saw in Walter Baxter?' Chilcott uttered to the chuckles of his team.

Foster stepped forwards and stifled the laughter. 'Come on. We've all heard that joke before. Let's crack on with these tasks. We've got a lot to achieve in a short space of time. I'm going to speak privately with DI Chilcott, and we'll all reconvene at the same time tomorrow.' She gave her team a stern look. 'It's time we made progress with this job. Make sure you each contribute to that.'

'Ma'am,' the detectives all answered and filed eagerly out of the room.

Foster took Chilcott to her office, closed the door behind him, and stepped within his personal space. 'What do you think?' she said quietly so that nobody outside of the room would hear their conversation.

'I don't know,' he replied blankly. 'I really don't know what to think?'

'I don't like what I just heard.'

'Me either… I mean, who agrees to a prenup like that?'

'Be serious, will you.'

'I thought I was.'

Foster gave her DI a *naughty boy* wiggle of the index finger.

'There's far more to this than meets the eye,' Chilcott said.

'I agree.'

Chilcott ran a hand down his face. 'It has to be financially motivated in some way. We need to run a thorough trawl of all phone records, bank transactions. You name it. But it's not just in the days before Debbie Williams disappeared; we are potentially looking at months before she vanished.'

'And what would you expect to find from such a detailed examination?'

Chilcott puffed air out through his lips, and they flapped against each other.

'I really don't know – a pattern of some sort? Something we can hook into and explore in further detail?'

'What do you plan on doing next? Knowing you as I do, I know you'll have something up your sleeve.'

'There's a beating heart to all that goes on down at the marina – Trevor Hicks. I'm going to remove him; take him out of his comfort zone and put a little pressure on him.'

The DCI scratched beneath her nose with a recently manicured nail and gave Chilcott a beady look.

'I do hope you don't intend to arrest him?'

Chilcott pouted. 'Nah, nothing that extreme.'

He twitched a shoulder. 'That's not to say I won't threaten it if I feel he is deliberately obstructing me.'

Noticing the displeasure on the DCI's face, he felt obliged to cover his tracks. 'But I won't follow through. We need him on our side.'

'Make sure you don't. You've done quite enough to undermine this case as it is.'

'Come on. This is me you're talking to.'

'Precisely!'

CHAPTER TWENTY-FOUR

Trevor Hicks was reluctant to leave the marina with Chilcott, but in the end, Chilcott's persistence and scampish charm had worn him down, and now they were a short distance away at Battery Point, looking across the Bristol Channel at the Welsh coastline and the hazy outline of the Severn Bridge far off in the distance. Chilcott knew this area well, easily recognisable from the stumpy lighthouse tower perched on the precipice of a jagged outcrop, with its long metal access gangplank from the grassy headland. As a younger man, he enjoyed a spot of sea fishing, and this was prime cod country due to the deep waters close to shore.

They sat aside one another on a beauty-spot bench, and Chilcott took his time to sip a hot brew from a cardboard coffee cup liberated from a nearby fast-food kiosk. He was in no hurry to pressure Trevor Hicks. If anything, he was enjoying the view as he reminisced about days gone by with his father down at the rocky water's edge.

'Are you actually going to ask me something?' Trevor asked.

Chilcott slurped loudly several times and continued to squint off into the distance. He had chosen this area carefully; if he had taken Hicks to the station or too far away from familiar surroundings, it might well have unnerved him or made him feel threatened. But this was perfect. The marina was a stone's throw behind them, and they were still in Trevor Hicks' comfort zone. But most importantly, here, Chilcott hoped, he could speak to Hicks candidly and without the distractions of listening ears.

'Nice here innit,' Chilcott said finally. 'Very nice, indeed.'

Hicks didn't answer but shuffled his bottom on the bench. Chilcott could see his leg was bouncing up and down with nerves.

'Do you bring the missus up here much?' Chilcott asked.

'No, we tend to stay at the marina. We've got no cause to come here.'

'Hmmm,' Chilcott groaned. 'Then you're missing out on the simple pleasures in life.'

'Who needs the simple pleasures when one can afford the not-so-simple?' Trevor remarked smugly.

'Hmmm,' Chilcott groaned again. 'I keep forgetting; you lot are minted, aren't you.'

He brought the paper cup to his lips and blinked away the rising steam from his eyes.

'Why do they make these drinks so bloody hot? Do you ever notice that? Go to a McDonald's drive-thru, get a black coffee, you can drive for half an hour, and it'll still scald your bloody tongue.'

'You said you needed to talk privately to me,' Hicks said, not entertaining Chilcott's attempts at small-talk.

'We are, aren't we?'

'Yes–I… I suppose we are, but I thought this was to do with Debs?'

'Ah, Debbie Williams,' Chilcott said in a reminiscent way.

'Who?'

Chilcott faced Trevor Hicks for the first time since they had sat down.

'Debbie Williams.'

Hicks blinked with hesitation. 'Don't you mean Deb Baxter?'

'Nope. Debbie Williams.'

'I'm sorry, I've never heard that surname used before.'

'Who told you she was called Baxter or did you just assume she shared the same surname as Walter?'

'Uh, I don't know?'

'Who met them first when they came to the marina?'

'Out of?'

'Your little group of friends. You know, the party crowd. Who was the first to make that initial approach or contact with Walter Baxter or Debbie Williams?'

'Uh… it was probably me.'

'And why would you do that?'

Hicks wiggled his head; confusion displayed on his face.

'What would you have in common with Walter Baxter?'

'Very little.'

'But you did with Debbie Williams.' Chilcott said this more as a statement than as a question.

'Yes– I… I suppose so.'

'She was much younger, wasn't she? Closer to your age than he was.'

189

'Yes.'

'Yes.'

Chilcott looked back out to sea and took cautious sips from his cup.

'I'm sorry,' Trevor Hick's said, stiffening his shoulders. 'Are you insinuating something?'

Chilcott looked back at him. 'Me? No. Just stating facts.'

He cast his eyes once again far off into the horizon and two container ships moving slowly down the channel.

'Do you think I had something to do with Deb's disappearance?'

'Did you?' Chilcott said, turning back to Hicks.

'No, I most certainly did not.'

'Okay.'

Hicks wiped building moisture from his top lip. 'You do believe me?'

'If you say you had nothing to do with her disappearance, then that's good enough for me.'

'What's this about? I don't understand why we're here?'

Chilcott scratched the back of his neck with his free hand.

'I'm just fact-finding, that's all. Did you know she had a car?'

'Of course, I did.'

'What was it?'

'A Porsche Carrera 4S.'

'Very nice too. Did you ever go in it?'

'No.'

'Did you see it?'

'Of course, I saw it. It was parked at the marina. You couldn't miss it. It was bright orange.'

'What about when they sailed somewhere? What did they do with the car then?'

'It stayed at the marina, I assume.'

'I understand Debbie would often stay away from the marina with friends. Did you know that?'

'I knew she had close friends that she would visit from time to time.'

'Did you ever meet them?'

'No… I–I don't think I did.'

'Would that be mostly weekends or weekdays?'

'I didn't really… Look, I don't know. Weekdays I suppose if you had to push me.'

'Meaning she was at the marina most weekends then?'

'Pretty much, I guess. There would be the occasional weekend when any of the group might be away.'

'And you'd know that better than most because of your parties.'

'Yes, I suppose so.'

'Did you always invite the same people, or could anyone come to one of your parties?'

'Well, not just anyone.'

'But also, not exclusive to those of you who were there the last time you saw Deb Williams?'

'Um no, within reason, anyone could join us.'

'Like marina staff and such?'

Hicks shrugged and bobbed his head with agreement. 'Yes, sometimes.'

'That is very convivial of you.'

'I like to enjoy life. That's not a crime, is it?'

'No, it certainly isn't. Good for you, that's what I say.'

Chilcott stopped talking and looked out to sea once

more. In his peripheral vision, he saw Hicks scratching the top of his head. He was clearly uncomfortable and confused by the questioning.

Chilcott leaned his body towards him.

'What did you make of Debbie Williams, you know, man-to-man. Did you fancy her?'

'I beg your pardon?'

'Would you… you know… stray if given half the chance?'

'No, I most certainly would not.'

'She was a looker though.'

'I'm not going to disagree, but—'

'That's okay, son, no need to explain anything to me. I'm just trying to get a feel for the lay of the land because obviously, I never met her.'

Chilcott noticed Hicks fiddling with his hands. 'Um…' he uttered.

'Yes?'

'I did overhear others talking about her, though.'

'Did you? Who would that be then?'

'Uh… pretty much everyone at one time or another.'

'Hmmm. And what might they have talked about?'

'Well, the odd relationship between Debs and Walter.'

Hicks leaned forwards, directing his weight through his knees. He was feeling uncomfortable with the conversation.

'Ever see anyone else with Debs, you know… in a *friendly* way?'

'Uh, no, no, I don't believe so.'

'Last question for you, Trevor. If you had to sum up Walter and Debs as individuals using only three words, what would they be?'

Hicks drew in a deep breath as he thought about the question.

'Uh… Walter would be; odd, individual and unfriendly.'

Chilcott nodded. He was expecting Hicks to say something like that. 'And Debs, how would you describe her?'

Hicks licked his top lip and answered much freer. 'Fun, young and… sassy.'

'Thank you, Mr Hicks. I've enjoyed our little chat.'

Hicks leaned back, clearly relieved that the questioning was over.

'I like it here,' Chilcott said. 'Maybe I'll get myself a boat, and then perhaps I'll get an invite to one of your parties?'

Hicks recoiled with a shocked expression.

'It's all right. I'm teasing you.'

CHAPTER TWENTY-FIVE

Tuesday 7th September

12:17 p.m.

DC Phillips bounded across the incident room towards Chilcott. She was full of determination.

'Sir, I have an update regarding the ANPR and PNC checks on our victim.'

'Good – go on.'

'PNC shows no previous criminal history. We have, however, traced a couple of historic calls from the intelligence databases but with different phone numbers. She appears to have been living in Southampton between 2008 and 2015. She was having issues with a stalker for a while, but nothing more than low-level pestering. Strong words of advice appeared to do the trick, and he vanished off the scene.'

'A stalker, eh?'

'And I took the liberty of calling her sister again.'

'You're brave.'

'I think the seriousness of the situation has sunk in. She was fine with me. Apparently, Debbie worked as crew on boats chartered around the Mediterranean for private clients, and from there took a job promoting luxury yachts at boat shows all over the world.'

'I can see why that must be a bit raw for Alison.'

'Yes, and in fact, it was at a boat show when she first met Walter Baxter.'

'Hmmm. That sounds like an interesting conversation I'd like to have with him.'

'As for the Porsche, DVLA reports that she sold it eleven days prior to her disappearance.'

Chilcott scowled. 'Really. That's a bit of a coincidence, wouldn't you agree?'

'It could account for the large wedge of cash in her bank account?'

'It could. What's the latest on those enquiries, do you know?'

'Penny Chiba has made the relevant requests; we're just waiting on the banks to get back to us with recent transaction history. It shouldn't be much longer.'

'Good – anything else I need to know about?'

'No, I think that's everything, for now, sir.'

Chilcott thanked DC Phillips, continued through to his office, and took his seat. He swivelled his chair back and forth as he stared through the glass walls into the incident room, watching his team going about their duties with increased enthusiasm. At that moment, his desk phone rang, and he debated whether or not to answer the call. If it were something important, they'd call back, but whoever it was, they were persistent. He rolled his eyes and answered.

'Chilcott.'

'Robbie, it's Jeff Graham over at the airport.'

Detective Superintendent Jeffrey Graham was an old pal of Chilcott's from their days on the beat at Wells and Glastonbury. Like Chilcott, he'd gone far in his career, and now he was the detective superintendent at Special Branch, based at Bristol International Airport.

'Jeff, you old bugger. What are you up to, mate?'

'I have some information that I think might just pique your interest.'

'Oh?'

'I've just had a quick look at your current investigations and see you're dealing with a high risk missing person case.'

'Yeah, well, it's not all international mystery and crime like it is for you guys.'

'Maybe, maybe not once you've heard this?'

Chilcott sat forwards. 'You're right; you do have my interest piqued.'

'I've been contacted by our counterparts in Port De Cassis, Marseille. They are investigating a murder at the port.'

Chilcott shrugged and shook his head. 'Okay.'

'They have a suspect in custody. He provided an account during an interview this morning and has demanded the officers dealing with the murder case make contact with you.'

'Contact me?'

'You.'

'I'm sorry, Jeff, I—'

'The suspect is one David Reynolds.'

Chilcott sprang upright in his seat. 'Say that again?'

'The person they have in police custody is a David Reynolds. I've cast an eye over your case, and I see he's named as a witness.'

'That's right. Are we sure we're talking about the same David Reynolds?'

'I looked at his date of birth on your crime report. It's the same person.'

'And he asked them to speak with me?'

'That's correct.'

'Why?'

'Are you sitting down?'

'Uh…yeah.'

'The victim of the murder is your MISPER, one, Debbie Williams.'

Chilcott shot up from his seat. 'What?'

'They confirmed her DNA at the scene.'

'Hold on,' Chilcott said, attempting to make sense of what he was hearing. 'David Reynolds is in French custody for murdering Debbie Williams?'

'Yes.'

'Are you sure? I mean… really?'

'I'm sure.'

'Have you got a name for your source?'

'Raphael Le Roux is leading the investigation. I got off the phone to him about ten minutes before I called you.'

'Is he a detective?'

'He is the most senior detective on this investigation.'

Chilcott fell silent.

'I thought I'd call you to give you an early heads-up. They are interviewing Reynolds for a second time this afternoon.'

'Yeah, thanks, Jeff – I think. Are they going to let you know how the next interview goes?'

'Absolutely, I'm going to stay in contact with Raphael and see if we can assist them with their investigation or vice-versa, but it's obviously still early days.'

'Thanks for letting me know. Well, that certainly puts the cat amongst the pigeons.'

CHAPTER TWENTY-SIX

Chilcott had to repeat himself several times before the DCI would believe what he was saying.

'But you can't die twice,' she said.

'Exactly! She clearly set it up to look like Walter Baxter had killed her in the UK. I don't know, maybe they planned it together, her and Reynolds. If you look at the timeline, it makes total sense.'

'I disagree. It simply doesn't work. It would take multiple days, if not weeks, to sail to the south of France.'

'I know that part of it doesn't add up, but who's to say they sailed? A flight would get them there in no time at all. David Reynolds has arrived in the last forty-eight hours or so, but Debbie Williams has had weeks to get there. We can't assume anything right now.'

The DCI walked through to the incident room and studied the timeline as Chilcott stood silently at her side.

'Okay, we need someone to trace the passport movements of Williams and Reynolds,' she said, turning to Chilcott. 'Quite frankly, this is an embarrassment to the department. How could we let Debbie Williams slip through our net?'

'With all due respect, Julie, when have we ever checked the passport movements of dead people? And remember, we've been concentrating on Debbie Baxter, not Debbie Williams. We didn't know her real name at the time she travelled.'

'That's not the point, Robbie. We should have checked, and we didn't. We have a live investigation, and one of the key named persons has subsequently died. Had we done our jobs, she may still be alive. This will probably have to be reviewed by the powers that be.'

'I want to speak to David Reynolds. I want to know exactly what went on at Portishead Marina and how he came to be in Marseille with Debbie Williams.'

'I agree he has questions to answer.'

'Too bloody right he does.'

'I suppose we need to consider releasing Walter Baxter from our investigation with no charge. And we'd better hand over details of our investigation to Special Branch.'

'Sod that. Not after all the running around, I've done. I'll go to France myself and ask him what we need to know.'

The DCI flipped him a parental-type gaze. 'Not on your Nelly. We haven't got the budget.'

He chomped down tightly and spoke through clenched teeth. 'I'll pay for the bloody flights myself. I hate being done over.'

Foster put a hand on his shoulder. 'I know. I know you do, Rob. I'm as angry about this as you are.'

'Then let me finish it.'

Her face cringed. 'I'm not going to promise you

anything, but let me chat to the detective chief superintendent and see if we can spare you, and a few hundred quid.'

As the DCI walked off, Chilcott turned back to the team of detectives diligently going about their tasks.

'Everyone, listen up,' he boomed.

Faces peered up at him from behind computer terminals, and telephone conversations were quickly placed on hold.

'Everything we thought we knew about this case has just been turned on its head. Debbie Williams is dead.'

Puzzled expressions and respectfully murmured queries bounced from one side of the room to the other.

'We've had game-changing information from Special Branch,' Chilcott announced, peering at his team individually.

'Debbie Williams was murdered at some point yesterday in the south of France.'

The puzzled expressions from the detectives grew even more bewildered.

'David Reynolds is currently being held by French police in Marseille under suspicion of the murder. I don't have any more detail at this time, but I do know that it appears that up to this point, we've been had over by Reynolds and Williams at Portishead Marina.'

'Richie,' he said to DC Allen. 'We now need to treat Walter Baxter as a witness. We need to establish what he knows about the relationship between his wife and David Reynolds. Fleur,' he said to DC Phillips, 'get back on to the CCTV from the marina. I want to see a detailed timeline of David Reynolds' comings and goings for the last month, but particularly the time from when Debbie Williams was last seen to the point Reynolds packed up and left the marina. Find out if he had a car and check automatic number plate recognition for any movement. My suspicion is that we'll see both Reynolds and Debbie together at some point after she left the marina with Walter.'

'Sir?' A hand rose from behind a desk partition.

'Yes.'

'If the French police are dealing with Debbie's murder, what are the chances they will allow us to investigate David Reynolds?'

'A good question that I can't answer right now. All I know is; I want to see the whites of that bastard's eyes.'

CHAPTER TWENTY-SEVEN

It was almost 6 p.m. when Detective Superintendent Jeff Graham got back on the phone to Chilcott. The incident room was now an environment of heightened tension and anxiety. Most of the detectives would have usually been off to their homes by now, but these coming hours could drastically change the course of the investigation, so long as red tape wasn't about to hold them back.

'Robbie, it's Jeff.'

'Hello, mate. What's the latest from France?'

'My source says that David Reynolds has been interviewed, but he's not having the murder.'

'Sounds familiar.'

'However, he did make full and frank admissions to assisting Debbie Williams in the faking of her death in the UK.'

'You're kidding?'

'He won't take full ownership, though. He says that Williams came to him, pleading to help her escape from Walter Baxter. She then apparently came up with the plan to frame Baxter for her murder on the premise that she and Reynolds run off into the sunset and start a new life together.'

'Hmm,' Chilcott murmured. 'That's ironic.'

'Isn't it just.'

'Did he confirm that they had a relationship?'

'He did. It seems that was just part of the deal, though. He significantly financed the venture to frame Walter Baxter and make a new life for themselves in France.'

'Such as?'

'For starters, he put Debbie up in a five-star hotel near Port De Cassis until she could transfer to the luxury yacht he rented. He paid for her flights out of Bristol. He bought her a new wardrobe and practically reinvented her identity.'

'What were their plans once they both got to Marseille?'

'He said they were going to explore the Mediterranean, from France to Italy, from Italy to Greece; you name it.'

'So, the boat is on a long-term lease?'

'Yeah, at twelve thousand Euros per week.'

'Wow!'

'It's fair to say Mr Reynolds leads a comfortable life.'

'It seems Miss Williams had an uncanny knack of finding that particular quality in her men.'

'You might also find this interesting? He mentioned about a piece of jewellery wrapped around a propeller shaft.'

'Yes, I know what that relates to.' Chilcott drifted off. There was no way Reynolds could have known about the jewellery unless he was directly involved. This was real.

'Reynolds set it up,' Jeff Graham said. 'Williams gave him the chain and told him to wrap it around the propeller.

He says he used his own diving equipment under cover of darkness to tangle it around the bottom of her husband's yacht.'

'That's right. We found that piece of jewellery, but it was on the wrong yacht. She didn't go missing from *Death Do Us Part*. She went missing from *AWoL*.'

'Apparently, she knew it would distract the investigation for long enough to allow the pair of them to leave the UK without detection.'

'The sneaky bitch.'

'Quite! The problem is we're on sticky ground now that we're out of the EU judicial cooperation policy. Although we are dealing with British nationals, our French counterparts have no obligation to co-operate or share their findings with UK law enforcement.'

Chilcott banged the table with the ball of his fist. 'That's bollocks.'

'It's okay, it's okay, Robbie. I have a good connection in that region, and I'm hopeful we'll get everything we need through them. They've already told me more than I'd anticipated at this stage of their investigation.'

'How long before we can see Reynolds?' Chilcott asked.

'Who knows? They certainly won't deport him while investigating a murder on their territory.'

Chilcott turned his book to a clean page. 'Just run me through the full circumstances, would you. What made the French authorities arrest him for murder in the first place?'

'It looks like Reynolds called the job in himself. He claims he returned to the rented yacht and found Debbie missing and a scene of a disturbance. He provided detectives with all the information they required, but they still formed the opinion that he had killed her, despite the fact he raised the alarm himself.'

'Any ideas where the body is?'

'The yacht was moored to a buoy several hundred metres out from the port itself and quite some distance to the nearest boat, which means there are no independent witnesses. Divers are still scouring the sea bed for her body.'

'I don't understand,' Chilcott said. 'If Reynolds killed her, why did he then call it in? Did he murder her and then succumb to a guilty conscience?'

'Not according to his account. He says he only met up with her the day before, having travelled from the UK. He went ashore for additional provisions, and it was upon his return to the yacht that he found the scene, and Debbie was missing.'

'So, she was alone on the yacht for a while?'

'That's what he says. And then, on his return to the boat, he found what he found. The police saw enough to arrest him there and then. He had blood on his hands and clothing, but he claims that was from tidying up the scene.'

'Why would he tidy the scene?'

'He says it was instinct, due to the fact it was a rental.'

'Okay. Any suggestion of a weapon?'

'There was nothing obvious at the scene, but they are keeping an open mind. Assuming there was a weapon, it probably went over the side into the drink. I guess that will materialise during the search of the seabed.'

Chilcott pinched the lobe of his ear until it hurt.

'What are the chances of seeing photographs of the scene?' he asked.

Graham puffed air into the receiver. 'I doubt it, Robbie.

I'll ask, but it's highly unlikely they'll share evidential photos with me.'

'Could you get someone to at least describe the scene in clear detail?'

'I'll try. Why what's so important about the scene?'

Chilcott shook his head. 'If it happened here, I'd be examining the scene. I obviously can't do that in France, so photos or a detailed description would be the next best thing.'

'Leave it with me.'

'Also, I don't know if you can do this, but is there any chance you could send me details of their passport movements, both Reynolds and Williams?'

'Well, there's a thing.'

'What is?'

'We have no record of them entering French territory or leaving the UK.'

Chilcott scowled. 'Okay… why France, why Marseille, do we know that much?'

'Reynolds claims that Williams was fluent in French, and it was her suggestion to move there. There's just one other thing you should know, Robbie; Reynolds says he set up a bank account for Williams. He claims he lent her three million Euros before they faked her disappearance from the UK so that she could get herself set up before he joined her. He says now that he wants that money back.'

CHAPTER TWENTY-EIGHT

DCI Foster sat in disbelieving silence as Chilcott updated her with the details of his conversation with Jeff Graham. And when he had finished, she still didn't speak.

'What are you thinking, Julie?'

She raised herself in her seat and cleared the back of her throat.

'Isn't this all a bit, *Gone Girl*?' she said.

'I don't know? I've never seen it.'

'How could what you've just told me be possible in this day and age?'

Chilcott shrugged. 'I dunno?'

'Where's the motivation to fake your own murder?'

'She was living an unhappy life with Baxter and saw Reynolds as an easy way out.'

'Why didn't she just file for divorce like everyone else manages to do?'

'Again, I don't know? Maybe we could get Baxter's take on that?'

'I think we need to ask Baxter a lot of questions about this situation.'

'We're already on it,' Chilcott said. 'Richie Allen is setting it up as we speak. I thought, given the news we've received, it would be better to notify Baxter of Debbie's death in company with his brief.'

'Will you be present at the interview?'

'Damn right, I will. He can hopefully shed some light on a whole host of questions spinning uncontrollably through my mind.'

'Why would Reynolds kill her so soon after liberating her from Baxter?'

'That's another topic I'd love to get my teeth into. Maybe he had a change of heart, or perhaps he realised what a high-maintenance nightmare she was?'

'I don't know. I don't like it.'

'I haven't liked this case since day one.'

'We don't pick and choose our cases, Robbie.'

'*"It's a nice simple case,"*' he mimicked Foster saying at the outset of the investigation. '*"It'll do you good. A pleasant change of scenery..."*'

'Okay, enough of that.'

Chilcott allowed himself an impudent grin. 'To be fair,' he said, 'this is why I joined the cops in the first place. Simple cases are boring and monotonous. I love a good mystery like this. It's a game; them against me.'

'And you haven't lost yet.'

He raised himself from his seat and stood tall. 'And I have no intention of losing now.'

· · ·

8:36 p.m.

Walter Baxter was seated alongside his solicitor, Miss Holman when Chilcott arrived at Patchway custody unit. DC Allen was already there, having escorted Baxter to the unit, and he certainly appeared more chipper to see Miss Holman again.

'I've had no disclosure, officers,' Leah Holman said to them both. 'Mr Baxter has been advised not to answer any of your questions until we have full sight of the evidence you are bringing against my client.'

'I understand,' Chilcott said. 'Quite right too.'

'But the interview has started,' she complained.

Chilcott interlocked his fingers and stared reflectively at Walter Baxter sitting pensively opposite him.

Leah Holman waited expectantly. 'Well?'

'Yes, I'm fine, thanks.'

'No, I don't mean *are you* well. Are you going to provide my client and me with full evidential disclosure before this interview goes any further?'

Chilcott put a hand to his mouth and puffed out air as he gently stroked his top lip with his thumb and forefinger.

'Thing is,' he said. 'There's a bit of a problem.'

'A problem?' Miss Holman repeated.

Chilcott nodded and pinched the bridge of his nose, creating a dramatic pause to the conversation. He held the position for a count of ten and then peered back at Miss Holman.

'We don't think your client killed his wife.'

Miss Holman leaned back, obviously surprised by the revelation.

'Oh, thank God,' Baxter said, flopping his body onto the desk, with his arms outstretched before him.

Chilcott observed him quietly as the signs of relief oozed out.

'No,' Chilcott said casually, still watching Baxter draped across the tabletop. 'Unfortunately, earlier today, we were notified that Debbie had been murdered in the south of France.' He cocked his head and waited for the fallout.

Baxter slowly lifted his head. 'What?' he breathed.

'Please don't comment,' Miss Holman said and quickly making a note on her pad.

'No,' Baxter said forcefully, shoving Miss Holman's outstretched hand away from his. 'What the hell do you mean… Debbie is dead?'

Chilcott raised his brows but remained indifferent to Baxter's reaction.

'Uh, we have reports that she was murdered yesterday.'

Chilcott watched as anguish built up and passed through Baxter, much like his own sea-sickness had overcome him. He waited and watched, and then he continued. 'We were notified earlier today by our colleagues in Special Branch that detectives in Marseille were investigating the death of your wife.'

'Marseille?' Baxter questioned.

'Yes. Marseille. Why, is that significant, Mr Baxter?'

'We… we lived in Marseille. We have property and connections there.'

Chilcott covered his mouth with a hand. That didn't ring true to what Jeff Graham had told him. If they had property there, why was Dave Reynolds shelling out to keep Debbie in a hotel? He leaned back in his seat and looked up at the small video camera over the door to check the little red light was glowing.

'And do you still have properties there?'

'Yes, that's what I just said. Well, Debbie does. I bought her an apartment in the city a few years ago.'

Baxter gripped his face between his hands and spoke through his fingers. 'How? How did she die?'

'She was murdered on a boat,' Chilcott replied blandly. He waited a few seconds for the information to reach its full impact. 'On a boat, she was sharing with David Reynolds.'

Baxter unpeeled his fingers from his face, and his eyes slowly moved up to meet Chilcott's. 'David Reynolds?' he whispered.

'That's right – your old mucker from the marina.'

'He wasn't my friend,' Baxter said as pain creased his brow. His head began to rake from left to right, and his mouth tightened. 'I knew it,' he quietly seethed.

'Mr Baxter,' Leah Holman said, attempting to calm her client. 'May I suggest you do not comment any further and we listen to what the officers have to say? We can then talk about the new information privately before you make any further comments.'

'That bastard,' Baxter spat, ignoring the sage advice of his solicitor.

'We still don't know what happened,' Chilcott said. 'The French authorities haven't told us the full story, but I can tell you that David Reynolds is being held in police custody on suspicion of her murder.'

'Did she suffer?' Baxter breathed, much to the evident frustration of his solicitor.

'We don't know.'

'But presumably, there was blood?'

Chilcott brought a hand to his face. 'There was.'

Baxter locked eyes with him. 'Then surely, she suffered in some way.'

He buried his face into his hands and started to hyperventilate.

'Come on, Mr Baxter.' Miss Holman placed an arm around his shoulders and, shooting a penetrating stare at Chilcott, said, 'Let's not speculate. Let's wait until the French police have finished their investigation before we jump to conclusions.'

Baxter's reddened eyes lifted from his hands and darted around the tabletop. 'I bet she was with him. I bet she was with him when she said she was going to London—'

'Mr Baxter, please,' Miss Holman spoke over the top of him in an attempt to disrupt her client's overwhelming desire to talk.

'He killed her?'

'That's what our French colleagues believe.'

Chilcott silently watched Baxter squirm in his chair. The torment he was suffering was clear to all.

'How well did you know Dave Reynolds?' Chilcott asked after a moment or two of listening to Baxter's whimpering.

'Not as well as my fucking wife,' Baxter spluttered.

I'll give you that one.

'Did you have any indication that something was going on between them?' DC Allen asked.

Baxter wiped his nose with a tissue before speaking. 'Perhaps,' he answered as if to himself.

'How so?' Chilcott asked. 'You said at an earlier interview that you knew he fancied your wife. How did that show itself?'

'I'm not blind. I saw the way they'd looked at each other. I could see the way she became all *girly* around him.'

'He was there, the night of the party, wasn't he?'

Baxter did enough to nod once or twice.

'Did they speak together alone?'

'Not that I saw.'

'Why do you think they set you up?'

Baxter thought about the question but didn't respond.

'They planted that jewellery on your propeller to make it look like you killed your wife. Why?'

'You'd have to ask them.'

'I'd love to. But your wife is dead, and I'm not sure I'll be getting the chance to speak with David Reynolds any time soon.'

Baxter drew a hand slowly across his face.

'What should I do…?' he muttered from behind his fingers, 'about Debs? I mean, who do I need to inform about our joint accounts and stuff?'

'Don't do anything yet,' Chilcott said. 'Let's wait for a formal identification once they have a body.'

Baxter stopped squirming. 'They haven't found her body?'

Chilcott shook his head. 'Not yet.'

Baxter looked towards his solicitor as Chilcott turned studiously through the pages of his daybook.

'Um, just one question that springs to mind, Mr Baxter,'

Chilcott said, scratching the side of his temple with an index finger. 'Did you know that your wife sold her car two weeks before her disappearance in the UK?'

Baxter wiped his eyes. 'Of course, I did.'

'Did she say why? I mean, what did you think about that?'

'I wasn't happy. That car cost me an arm and a leg.'

'But she must have given you a reason for selling it at the time? We all know what that reason is now.'

'She said she would no longer need it once we had the Amel Sixty, as we'd both be spending more time at sea rather than on land. We had plans to sail to other parts of the world, so it sounded reasonable enough to me at the time.'

'Hmmm.'

Baxter rubbed the skin behind his ear. 'We planned to leave Portishead. I–I still do.'

'Where will you go?'

Baxter flicked the side of his nose with the stub of his thumb. 'I don't know? Somewhere hot and more accessible for sailing.'

'Can't say I blame you.' Chilcott looked over to his colleague. 'DC Allen, any questions for Mr Baxter before we wrap up this interview?'

DC Allen looked through his notes for a few seconds.

'When did you first notice that your wife and Dave Reynolds were paying more attention to one another?'

Baxter shook his head and glanced distantly away. 'I don't know. I suppose it wasn't long after we arrived at the marina. Could only have been weeks rather than months into our stay.'

'He was there first, though, wasn't he?' DC Allen said.

'Yes, but he only stayed at weekends. He wouldn't normally be at the marina through the week.'

'Did you ever see him during the week?' DC Allen continued.

'No–I… I don't think so.'

'Were your suspicions raised in any way before you both left to collect your new boat?'

'None more so than usual.'

'And how does that make you feel now. Now that you know they've both set you up?'

Baxter stared for a long minute at DC Allen.

'I'd kill them both, If I could.'

'Okay, that's more than enough,' Leah Holman jumped in. 'My client has been more than cooperative with you. I assume, given your earlier acknowledgement about my client's status, he will be released from this investigation, and all matters dropped without further delay?'

'Yes, I'll get onto that personally myself,' Chilcott said. 'But we may need to speak again in the coming days, so I'd request that your client doesn't sail off into the sunset just yet.'

'Of course, on the proviso that my client has his full liberty.'

'Without question,' Chilcott smiled. 'Right, Mr Baxter. Is there anything you'd like to ask us before we wrap this up?'

Baxter raised his chin and glared at Chilcott. 'Who do I sue for wrongful arrest?'

'I'll talk to you about that outside, Mr Baxter,' Miss Holman said with muted tones. 'C'mon, let's not hold these officers up from releasing you any longer than is necessary.'

Chilcott watched Baxter leave the interview room with Miss Holman, who was being watched equally as closely by DC Allen.

'What do you think?' Chilcott asked his colleague once they had left the room.

'Fit as fuck, boss.'

'Not his brief, you idiot. Baxter?'

'It's a gutter.'

'Yeah. I kind of feel for the old bugger in some small way. He loses his wife to a younger man who then turns around and kills her no sooner than he wins her freedom.'

'Yeah, but it's also quite funny in a way if you think about it?'

Chilcott turned with surprise. 'Funny, how so?'

'Baxter's minted to the max and can afford anything in life, and here is his wife who's been murdered twice. Not many people can say that.'

Chilcott pondered the statement for a second or two. 'Baxter...' he said.

DC Allen waited for Chilcott to elaborate.

'He's something of a contradiction, wouldn't you say?'

'I suppose so.'

'As you say, he's a man with wealth far greater than our entire department put together, and let's face it, he has a trophy wife that most men would be only too pleased to show off.'

Allen agreed with a firm nod of the head.

'But what's the point in having a trophy wife if you don't have anywhere to show her off? By all accounts, Baxter is an anti-social, misogynistic control freak who likes nothing more than his own company—'

'Who also happens to live on one of the most expensive yachts on the marina,' DC Allen chipped in.

'Exactly.'

Chilcott silently applauded his underling's quick grasp of where he was going with this train of thought. He leaned forwards on his elbows and steepled his fingers into a triangle.

'None of it adds up,' he said. 'None of it; the boat; the beautiful wife; the allegation… even the new murder.' He frowned. 'And what does Baxter leave us with at the very end of the interview?'

DC Allen shrugged. 'Uh…?'

'*"Who do I sue?"*'

DC Allen shook his head in misunderstanding.

'Money,' Chilcott said. 'He is trying to turn this shitty situation into a cash cow for himself. Who does that when they've just been told their wife has been murdered?'

'Walter Baxter does.'

Chilcott stood up and walked to the open door and looked down the corridor, but Baxter and his brief were already out of sight.

'In life, there are winners and losers, Richie. And Baxter is clearly a winner.'

'Despite his wife being murdered?'

Chilcott rocked his head. 'Even when his wife has been murdered.'

CHAPTER TWENTY-NINE

Back at the incident room, Chilcott peered up at the timeline. It was reading like a *Netflix* drama. What started as a simple missing person report had escalated so rapidly into a full-blown, detailed murder case with its strands of suspicion pointing, if not proving, Walter Baxter had been "the killer." As he silently considered the weave of evidence, all he could hear repeating in his head was, *who do I sue?*

Deceit had been the route of this particular evil, but not for David Reynolds. His motivation was good old-fashioned lust. So, what would drive a man to kill his prize just days after he got exactly what he wanted? It didn't make any sense? He'd gone ashore, leaving Debbie Williams aboard their luxury hired yacht, and upon his return, she had come to significant or fatal harm. It was conceivable that being so far out from shore, third parties on another boat boarded the rental, killed or maimed Debbie and took her with them. But who? And why?

Chilcott drew in a lung full of air and sighed. And what

of David Reynolds' three million Euros of cash sitting in Debbie Williams' bank account?

Who do I sue?

He went through to his office and rang Jeff Graham.

'Jeff, it's Robbie. Do you think the French will provide us with a few basic details?'

'Like what?'

'Access to Reynolds' bank account details. The bank account he set up for Debbie Williams and put the three million Euros inside. Local crime reports relating to marine crime, piracy and the like – those sorts of details.'

'It's unlikely, but I can try?'

'It's not going to interfere with their investigation. I need it for my peace of mind.'

'Robbie?'

'I just need to be sure I've covered all angles.'

'What are you hoping to see?'

'I hope to see three million Euros. It's a simple test of the account Reynolds gave in his interview. If he's telling the truth about that, then maybe he's telling the truth about the rest of his story, and he didn't kill Debbie Williams.'

'Okay. Give me a bit of time, and I'll get back to you.'

'Appreciate it.'

Chilcott called DC Allen into his office and asked him to close the door. He took general pride in having an open-door policy for his detectives, both sergeants and constables alike. It provided a safe environment for the troops to chew over any issues and concerns. Win the hearts and trust of the team and, in return, foster an environment of proud and eager bloodhounds. There was a fine line to tread, though; too relaxed and the troops may take the piss and lose their respect; too stand-offish and create a fragmented workplace where important issues might get lost in the void of non-communication.

DC Allen looked nervous as he closed the door behind him. This was the reversal of the open-door policy. Allen had been summoned and then asked to close out the rest of the team. This was for his ears only.

He edged forwards, and Chilcott didn't look up from his computer screen.

'Take a seat,' Chilcott said.

DC Allen perched tentatively on the edge of the soft, comfy chair adjacent to his boss. Chilcott continued tapping on his keyboard and didn't look over or speak to Allen for what felt like minutes.

DC Allen eventually plucked up the courage to speak. 'You wanted to speak to me, sir?'

'Yes,' Chilcott replied and finished typing an email which he then sent off with a firm press of the send button. He sat back and swivelled around to face DC Allen.

'How's it going, son?'

'Um, okay, thanks, boss?'

'Good. I've been impressed with your work over the last few days. It hasn't been an easy case to nail down.'

'Thanks, sir. I appreciate that.'

Chilcott sucked in a deep breath through his nose and huffed as he exhaled through his mouth.

'I'm sure you're as disappointed as I am to see Walter Baxter walking away from this.'

DC Allen nodded but appeared slightly confused.

'We had no choice in the matter. Whether I like it or not, we can't ignore what has happened in France.'

DC Allen nodded in agreement.

'I was just wondering if there were anything you would have done differently?'

'Sir?'

'You've been as involved with this case as anyone. Is there any element that could have been handled differently?'

'I don't think so, sir.'

'Forget rank. We all make mistakes and overlook things that maybe shouldn't have been missed.'

DC Allen shook his head. 'I uh…'

'I can't help but feel I've missed something, and you've been at my side this whole time, so I'd appreciate any feedback you might have.'

'There wasn't a thing you or anyone could have done differently, sir. If it weren't for the French incident, Walter Baxter would be facing a charge of murder.'

'And that's what bothers me, son. I wonder how many cases have resulted in conviction because a *"French incident"* didn't happen?'

DC Allen frowned. 'Are you okay, sir?'

Chilcott smiled through thin lips. 'Yes, Richie. Thank you.' He slowly massaged away building pressure in his forehead as he drifted off again into his thoughts.

'You didn't miss anything, sir… and it's been a pleasure to work alongside you.'

Chilcott gently bobbed his head. 'Thanks, Richie. Hey, can you do me a favour?'

'Of course, boss. Anything you want.'

'Give that nice young solicitor a call. You two look good together.'

CHAPTER THIRTY

Wednesday 8th September

Chilcott had endured a restless night as details of the investigation plagued his waking and sleeping mind. Similar to how a writer might get inspiration at the most inopportune of moments, so his thoughts had pulled him in a myriad of directions as various scenarios played out in full, resonating detail. But the more he thought about one such theory in particular, the closer he believed he was finally getting to the truth. It had first crossed his mind a day or two back, but he wasn't confident enough to suggest it. Now, he felt certain more than ever that this hypothesis was one worth pursuing. But first, he had to get it beyond the guardianship of his boss.

DCI Foster faced Chilcott with an open mouth. 'You're kidding, aren't you?'

'I'm not, Julie. I haven't slept all night thinking about it. Look at the evidence.'

'What evidence?'

'Exactly my point.'

'You know what I mean.'

'Look at it. Just look.'

'It's a bit far-fetched, Rob.'

'Is it? Can you honestly sit there and say with absolute certainty I'm not on to something?'

'Granted, they don't have a body yet—'

'And they won't find one for as long as they focus on Reynolds and the other evidence.'

'I don't know.'

'Tell me how I'm wrong?'

'Rob, Debbie's blood is at the scene.'

'Ever dropped a cup of tea?'

Foster cocked her head.

'It makes a hell of a mess.'

Foster nodded in agreement.

'What did Debbie do for a profession before she married Baxter?'

'She worked on boats.'

'No. She was a nurse. And what do nurses do regularly? They draw blood.'

Foster narrowed her stare.

'She would have the know-how and possibly even the tools to bleed herself enough to make it look like she'd been carved up and come through the process unscathed. It would take no more than a cup of blood to make a hell of a mess of that yacht.'

Foster scowled.

'It's a mirror image, Julie. Debbie Williams isn't dead, and she has been gifted the valuable commodity of time.'

'Time to do what?'

'Time to get away. Time to put distance between herself and Marseille. Time to move three million Euros and launder it in other commodities. Before we know it, she would have vanished along with the cash. She's probably already gone, to be honest.'

'Why would she do that?'

'Three million Euros would be enough of a *why* from where I'm sitting.'

'It's an interesting theory.'

'It's the most compelling theory, and that's why we need urgent access to the bank account holding David Reynolds' three million Euros. And I bet when we see the account, you'll find it's all gone.'

'Well, what did your mate at Special Branch say? Can't he get this?'

'He's looking into it but doesn't hold out much hope of the French authorities giving up their information that easily.'

'So, let's just say, for argument's sake, we discover the three million has moved; what then? What does that prove?'

'If it has moved after her alleged murder, it will prove that Debbie Williams is still alive. And we'll have a paper trail to lead us to her.'

The DCI looked distantly out of her window. 'And on the flip side,' she said. 'What if it's still there. What will that prove?'

'Money and greed are the motives for this crime – correction, for both of these crimes. Debbie Williams' only reason to be with Walter Baxter was for his cash and the life-style it afforded her to enjoy. There aren't many young women who live on a million-pound yacht and drive around in a flash Porsche.'

'I don't know? It's also not the kind of crime that someone can just wake up one day and decide to commit. What you are suggesting would take significant planning to execute so smoothly.'

'How about six years' worth of planning? What if she was crafting this from the moment she first met Walter Baxter at the boat show? What if she identified Dave Reynolds as a target from the moment she and Walter Baxter first arrived at Portishead Marina? Think about it. Of all the people she escapes with, it's the young, single, sole heir to a multi-million-pound pharmaceutical fortune. Baxter was older, Reynolds is younger, but the money tastes just as sweet regardless of where it's coming from.'

Foster stared blankly at Chilcott. 'Debbie Williams has no previous convictions. She's not a career criminal. You're talking about her like she's the bloody *Wolf of Wall Street* or something?'

'And people only knew about him once he was caught. Who's to say she hasn't got a list of unsolved crimes under her belt; a small deception here, a larger fraud there, all of them undetected and all of them good practice for the main event.'

'Oh, please spare me.'

'Come on, don't just dismiss it out of hand. We've had loads of frauds where we haven't been able to secure a conviction. That's not to say the crimes didn't happen. We just didn't nail them down tightly enough.'

'Ahhh, Rob… but what you're talking about is on a whole different level. You are suggesting that young woman faked her death – twice, and all in the name of money.'

'Absolutely.'

'So where is she now? Where could she possibly go undiscovered? She'd need a new identity to travel. Her accounts would need changing, and how easy is that to do in this day and age?'

'Death do us part,' Chilcott replied.

Foster shrugged. 'That's the name of the boat, so what?'

'Baxter said Debbie Williams came up with the name, despite their sailing buddies saying it was tempting fate.'

'And?'

'It's just part of the set-up. She names the boat something that instils togetherness, unity, an unbreakable bond, and then she buggers off at the first opportunity. She makes it look like she's been murdered by her husband, so in turn, he gets nicked and so creates the perfect buffer in time for her to take the plan to the next level.'

Foster pinched her lips together and pulled a pained expression.

'Come on,' Chilcott said. 'You have to admit, it's plausible?'

His boss bunched her lips tighter.

'And that's why the alleged murder in France didn't happen. She's done exactly the same again. She has created the perfect buffer in time.'

'To do what?'

'That's where I'm guessing the three million Euros will point us.'

Foster screwed her eyes and peered at Chilcott for a long

and troubled moment. 'I'll make some enquiries,' she eventually said. 'But you must promise me that if three million Euros are sitting in Debbie Williams' Marseille bank account, you leave this case well alone and step away.'

Chilcott crossed his hands over his heart.

'One last thing, Rob, before you go.' She gave him a serious look. 'You are a great detective, possibly the best I've seen. But sometimes, just sometimes, for your own sake and well-being, you've got to realise that you can't win them all.'

Chilcott stood up and walked towards the door but stopped halfway. He sniffed the air and turned to face his boss.

'You forget something, Julie. When have I ever put my well-being before the job? And when have you ever seen me lose?'

CHAPTER THIRTY-ONE

Seventy-two hours later, and David Reynolds had been offi-cially charged with the murder of Debbie Williams. He was still languishing in a sweaty French prison cell, regardless of the fact repeated dredges of the ocean bed beneath Reynolds' hired yacht had failed to locate her body or murder weapon. French investigators were satisfied that Reynolds' vessel provided enough forensic evidence in the shape of Debbie's blood and the scene of disturbance to suggest she had come to significant harm. And he was being remanded in custody for an unspecified time while he awaited trial, all of which was frustrating the hell out of Chilcott's investigation.

Sitting in his office, despite it being a Saturday and all the other detectives on his team having a well-earned day off, Chilcott stared vaguely down at the car park below. The rain was lashing down so hard he could see it bouncing back up from the rooftops of the few cars parked there, like millions of ball bearings off a trampoline. But crime, just as time, stopped for no man, and he was already onto a new case; a daytime stabbing in the Cabot Circus Shopping Centre. Thankfully, the injuries weren't as severe for the victim as they could have been. Although his officers weren't directly involved in the investigation, Chilcott was overseeing the district response, ensuring they investigated the case appropriately and with due diligence. That said, Debbie Williams remained very much in the foreground of his mind, and she was eating away at his psyche.

His desk phone rang, and he immediately picked up.

'DI Chilcott.'

'Robbie, it's Jeff Graham.'

'Hello, Jeff. What are you doing working on a Saturday? I thought you gave that lark up with your uniform.'

'Yeah, well, no rest for the wicked as they say.'

'Do you have some news for me from Marseille?' Chilcott asked in hope rather than expectation.

'As a matter of fact, I do.'

Chilcott sprang to attention and fumbled for a ballpoint pen and his daybook.

'Shoot,' he said eagerly.

'I've got those bank account details you asked me for.'

'Fantastic! How did you get them so quickly?'

'Don't ask, but you owe me.'

'Not a problem – I'll buy you a pint sometime.'

'It'll take more than a pint. I'll ping over the details. The French detectives have run their own financial checks, and I have that report too. I'll share that with you, but if anyone asks, it didn't come from me.'

'You're a star.'

'You'll see details of a holding account in Marseille belonging to Debbie Williams containing the large cash deposit from David Reynolds. You'll see that entire amount was sent to another account along with several other smaller deposits in recent days and months.'

'To the same onward account?'

'Yes.'

'Is there a name attached to that account?'

'It's a French-held business account.'

'Can't we just dig deeper to see who runs the show?'

'It's not the same as conducting a Companies House enquiry. I'm afraid there's a little more to it.' Graham paused. 'But…'

'But?'

'You're not going to believe what these reports show.'

'Come on, Jeff, don't keep me in suspenders.'

'The source destination is a Credit Agricole account on the island of Réunion in the Indian Ocean.'

'Never heard of it.'

'It's close to Mauritius.'

'Oh, okay, I've heard of that. It's a place I can't afford to visit.'

'Yeah, me too, anyway, it's not a new account, but the entire three million Euros was wired remotely on Tuesday the sixth.'

'That's after Deb Williams was murdered for the second time.'

'That's correct.'

Chilcott rubbed his jawline as he digested the information.

'So, let me get this right to make sure I've interpreted this correctly. David Reynolds says in the interview that he gifted three million Euros to Debbie Williams and that sat in a Marseille bank account in her name until they both arrived sometime before Monday the fifth of September.'

'Correct.'

'She then disappears and is suspected of being murdered by Reynolds, who in turn gets arrested for said murder. The location of her body remains outstanding. And, in the meantime, the three million Euros gets transferred from her account in Marseille to another account held on an island in the Indian Ocean. Is that right?'

'That's about the size of it.'

'Fantastic.'

'But we don't yet know who controls the bank account on the island of Réunion.'

'You might not, but I sure as hell think I do.'

Chilcott ended the call and rushed to the DCI's office in the hope that she was also at work on a day off. He was in luck.

Tapping loudly on the door, he entered.

'Julie, have you got a moment, please?'

'Yes, do come in, Robbie. Couldn't stay away either? Everything okay with the Cabot job?'

'Yeah, yeah, that's all fine. Look, I'm not here about that. I've just heard from Jeff Graham; David Reynolds put the three million into a holding account in Marseille controlled by Debbie Williams. That three million was then transferred to an as yet unidentified account after Debbie Williams was allegedly murdered, for a second time.'

The DCI leaned slowly into the back of her chair.

'Close the door, would you.'

'There's no one else here, Julie. It's just the two of us.'

Foster studied his face.

'It's her. I know it is,' he said.

'Who?'

'Debbie bloody Williams, that's who. She's mucked up this time. She should have kept it there for longer. We may never have known.'

The DCI held up a pair of pausing hands. 'Just wait a moment.'

She lowered her hands, creating a calming minute to think.

'Who has control of that Marseille account?'

'Debbie Williams.'

'Okay,' the DCI said, trying her best to dampen Chilcott's exuberance. 'Does anyone else have legal access to it?'

'I don't know.'

'And where is this other account held?'

'You're going to love this.' Chilcott moved towards her desk. 'Can I just use your keyboard?'

'For what?'

'You'll see.'

She looked at him suspiciously but then wheeled her chair back to allow him to lean over her desk and tap something into the keyboard. A map came up, and Chilcott drilled down to a small island in the middle of the ocean.

'There,' he said, clicking the mouse button in triumph.

The DCI leaned forwards and stared at the screen. 'Réunion?'

'It's an island in the Indian Ocean, not far from Mauritius.'

Foster dipped her head and looked at Chilcott from beneath the lids of her eyes. 'Mauritius?' she repeated.

'No – Réunion. Mauritius is the next closest island.'

He prodded the screen with his fingertip.

'That's where we'll find Debbie Williams.'

Foster didn't speak and moved closer towards the screen.

'Robbie?'

'I don't lose,' he said, folding his arms defiantly.

'And you don't have holidays on the MCIT budget either.'

'Come on. Look at the evidence.'

'Circumstantial.'

'No, it's not. It's the strongest link we've had since this entire debacle of an investigation started.'

'I need more.'

'And I'll get you more. Jeff is sending over the French financial reports. You'll be able to see for yourself. The Réunion account has been open and lying dormant for two years until money started flowing through several months ago when Reynolds started feeding Debbie Williams' Marseille account.'

'I'll go back to a comment I made to you days ago; it's all a bit too... *Hollywood*, this theory of yours.'

'That may well be the case, but fact is often stranger than fiction. We have to be open to the possibility that she is still alive and living the high life on some paradise island.'

'Online financial crime occurs all over the world. Debbie Williams doesn't have to be in the same location as the deposited funds. If anything, that would be a stupid move.'

'It would. And perhaps it would be the stupid kind of move that gives the cops a break they've been looking for.'

'Why would she plan her death so meticulously here, only to slip up at the vital time?'

'As far as she's concerned, the French police have their man in custody for her murder. She's dead, and she's also scot-free. Probably got a new name, probably already trapped some poor loaded bastard, and she'll take him for everything he's got in the future too.'

Foster sighed and folded her arms.

Chilcott could see from the amount she was blinking that she was coming around to his way of thinking.

'I don't know,' she said, not immediately giving him the satisfaction of her agreement.

'The French detectives aren't going to pursue the case. They think she's dead. It's up to us to finish this.'

Foster glanced around the room at anything other than him.

'There's one thing Debbie Williams didn't bank on.'

Foster looked back at him.

'And what might that be, Robbie?'

'Me.'

CHAPTER THIRTY-TWO

Even though DCI Foster seemed to be softening, Chilcott felt the need to turn the screw still further.

'I'm not just talking about me going. Richie Allen needs to come too. We've both been had over, and it will be good for the youngster to see justice prevail.'

Foster laughed aloud. 'Oh please, spare me the melodramatics, Robbie.'

Chilcott grinned. 'You know it makes sense, Julie.'

'How much are tickets going to cost to send you two jokers on a jolly to paradise?'

'Don't worry about a small detail like that. Think about the kudos we'd get for smashing an international money laundering syndicate.'

'Now you're really pushing it, Robbie,' Foster glared. 'We aren't talking syndicates. We're talking about a strong, young, resourceful woman who has got the better of you.'

'Ah! So, you finally admit that I'm right?'

Foster began to reply and then clearly realised Chilcott was playing her.

'Get me some prices for tickets, and I'll consider going to the detective chief super' about it all. In the meantime, you and I are going back to see Walter Baxter. Let's run your theory past him and see what he thinks about it? Who knows, he might even have supporting evidence for your *hair-brained* idea?'

'You want to come too? You are suddenly taking this seriously.'

Foster began to bob her head but then slowly started to shake it.

'I can't decide?' she said.

'Can't decide on what?'

'Whether getting you back into this department was a good or bad thing?'

Chilcott laughed. 'What would you do without me?'

Foster planted him with an uncompromising stare. 'For one, I'd sleep at night!'

It was dusk at the marina, and the sky was low with foreboding dark clouds. The earlier rain showers had pushed through, and now the paved walkways around the edge of the marina were wet and shiny. Rain canopies of the motorboats were fixed down tightly, and Chilcott imagined anyone living onboard their boats would be inside with a warm brew in their hands. The manager's office was closed for the night, but Chilcott had the code for the security gates, and he and DCI Foster made their way towards jetty seven without seeing another soul.

As they neared the end of the jetty, Chilcott could see

illumination from within Trevor and Jane Hicks' boat, but there was no light from inside Walter Baxter's yacht.

As DCI Foster took a closer look, Chilcott checked the time. It was only 8.11 p.m.

He removed his mobile phone. 'I'll give Baxter a call and ask him to meet us here.'

But the phone rang off immediately, without an answer.

'Could you hear his phone ringing?' Chilcott called out to DCI Foster, who was now leaning as far over the jetty edge as was comfortable.

'No, nothing from the inside.'

'You won't get him,' a voice came from behind.

Chilcott turned with a start. It was Trevor Hicks wrapped tightly in a camouflaged surf-style Dryrobe.

'I saw him leave here two days ago. He hasn't come back.'

'Leave?' Chilcott said. 'Did he have anything with him?'

Trevor Hicks nodded. 'He certainly did. Two suitcases and a holdall.'

Chilcott frowned, and DCI Foster joined alongside him.

'DCI Foster,' she said, extending her hand to shake.

'Oh, sorry,' Chilcott said, breaking from a momentary gaze. 'This is Trevor Hicks, whose name you'll know from our enquiries.'

'Ah, yes, a pleasure to meet you, Mr Hicks. What were you saying, Walter Baxter has gone somewhere?'

'I assumed you lot knew. I guessed you'd given him the green light to go.'

Chilcott cut his boss a sideways glance.

'I just tried calling him, but he didn't answer. Any ideas where he may have gone?' Chilcott asked Trevor.

'Nope, but as I say, he wasn't packing light.'

'You've known of him for a while now. Have you seen him do this before; leave with so many belongings?'

'No, but good riddance to the bloke. I hope he stays away. He's ruined what was once a great place to live. Now even Jane wants us to move somewhere else.'

'Don't,' Chilcott answered quickly. 'Trust me, you're in the best place here, and Walter Baxter really isn't a concern any of you need to have.'

Trevor closed the gap between them and spoke in a quieter voice.

'What, you mean he didn't kill Debs?'

Chilcott rocked his head. 'All I'm saying is, things are rarely as they seem.'

Hicks scratched behind his head and scowled.

'Do you know if Simon Dupont-Avery is aware that Baxter has gone somewhere?'

'I wouldn't know? But to be honest, all he needs to worry about is if the mooring fees are paid. We can come and go on land wherever and whenever we like.'

'Hmmm,' Chilcott mused, staring off distantly. 'Okay, thanks for the info. Would you do me a favour and let me know if Baxter returns?'

'Yeah, of course.'

'You've still got my business card?'

'It's never far from Jane's side.'

Chilcott smiled. 'It's good to know someone wants me.'

'Actually, I want to thank you for what you've done. You've driven him away, and that's all any of us wanted.'

Chilcott lingered on Hicks' face for a moment.

'Right,' DCI Foster said. 'There's not much point in us being here any longer. Perhaps we'll get off home tonight.'

She thanked Trevor Hicks and grabbed Chilcott's arm. 'Come on, Robbie, let's get going.'

Driving back to the office, DCI Foster tried Walter Baxter's phone a further four times, but the phone was switched off each time.

'Why do you think he's not answering?' she asked.

'I don't know. But I don't like it.'

'Where was he going with his bags?'

'I don't know that either, but I suggest we find out.'

'How are we going to do that?'

Chilcott didn't answer, but his mind was formulating all sorts of undesirable scenarios.

•

CHAPTER THIRTY-THREE

Monday 13th September

7:59 a.m.

Chilcott had already been in the office for over an hour. He must have looked at his desk phone a hundred times as he waited impatiently to phone Simon Dupont-Avery. He'd done his homework, the tide had been low, so there wasn't any point in calling before now, as Dupont-Avery wouldn't have been required to operate the lock gates.

He watched the second-hand tick beyond the thirty, and so began his countdown. And on the stroke of eight, he dived in his seat and punched in the number.

'Good morning, Portishead Marina. How may I help you?' the familiar and breezy voice of Dupont-Avery said.

'Good morning,' Chilcott answered. 'It's DI Robbie Chilcott here.'

'Oh, good morning, Detective Chilcott.'

'How are you?'

'Um, I'm fine. Thank you for asking.'

'I came down to the marina on Saturday evening, but unfortunately, you weren't around.'

'No, I was actually out celebrating my wife's birthday.'

'Lovely – I hope you had a nice time.'

'It was very pleasant, thank you. We went to the theatre—'

'Anyway,' Chilcott said over the top of Dupont-Avery, not giving two shits about his theatre experience. 'I let myself onto the pontoon, and uh… well, I was really there to speak with Walter Baxter.'

'Ah.'

'Ah?'

'Uh, Mr Baxter won't be there.'

'So I discovered. Any idea where he has gone? He's not answering his phone.'

'No, sorry. But Walter has asked me to email him should a buyer put in an offer.'

Chilcott didn't speak.

'Hello?' Dupont-Avery said.

'Just run that by me one more time; he's putting his boat up for sale?'

'His yacht, yes. I'd imagine it will go very quickly; he's offering it at a ridiculously low price.'

Chilcott fell numb and glanced out of the window as he attempted to correlate the information.

'In fact, I have already emailed three potential purchasers who I know for certain are specifically looking for an Amel.'

'How much?'

'I'm sorry?'

'How much has he put it up for?'

'Ah, I really don't think—'

'Just tell me how much he's put it on for – it's not a difficult question.'

Dupont-Avery stalled for a beat but then answered.

'Seven hundred and fifty-thousand pounds.'

'Seven-fifty, and he bought it just over a month ago for over one million?'

'One million two hundred and seventy-five-thousand Euros.'

Chilcott's eyes glazed over, and he ended the call.

'Delay the briefing,' he told DCI Foster, interrupting a conversation she was having with one of the team.

She looked at him, about to scald him for the interruption, but thought better of it when she saw the look on his face.

'Thank you, Sam. We'll chat again later.'

The detective left the room, giving Chilcott a quiet, 'Morning sir,' on her way out.

Foster looked at her DI, and her shoulders sank.

'Problems?' she asked.

'I've just got off the phone to Simon bloody Dupont-sodding-Avery, and he's just told me *Death Do Us Part* is up for sale.'

'What?'

'Not only that, Baxter is practically giving it away.'

DCI Foster had a deep look of concern ridged into her brow.

'Right, calm down and tell me exactly what he said.'

'He's selling his fucking boat. He's gone.'

'I don't understand?'

'He bought it for one million, two hundred and seventy-five-thousand Euros a matter of weeks ago, and he's now selling for seven hundred and fifty grand.'

'That's about right, isn't it?'

'You haven't been abroad recently. The exchange rate with the Euro is practically one-for-one these days. That's a hell of a loss.'

'Why would he do that?'

Chilcott shook his head. 'I'm not getting a warm and fuzzy feeling about this.'

DCI Foster stood up from her chair.

'Okay, let's think laterally about this information.'

Chilcott folded his arms.

'We don't know where he's gone, and we don't know why he's selling his boat? We can only assume it's because we have told him his wife is dead.'

'Or something much worse.'

DCI Foster stared at Chilcott.

'What if he knows she's in Réunion?' Chilcott said. 'What if he's going out there to track her down?'

DCI Foster's eyes flickered. 'You don't think he's…?'

'She's ruined his life. Remember what he said in his interview *"I'd kill them both".*'

'Oh shit. Have you got his number to hand?'

'Of course.' Chilcott thumbed through the pages of his

daybook and read out the number as Foster dialled it in her desk phone and put the loudspeaker on full volume.

This time, Baxter's phone rang, but Foster ended the call after only three rings.

She tapped in another eleven-digit number and waited.

Chilcott pulled a face, and then Foster's own mobile phone began ringing in her pocket to the tune of *That Don't Impress Me Much*, by Shania Twain.

Just as quickly, she ended the call and looked at him with hollow eyes.

'It's a different ring tone. He's already abroad.'

'I do not like this one little bit,' Chilcott glowered.

'Have we documented his passport number?'

'Yep.'

'Get on to your mate over at the branch. Let's find out exactly where he's gone. You have my authority to do whatever checks are necessary to find Walter Baxter's current location.'

Chilcott stormed out of the office with a visceral purpose and returned in less than fifteen minutes.

Walter Baxter had flown from Bristol Airport to Paris on Thursday evening. From there, he had taken a direct flight with Air France to Réunion on Saturday, arriving in the small hours of Sunday.

'He was on the flight when we were trying to call him,' Chilcott said. 'That's why his phone was turned off.'

DCI Foster sat flaccidly and with an open mouth.

'How did he know she would be there?' she finally asked.

'Beats me? Perhaps they talked about it in the past. Maybe Debbie always said it was a place she'd love to visit or live? Either way, I'm now sure she's there, and so is he.'

DCI Foster cradled her forehead in her hand and didn't speak for what seemed like minutes.

'Okay – expedite a triangulation on Baxter's phone,' she said. 'If he's on that island, I want to know exactly where he is.'

'It's not a huge island. I'll see what I can do.'

'Did Jeff say if there was any accommodation booked through the airline?'

'No, that was all he had.'

'Get on to High Tech Crime, I don't care how they do it, but I want those triangulation results by lunchtime.'

'Sorted.'

'I'll speak directly with Jeff Graham and see who we need to notify over in Réunion. We've got to stop Walter Baxter from killing his wife.' She gave Chilcott an ironic stare. 'Again!'

They got what they were looking for before 2 p.m. Réunion Island was less than one thousand square miles in size but had a population of nearly eight hundred and fifty-thousand people or roughly a quarter more than the population of Bristol. That was a lot of phones to service, and their triangulation narrowed the search down to a region west of the capital, Saint-Denis.

Chilcott, Foster and DC Allen stood in his office as Chilcott tapped the details into a google search browser.

'There,' he said. 'That's where he is.' He tapped the screen, and the others looked in closer.

'He'll be at the marina, I guarantee it.'

'Ponton Darse de Plaisance Port Quest,' Foster read from the screen. 'I'll ask Special Branch to notify the local cops, and we'll see if he's booked into any hotels.'

Foster drilled down deeper into the results.

'It's perfect,' she said. 'Close to the main city, transport systems—'

'Banks,' Chilcott said over the top of her.

Foster looked up from the computer screen back at Chilcott.

'What if he's not going there to kill her?' he said. 'Saint-Denis is the location of the bank containing David Reynolds' three million Euros. What if he's going out there to live with her?'

Foster straightened up. 'I hadn't thought of that.'

'The way this investigation has gone, I wouldn't put it past him.'

'I need to call Jaz Chowdhury,' Foster said. 'He's going to run the department for a few days.'

Chilcott raised a brow.

'What, you think I'm letting you two go out there alone?' She looked at the paradise image of Réunion on Chilcott's computer screen. 'Someone has to look after you.'

CHAPTER THIRTY-FOUR

Tuesday 14th September

Chilcott arrived at the airport first, followed soon after by
DCI Foster, who was in company with Detective Superin-
tendent Jeff Graham, who had met her outside the terminal.
They had arranged to all meet beside the Bureau De
Change desk before checking in together.

'Where is Richie?' Chilcott said, checking his watch.

In reality, they still had loads of time before the flight
was due to take off, but Chilcott liked to sample a fully-
loaded cooked breakfast before he flew, and DC Allen's
tardiness was narrowing his eating time.

Even though the schools were back from their summer
holidays, Bristol Airport always seemed to be busy, and the
easyJet queues were already long, despite the time only
being seven fifteen in the morning. One large group of lads
had already caught Chilcott's attention. Going from their
loud regional accents, large kit bags and general over-

exuberance, they were a touring Welsh rugby team. Lads being lads, they were by far the loudest group at the terminal, and one of them in particular, with a personalised shirt, aptly named *"Nobber"*, was doing a fine job of pissing Chilcott off.

DC Allen walked in through the swivel doors and made towards the desk. Chilcott looked him up and down and turned to DCI Foster with raised eyes.

He was wearing camo-cargo shorts, a white T-shirt, white Nike trainers, and a pair of Ray-Bans slung on top of his head.

'All right, Richie?' Chilcott asked.

'Hi, boss. Sorry, I'm a bit late. My bus was delayed from the car park.'

Chilcott gave him another up and down. 'I see you didn't get the email about the dress code.'

'Email? No, sorry, I—'

'He's joking,' DCI Foster said. 'But remember, we are on work business, so I do hope you've packed a suit?'

'Um, yes, Ma'am. I just thought as we were travelling—'

'It's okay, but perhaps wear your suit for the final leg from Paris.'

'Yes, Ma'am,' DC Allen said, his cheeks flushing red.

'Right, shall we get ourselves checked in?' Chilcott said, picking up his suitcase.

'I've had a word with the guys on security,' Jeff Graham said. 'You can go through priority searching, just drop my name, and they'll know who you are.'

'Any chance of a free pint too?' Chilcott asked.

'That's pushing it.'

'I thought you were coming too?' DCI Foster asked him.

'Afraid not, but we have a colleague based in Paris. They'll tag along on the final stretch, just to have a Special Branch presence, in case there are any problems on the French side. They won't interfere with your investigation but may be very handy to have along from a diplomatic standpoint.'

'I'm sorry you're not coming too,' Chilcott said, shaking his friend's hand. 'We appreciate your assistance.'

'I'll be here when you get back. There will be two interview-style rooms set aside once you get through passport control, and I'll meet you off the plane so you don't have to wait in line with any prisoners you may have.'

'I'm not coming back unless I've got a prisoner attached to my wrist,' Chilcott said.

'You bloody are,' DCI Foster corrected him. 'If either of them has already gone from Réunion, we are coming straight home.'

They said their goodbyes, checked in, and an hour and a half later, they were on the plane to Paris.

Chilcott was grateful for it being only a short flight time. Out of the three of them, he seemed to bag the short straw. They hadn't paid the extra to sit together, and as a result, he was alongside a very talkative and more than a slightly eccentric older woman with a large, oversized floppy sun hat that kept prodding him in the side of the head each time she turned to talk with him. He considered telling her to piss off to another seat but thought better of it and instead closed his eyes and pretended to fall asleep against the window panelling, but that didn't seem to stop the older woman from perpetually rabbiting on.

They arrived in Paris at the expected time, found their

way to the budget hotel at Charles de Gaulle airport, and arranged to meet up later at 6 p.m. for dinner. Jeff Graham had also agreed with the Special Branch operative who lived in Paris to meet them at the hotel's dining hall.

The room was small but comfortable enough; after all, it was only a short stop-over, and all he needed was a bed and bathroom facilities.

Chilcott kicked off his work shoes and lounged on the bed as he flicked through the TV channels in the hope of finding something in spoken English.

Before he knew it, five o'clock had come around, and he had a quick freshen up before heading down to the bar.

Apart from an attractive bobbed-brunette, he was alone sitting on a stool at the end of the bar. He noticed her reaction to his voice when he asked for a beer, and he doffed her a nod and smile.

'Evening,' he said, not knowing if she understood what he was saying.

'Good evening,' she replied in a strong French accent and lifted her glass of sparkling water in a greeting.

Chilcott looked around at the empty seats and back at the woman who smiled at him again.

'Do you mind if I pull up a stool?'

She had a look of confusion until he picked up one of the metal legged stools to show what he meant.

'Ah oui,' she said and slid her drink to the other side of her in a symbolic display of agreement.

The barman pulled Chilcott's drink, and he tried not to visibly cringe as he then took seven Euros fifty for the pleasure.

'You here on holiday?' the woman asked.

'Me? No. I'm here for work.' He lifted his glass and said, 'Cheers.'

'Santé,' the woman said, lifting her glass.

'How about you?' Chilcott asked. 'Do you live in Paris?'

'Yes.'

'Sadly, I'm moving on again tomorrow, but it would have been nice to take a look around. It's my first time here.'

'Ah, never mind,' she said. 'You can come again one day.'

Chilcott smiled politely but didn't imagine that was going to happen anytime soon. Other than on the return journey, when he hoped to be attached to a prisoner or two.

'What you do, for work?' the woman asked.

'Oh, boring stuff,' he said, wafting the question away with a hand.

'Ah.'

'How about you, do you work in Paris?'

'Oui.'

He looked over his shoulder and then down at his watch.

'Are you meet someone?'

'Yes, my work friends.'

'Ah.'

The woman turned her stool to face back towards the bar, and she took a sip from her drink.

'We...uh... we are having dinner here tonight.'

'Oh,' the woman said, taking note with a lift of her brow.

'It's not bad, is it, the food here?'

'Non, non, non.'

'Sorry, I just noticed you reacted when I said we were eating here tonight.'

'No, it's very good. Excellent French food.'

'Ah, great. I love a good steak.'

'It's just, I too meet someone here for food.' She gave him a long look.

'Someone English.'

Chilcott recoiled slightly and looked around the woman's face.

'You're not, um… I hope you don't mind me asking this, but you're not part of the police here, are you?'

She smiled. 'Shilcott?'

'Chilcott. Yes – wow! You are the Special Branch officer we're here to meet?'

The woman looked towards the barman and subtly dropped her head.

'Oh, sorry,' he said, realising his voice must have been relatively animated. 'I didn't mean to—'

'I wasn't expecting such a handsome man.'

'Me? No – really?' he asked, reaching for the tie he wasn't even wearing.

'I'm sorry, and you are?'

'Bette.'

'Bette. That's a lovely name.'

'Thank you.'

'Don't be shy, Robbie, get them in,' a voice came from behind. It was DCI Foster and DC Allen.

'I see it didn't take you long to make a menace of yourself,' Foster said beneath her breath as she came behind and rested her arms on the bar on the other side of him.

'Uh, this is Bette. She's who we are supposed to be meeting tonight.'

DCI Foster greeted her with a warm handshake and introduced her to DC Allen.

'Ah, Monsieur Shilcott has been very nice to me.'

'I'm sure Monsieur Shilcott has,' Foster said, giving him a teacher-like look.

They ordered their drinks and took them to a table at the edge of the restaurant, where they discussed the plan for the following day and about what they would do once they reached Réunion. It transpired that Bette was familiar with the island, having holidayed there with her parents many times through the eighties. She had already been in contact with the local Police Nationale, and they were going to greet them from the airport and take them to the port where they would stay in a local hotel, while further enquiries could be made regarding the location of Baxter and potentially Debbie Williams.

The meal over, it was time to go their separate ways, but through the course of the evening, Chilcott had discovered two things: firstly, there was no foregone conclusion that their plan would work, and secondly, he seriously had the hots for Bette.

CHAPTER THIRTY-FIVE

Friday 17th September

09:30 a.m.

They arranged to gather in the small foyer at the hotel they were all staying. It was the first full day they had with business on their minds. The overnight flight from Paris had taken just over eleven hours, and yesterday was written off as a result. Chilcott didn't sleep during the flight, and his limbs ached from altitude and inactivity. He managed to catch up on five hours kip, despite the thin brown drapes doing little to prevent light from pouring into his room. Bette had told him September was a good month to visit Réunion as it was cooler and dryer than the later months. But with a ceiling fan doing little except push 80-degree air around, when he awoke, he had to peel himself away from the bedsheets. They had enjoyed a relaxing evening meal, talking about anything but the job at hand. They even managed to see off three bottles of the local red wine, which to Chilcott's pleasure was probably better than wine he bought for himself back home, but for a fraction of the price. It helped that Bette was with them; she conversed in the local dialect of French Creole and seemed to have a good measure of what was going on. Chilcott had never been to this part of the world, but he liked it a lot.

Foster, Allen and Bette were already waiting for him as he stepped out from the old-fashioned lift. Chilcott had chosen to ditch his suit jacket, but he was still wearing a shirt and tie, and the cloth stuck to his back as he walked towards the others.

'How are we all?' he asked.

'Good thanks,' Foster replied. 'Sleep okay?'

'Yeah, you know, I'm not used to the heat.'

Bette laughed. 'Welcome to Réunion. You'll get used to it.'

'I wish I was here for long enough to get used to it.'

'Maybe you come back for a holiday?'

'I'd like that.' He held her gaze for a little longer than was necessary.

'So, what's the plan?' Foster asked Chilcott.

'First, I need coffee. Let's grab a brew and go through a plan of attack.'

They walked through to a separate lounge area with several large ceiling fans spinning at a high velocity above their heads. The walls were dark varnished wood, and the décor was a throwback to the seventies, but the coffee tasted superb.

Chilcott spread several sheets out on a small round table beside them.

'These are the bank account details obtained by special branch. What I propose is that we go to this bank, the bank where Reynolds deposited the three million Euros, and we obtain an up-to-date report and try to establish who is in control of any movement.'

'I doubt it will be that simple,' Foster said.

'But we've got our secret weapon.' Chilcott looked to Bette. 'Do you think you could wrangle that information for us?'

'I don't know. I don't have jurisdiction here.'

'But we could try?'

Bette rolled her head and shrugged. 'We can try.'

'You seemed to get on well with the police commander yesterday,' Foster said.

'Yes,' Bette said.

'Maybe we should go back to the station and see if they could help us?'

'Yes, okay.'

'What are you hoping to see?' Foster asked Chilcott.

'I'd like to see some local transactions. Perhaps a hotel charge or something like that. It's a small island.' Chilcott prodded a colour tourist leaflet showing the coastal town to the west of their location. 'We already know from Baxter's phone triangulation that he's in this area. They have to buy something at some time, and he's unlikely to use his UK bank account through fear of being located.'

'And as far as Debbie Williams is concerned, she's home and dry,' DC Allen added.

'That's right. I think we should concentrate on getting a result at this bank. We know they're here or have been here. Let's track their movements from their spending and see if we can identify any specific locations where we can follow up with CCTV enquiries.'

'We'll need the local police to assist us,' Foster said. 'I'm not comfortable doing this without their authority.'

Chilcott looked to Bette, who nodded. 'I can call them. I have the commander's number.'

'Good,' Chilcott said. 'I've got a good feeling about this.'

CHAPTER THIRTY-SIX

They waited at the lobby for almost two hours before several local police officers, including the station commander, arrived to take them to the Credit Agricole bank in the island capital, Saint-Denis. It was a short journey from the hotel, which was just as well, given the bank was due to close for the entire weekend at 4:00 p.m.

The seven of them entered the modern open-plan foyer, and to Chilcott's delight, the air conditioning kept the temperature to an icy-cold and far more comfortable level.

The officer in charge had called ahead, and the most senior staff members at the bank were waiting to greet them and quickly whisk them away to a side room.

Bette spoke first and explained the reason for their visit, giving Foster, Chilcott and Allen an interpreter-style summary of the conversation as she went along.

The manager looked at the British officers with a concerned expression and then spoke to Bette in an animated fashion.

'Everything all right?' Chilcott asked. 'What did he just say?'

'He says you have no jurisdiction to obtain such information.'

Chilcott and Foster gave each other a look that each of them understood.

'Tell him he might wish to reconsider,' Chilcott said. 'The bank wouldn't want to go through the stress of a thorough and detailed audit of their business actions, knowing as we do, this bank has authorised three million Euros worth of fraudulent money.'

Bette relayed the message, and to Chilcott's surprise, the police commander followed that up with his own words of advice. Chilcott had no idea what he said, but it seemed to do the trick.

'He says he will show you information on the screen, but he will not provide you with a hard copy of anything to do with the account.'

'So long as we can make our notes, I'm happy with that,' Chilcott said.

After a further short conversation between Bette and the manager, all police officers were on the other side of the desk and looking down at the computer screen. The manager brought up the relevant account details.

Looking closer, the manager turned to the police commander and said something that he then fed back to Bette.

'It appears a large quantity of the finances has moved,' Bette said.

'Where?'

'He doesn't know. He would have to check on another system.'

'Is there any recent activity on the account from the island – we're talking over the last few days?'

Bette asked the question, and the manager pulled up a detailed statement and pointed down the list as he relayed the information to Bette.

'Yes,' she said.

Chilcott balled his fists in triumph.

'There is a cash withdrawal from an ATM at Ponton Darse de Plaisance Port Quest.'

'That's where we had the phone triangulation on Baxter's mobile.'

Foster nodded. 'How much was taken out?'

'Three hundred Euros.'

'When?'

The manager pointed something out on the screen to Bette, who then replied.

'That was the first recent transaction, but there have been others since.'

'Where?' Chilcott said leaning closer to the screen.

The manager pointed to the screen and relayed something to Bette.

'It looks like they have been eating at the same restaurant for the past three days, including earlier today.'

'That's it. That's how we get Baxter and Williams,' Chilcott said with excitement.

'Where is it?' Foster asked.

The manager, police commander and Bette had a three-way conversation and then Bette fed it back in English.

'They are on the west coast at a place called Saint-Gilles.

They have been at a hotel where it seems they have eaten lunch each day since Thursday.'

'Do we think they are staying at the hotel?'

'I don't know. There are no other payments.'

'What time are the transactions made? Can we see that, please?'

The manager wrote the details onto a sheet of paper and handed it to Chilcott.

'Thursday was 1:42 p.m., Friday was 1:57 p.m., and today was 1:37 p.m.'

He looked at DCI Foster and DC Allen with wide eyes.

'What are the odds on them being there between one and two o'clock tomorrow?'

'That'll be fifty-fifty, boss,' DC Allen said.

'That'll do me just fine, Richie. Can you ask the commander if we can borrow a few of his team to go to this hotel tomorrow, please, Bette?'

She spoke to the police commander, and he willingly agreed. Chilcott shook his hand and thanked him and then shook the hands of each of the other officers and the bank manager in turn.

He left the bank feeling a mixture of excitement, apprehension and wishing the next twenty-two hours would fly by in a flash.

CHAPTER THIRTY-SEVEN

Saturday 18th September

11:40 a.m.

The hotel was located on the seafront, backing directly onto the white sand of the picturesque bay. With a breezy open-plan lobby and a single large circular reception desk in the middle of the room, remaining covert here would be challenging. They still didn't know if Baxter and Williams were staying at the hotel. All they knew was that they liked to dine here at lunchtimes. Even though none of the officers had met Debbie Williams, Walter Baxter had been face-to-face with Chilcott and Allen. An overt police presence from the local constabulary might spook Williams and Baxter, but two women, DCI Foster and Bette, could come and go with impunity as two restaurant guests. It wasn't an ideal plan, but it was all they had at short notice.

As Julie Foster and Bette went into the hotel, Chilcott, Allen, the police commander and six of his team remained several buildings away and out of sight. Waiting was the most challenging part of any operation like this. With so many variables for it to fail, Chilcott knew they had one shot at success.

It was nearly thirty minutes before Foster and Bette returned to Chilcott's rendezvous location.

'Tell me the news,' Chilcott said impatiently as the two women approached.

'They can't tell us if Williams and Baxter are guests of the hotel.'

'Did they try?'

'Yes, of course, they tried. There are no staying guests in their names.'

'Do you think they're using aliases?' DC Allen asked.

'More than likely,' Foster said. 'But the good news is, Bette and I booked in for lunch at 1:00 p.m.'

'Lucky you,' Chilcott replied. 'Do you think they twigged you are cops?'

'No. We said we were friends of Williams and Baxter and thought they were staying, but we could be wrong. I don't think we gave anything away.'

Chilcott bunched his lips.

'So, here's the plan. Bette and I will arrive ten minutes early and see if we can have a table with a clear view of the rest of the diners. When Williams and Baxter arrive, I'll contact you by phone, and you can come en masse to arrest them.'

'Sounds like a plan.'

'Better still, lunch service is between 12:30 and 2:00 p.m., so we know we have a narrow window.'

'What's the time now?' DC Allen asked.

'12:07.'

Chilcott sighed. 'Good. Bette, could you update the commander and make sure he's okay to hang around?'

Bette did as requested, and although the police commander agreed, his body language betrayed a growing impatience.

12:51 p.m.

They found a table perfect for observing the other restaurant patrons. A wide wooden boardwalk ran from the hotel's rear exit in a straight line down to the water's edge. Tables with sun canopies made of a rigid weave were situated left and right of the walkway. A classic-looking paradise beach bar had its own separate chill-out area off to the side, and a warm on-shore breeze ruffled the brilliant white cloth of the tables. The restaurant was by no means full, but at least a dozen tables were occupied.

Bette ordered drinks and a 'light' lunchtime snack for them both, as Foster took in each of the tables like a hawk.

She had seen photos of both Williams and Baxter. Debbie Williams had a long blonde shock of hair, and Baxter, well, he looked like a serial killer. She was confident they would stand out. The problem was, they didn't.

Chilcott had already text three times for an update. She had declined to reply, but with the clock now beyond 1:40 p.m., Foster was resigned to the fact Williams and Baxter weren't coming.

Had they seen the officers? Did they recognise Foster in some way? She was wearing a large floppy sunhat and sixties-style sunglasses, so that was unlikely. Even her friends back home would struggle to recognise her in this situation.

She broke the news to Chilcott with a text. His response was immediate and a single four-letter word.

Bette paid the bill, and at 2:20 p.m., they re-joined Chilcott and the other officers.

Chilcott was pacing like a hungry lion.

'We need to go back to the bank,' he said. 'I need to know where they've gone today?'

'The bank is closed until Tuesday,' Bette said.

'That's no good. We're on a plane on Monday evening,' Foster cut in.

'Change it. Change the flights,' Chilcott said quickly.

'We can't change the flights, Robbie. This isn't Heathrow. We are on that flight, whether we've got Williams and Baxter or not.'

'This is bullshit,' Chilcott shouted. 'I can't fucking believe our luck. We were so close.'

Bette came up to Chilcott and put an arm around his waist. 'It's okay,' she said softly. 'We have tomorrow.'

Chilcott looked into her deep brown eyes, and her soothing voice pacified him in an instant.

'They may be sight-seeing today,' she continued. 'If they

are still here, then I am sure they will come back to this restaurant.'

'We'll do the same plan tomorrow,' Foster said. 'But it's the last throw of the dice.' She looked at Chilcott. 'I mean it; we're on that plane on Monday night, with or without prisoners.'

CHAPTER THIRTY-EIGHT

Sunday 19th September

Chilcott had hardly slept, and unlike him, he had barely touched breakfast. Having travelled almost halfway around the world, it seemed perverse that the success of his case rested entirely on luck. He didn't cope well with being at the mercy of fortune. Life had shown him all too often that he didn't excel in that particular department. He had thought long and hard about other options throughout the night, even calling Baxter to hand himself in. That was still an option, but that would be foolhardy and a final, desperate attempt for justice.

Just as yesterday, the officers gathered at the rendezvous point away from the hotel. This time, Julie and Bette had booked a table from 12:30 p.m., with there being an outside possibility that they had missed Williams and Baxter in the first half an hour of service yesterday.

The mood was sombre. If yesterday was a fifty-fifty chance of finding Williams and Baxter, the chances of success today seemed half of that again.

Chilcott had already packed his case, his hotel room was tidy, and he didn't want to overthink about another day of failure. He didn't cope well with coming second-best.

As the time came for Julie and Bette to head for the hotel, Bette turned to Chilcott, held him by the shoulders and gave him a peck on both cheeks.

'That's for luck,' she said.

Blinking, Chilcott struggled to talk and replied, 'Thank you.'

He watched them until they vanished out of sight, his heart racing beneath his hot and sticky suit.

'Are you okay, boss?' DC Allen asked.

'Yeah. Yeah, I'm fine. Why?'

DC Allen hesitated before answering. 'Nothing, boss.'

At 1:10 p.m., Chilcott received a text from Julie Foster. It was a photograph. And in that instant, Chilcott's luck appeared to be changing.

Tall beach palms swayed gently in the heat of the midday sun as small fishing canoes bobbed up and down on the lively turquoise waters of the lagoon. They sat beneath the shade of a champagne palm at a table that had already become "their own" at lunch times. Water lapped gently against a stone sea break just feet away from their dining table. If you could picture paradise, it would probably look, feel and smell something like this.

They held hands beneath the table and dug shallow trenches in the white sand with their toes as they looked out towards their gleaming new yacht at anchor beyond the breaking reef.

A waiter came to the table and presented them with a curry dish within a banana leaf.

'Madame, Monsieur. Cabri Massalé for each of you. Bon appétit.'

They cooed over their delicious-smelling lunch and clinked tall, slender glasses of the most expensive white wine the hotel restaurant had to offer.

'This is more like it,' he said. 'The finest wine, in the finest hotel, in the finest location.'

'Absolutely.' She took a long, satisfying sip from her drink. 'I could stay here forever, you know. It's a shame we have to leave.'

'It's a beautiful spot, but there will be others. The world is ours for the taking.'

He was disturbed by his phone ringing, and he apologised before answering.

'Hello,' he said sharply.

'Apologies, Monsieur, but you have a message waiting for you at reception.'

'Okay, thank you. I'll be there as soon as I can. I'll finish my lunch first, though if you don't mind?'

'Of course, Monsieur. Bon appétit.'

He ended the call and left the phone on the side of the table.

'Who was that?'

'Reception – they have a message for me.'

'Couldn't they tell you over the phone?'

'It's probably from Cecile. It'll be the property reports I asked for.'

'I'm so excited about the place in the hills.' She looked longingly out towards their yacht. 'It's so beautiful here. It'll be a fabulous place to return to.'

'Where next, have you thought about it?'

She rubbed her toes up his shin and smiled sweetly. 'I was thinking, Mauritius. It's the natural next stop from here.'

He chuckled and took a sip of wine. 'I was thinking the same. It's been a long time since I last visited.' He looked off regretfully into space.

'Did you go with… her?' Her voice became suddenly barbed in its tone.

'Yes,' he said at almost a whisper.

She withdrew her foot from his leg and turned her back to him. 'Did you bring *her* here as well?'

'No, tulip. I didn't.'

She crossed her legs and faced away from him.

'Come on, let's not ruin lunch. There's absolutely no need for it.'

'Why… because she's dead?'

He looked over his shoulder at the other diners. No one appeared to be paying them any attention.

'Come on, sweetheart, you know I only want you.'

She turned back to him with a menacing grin. 'You'd

better only want me, or else I'll cut your fucking balls off and shove them down your throat.'

'Everything all right with your meal, Monsieur?' a voice came from behind them.

He coughed into his napkin and nodded. 'Yes, yes. It looks delightful, thank you. We were just admiring the scenery before we begin.'

'Of course. Bon appétit.'

He caught her eye, and they both broke into a snigger.

'You could have told me he was behind us,' she giggled.

'I didn't know? Honestly, what are you like?'

She bumped his knee with hers, and he leaned in towards her for a kiss.

'Come on,' he said. 'This won't eat itself.'

They tucked into their meals and ordered a second bottle of wine. When they had finished, he called the waiter over and requested the bill. The remaining half-bottle would taste just as good on their yacht at sunset, if not better.

'I suppose I ought to go to reception, see what this message is.'

'Be quick. You never know, you might have a present waiting for you when you come back?'

He smiled broadly and clutched the top of her shoulders as he stood behind her chair. He leaned in next to her ear. 'I'll be back in a flash.'

She sniffed in the freshness of unpolluted air and felt the heat of the sun on her face. She smiled and unzipped her bag, removing her MacBook Air. She tapped a few keys, and a detailed spreadsheet came onto the screen. As she studied the data, she noticed a small bird, about the size of a European blue tit fly down and pitch itself on the edge of the table. A bright shock of red across its eyes and beak gave it the look of an avian outlaw.

'Is this a hold-up?' she asked the little bird. 'Are you here to steal my food?'

She held her hand out and rubbed her thumb and forefinger together, and made a quiet bird sound through her lips.

'Hello, little friend. Would you like some bread?' She broke off a crust from an uneaten roll and sprinkled crumbs onto the brilliant white table cloth. The little bird checked her over a couple of times and then bounced towards the bounty.

'There we go,' she said as the little bird pecked away at the morsels of food. Suddenly, it dipped its body and took to evasive flight.

'I hope you don't mind me approaching,' a male voice came from behind. 'But I noticed you from the bar. Could I buy you a drink?'

She watched the small bird vanish into the palm trees, and sadness replaced the joyful moment they had just shared.

'No,' she said, angling the screen of her laptop away from potentially prying eyes. 'You cannot.'

A well-practised smile replaced her spiky response, and she turned to face the man. 'But do allow me to buy you one.'

The man stood beneath the sun canopy. He was pale and clearly hot in his full grey suit and tie going by the perspiration on his brow.

'Hello, Debbie,' Chilcott said. 'It's so lovely to finally meet you.'

She quickly looked all around and then saw Walter Baxter beside the bar in handcuffs, flanked by local police officers and DCI Foster.

DC Allen stepped forwards and tossed an envelope onto the table in front of Debbie Williams.

'What's this?' she asked as if entirely bewildered by the entire episode.

Chilcott closed the gap between them and placed a firm hand upon her shoulder. 'My gift to you. A pair of one-way tickets to the UK. And you, my love, are under arrest for fraud and perverting the course of justice.'

He raised his free hand, and a further four uniformed police officers hurried forwards and took Debbie Williams into their custody, much to the disquiet of the other seated diners and staff.

As she was led away alongside a complaining Walter Baxter, Chilcott looked out into the bay. DCI Foster and DC Allen joined him, and none of them spoke as they lost themselves, just for a moment, in the beauty of the vista.

Chilcott looked down and noticed the half-bottle of wine in the chiller. He removed the serving towel and lifted the bottle to examine the contents.

'Bargain,' he said, turning an unused water glass the right way up on the table. He looked briefly at the wine label and shrugged before filling the glass. He turned to his colleagues and raised it in the air.

'The sweet taste of victory. Cheers.'

CHAPTER THIRTY-NINE

Three weeks later and Bristol seemed altogether bleaker and greyer than ever he'd viewed it before. Williams and Baxter were safely tucked up in custody, and this time, they were going nowhere. As a result of them being a serious flight risk, neither would be leaving the confines of a cell until their trial some eight or nine months further down the line. Debbie Williams' laptop was a veritable gold-mine of evidence relating to the movement of monies obtained through fraudulent activity over the course of ten years or more. Death Do Us Part was now police property having been seized under the Proceeds of Crime Act, along with the new yacht in the Indian Ocean and seven properties around the world to a total value of over fourteen million pounds.

The investigation had turned out to be an unparalleled success and both Chilcott and Richie Allen received Chief Constable Commendations for their work in bringing Williams and Baxter to justice.

Yes, he'd won. Yes, he'd outsmarted the baddies once

again, but he'd seen a side of life that left him feeling incomplete. And if he was being brutally honest with himself, he was missing the marina. He may have flippantly teased Trevor Hicks about attending one of his parties, but truth was; he would have loved it. However, something else was making him feel empty. Since Réunion, he couldn't stop thinking about Bette. Did they really have a mutual attraction? He hoped so, but he found it hard to believe. It had been a long time since any female had found him attractive and all the while he was in her presence, he felt an energy lacking for so long, that now they were apart, it physically hurt.

DC Allen tapped on the door and came inside.

'Hi, boss,' he said.

'Hello, Richie, how's it going, son?'

'All right, thanks. I just want you to know that I took Leah Holman out last night and we got along really well.'

Chilcott smiled sadly.

'That's good news, son. Well done.'

'Since she removed herself from the Baxter case, there's no longer a conflict of interest and we can see one another freely.'

'Good for you, Richie.'

DC Allen lingered next to the desk and Chilcott looked up at him.

'U… Um…' DC Allen stuttered.

'Yes?' Chilcott said.

'I don't want to pry or anything…'

Chilcott dipped his head. 'But…?'

'But I've noticed how withdrawn you've been since Réunion.'

Chilcott looked away.

'A very wise man once gave me some advice and I'd like to give it to you, sir.'

He turned back to face DC Allen with moistening eyes.

'Just give her a call, boss.'

Keep reading for a preview of *A Whisper of Evil*, the third DI Chilcott novel.

A WHISPER OF EVIL

A DI CHILCOTT MYSTERY
BOOK THREE

PROLOGUE

Saturday 5th March

10:23 p.m.

Madeleine Gilbert waited outside the closed stage side door for her new acting *crush* to emerge. It was a narrow street that ran alongside the famous old Theatre Royal in Bath. She wasn't alone, though. Several eager theatre fans were waiting for their heroes to come out through the doors. Some other actors had already left via the same exit, some of them quite well known to Madeleine. She recognised one of them from a TV series, one of those period costume dramas, but none of the actors had caught her eye in quite the same way as Travis Yardley. To her, he was simply adorable. And Madeleine had a quiet confidence that he would like her too if he was so inclined. She knew all about him, having googled his name repeatedly in the days leading up to the show. He had a wife, but according to a sensationalist three-month-old news report from one of the tabloids, their relationship had been rocky for years, and now, apparently, he was back on the market.

She had been waiting outside for just over thirty-five minutes, and her long dark hair had become drab and matted in the damp night air. She hadn't given the weather conditions a second thought; instead, her mind didn't have the capacity to think about anything other than Travis Yardley.

The outdoor covered seating areas of nearby bars and restaurants were buzzing with people seemingly oblivious to the super-talented cast who were still slowly trickling out through the side door of the theatre. She lingered in the shadows of the wall line so as not to draw attention to herself, and then she saw him.

A sudden rush of adrenalin made her half-stumble backwards; her cheeks flushing in wild anticipation of him walking in her direction. He was coming closer, and she stood taller, peeling herself away from the security of the wall. She stepped sideways by no more than a foot, but enough to make him break stride and, most importantly, glance at her as he passed.

If a heart could sing, hers would be screaming the *Macarena* at the top of its sodding voice. It was certainly making the moves, and now he was close; she didn't care who might notice.

'I think you're amazing,' Madeleine said breathlessly.

He turned his head towards her in recognition of her comment, and then, amazingly, he stopped walking.

'Will you sign my programme, please?' she said,

reaching out with a rolled-up glossy brochure that had set her back ten quid at the start of the night. She had already turned to the right page, and Travis's face had been staring back at her for the entirety of the show as she cradled "him" in the warm comfort of her lap.

He peered at Madeleine for a considered second, politely smiled and looked beyond her shoulder towards the noisy bar area.

'Sure,' he said, stepping back towards her.

He was utterly gorgeous. Those dark and expressive eyes were cutting right through the little personal barrier Madeleine struggled to maintain between them.

He waited for a beat and then gestured with a hand as if writing something in mid-air.

'Oh, sorry,' Madeleine fussed, digging a hand into her clutch bag and producing a Sharpie pen which she handed him slowly, keeping hold of it just long enough for him to look into her eyes one more time.

'Who shall I make it out to?' Travis asked in his deep velvety tone.

'Oh, um… Madeleine. I'm Madeleine. Can you make it to Madeleine, please?'

'Pretty name.'

He caught her eye, just long enough for Madeleine to know that he found her attractive.

Travis held the theatre programme out before him, and his phone began ringing inside his trouser pocket.

'Thank you,' Madeleine replied, desperate to keep his attention. She looked down at his masculine smiling lips and took in the rest of his face. Their eyes locked together once again.

'Do you mind…?' he said, drawing a circle in the air with his index finger for Madeleine to turn around.

'Are you going to answer your phone?' Madeleine asked him as the caller persisted in their attempts to get a response.

'It can wait,' he said, not taking his eyes from Madeleine. 'I know who it'll be.'

He repeated the twirl of his finger, and she willingly obliged, and a huge grin passed her lips as she felt Travis pressing down on her back as he signed the theatre programme.

Travis Yardley just touched me; her ecstatic voice bellowed inside her head.

She spun quickly back around, and he handed her the programme, but this time, he held onto the pen as Madeleine grabbed for it.

Another fan barged into the side of Madeleine, forcing her forwards, spilling the contents of her bag and brochure onto the pavement. As she looked back, hoping for Travis to still be there, a female fan was forcing a phone camera into Travis's face and grabbing a 'selfie' alongside him.

Madeleine swiftly scooped the spilt belongings back into her bag and readjusted her jacket. 'I suppose that's one way to do it,' she said, attempting to turn the embarrassing experience into humour.

Travis stood motionless for a second.

'It's okay,' Madelaine said. 'I'm okay. I suppose you get that a lot from your female followers.'

'Do you live here in Bath,' he asked. 'In this stunning town?'

'Yes, I do… well, not really. Well, almost. Not far away, anyway.'

His eyes lengthened, and he relinquished his grasp of the pen.

'Thank you. Thank you so much,' Madeleine uttered, adjusting herself once more.

'Aren't you going to read what I've written?'

Madeleine giggled nervously, and hurriedly opened the pages to the Travis Yardley biography taking up an entire side of the brochure. She scanned the words but didn't take them in as the warmth of another flush came to her cheeks.

'Thank you,' she said softly.

Travis looked down at his watch. 'Do you, maybe… have time for a drink somewhere, or do you need to—'

'Yes, absolutely,' she said, barely stopping herself from grabbing him. 'That would be…' Her breath ran out before she could end the sentence.

'Great. Where's a good place to go where we can hear ourselves talk?'

'Um, there's a small bar down on Kingsmead Square. We could go there if you like? It's really quite nice. It has beer and wine and everything.'

Travis laughed. 'That sounds perfect. I like beer and wine.' He touched her shoulder. 'And everything.' He raised a brow, and Madeleine tittered nervously.

'You'll have to lead the way; I have no idea where I'm going in this town.'

'Oh, yes,' Madeleine giggled. 'Um, it's this way.'

She began walking away from the theatre towards Monmouth Street, constantly checking over her shoulder that Travis Yardley was *really* coming with her. As they passed couples and groups walking towards them, she wanted to scream out with pride that she was with Travis Yardley, but she also wanted him just to herself. The last thing she needed now was a drunken floozy taking his attention away from her.

A few short moments later, they were entering a dimly-lit wine bar, recently refurbished with tall, leather burgundy-coloured half-moon booths, just perfect for a private tete a tete.

Travis ordered a double rum and coke and a raspberry Bellini for Madeleine. They clinked glasses and said "cheers" in unison.

'What is it?' he asked her after a few moments as Madeleine struggled to make conversation.

'No one would believe me. No one would believe *this*.'

'Why not?'

'Because…'

Travis dipped his head provocatively.

'Oh, come on. You're gorgeous. And famous. And gorgeous, and you're in here with me.'

'Yes, I am… here with you.'

Madeleine giggled again.

His phone rang again, and he waved a dismissive hand as it rang off after the twentieth ring.

'So,' he said, looking around at the other booths. 'What brings you out tonight… alone?'

'I love the theatre. You just cannot beat the intensity of a live performance.'

'I agree. There's nothing more invigorating than feeling the passion and emotion.'

They shared a smile.

'Can I ask,' she said? 'Do you mind playing a baddie?'

Travis smiled with his lengthening eyes and took a long sip from his drink as he held her stare. 'Do you like bad boys?'

Madeleine hooked fallen hair away from her face. 'Well, I like your bad boy,' she blushed.

'Good.'

'Um, do you mind me commenting on something?'

'Be my guest.'

'I thought you were from London?'

Travis brought his glass towards his lips, and he licked the rim of the glass with the tip of his tongue before he took another gulp. 'Are you going to answer my question?' he asked.

Madeleine rubbed the side of her neck. 'Which question?'

'Why are you out alone?'

'I… I didn't have anyone to come with.'

His eyes narrowed. 'You live by yourself?'

'Yes…' she said hesitantly. 'Well, kind of.' She rubbed the side of her neck and looked away.

'Kind of…?'

'I look after my mother. She's got dementia. We live together.'

Travis turned his face.

'She lives in the main house,' Madeleine quickly qualified. 'I live in the annexe… by myself.'

'I see.'

He stared at her intently with his dark chocolaty eyes. 'If you don't mind me saying?'

She nodded eagerly.

'I thought you were a little too old to be still living with Mum and Dad.'

'I'm twenty-nine, I'll have you know,' Madeleine bit playfully.

'And incredibly beautiful with it.'

Madeleine looked down at the table and felt the flush of embarrassment once more.

'How about you?' she braced herself to ask. 'Do you live with anyone?'

'Me? No. I'm always… transient.'

'I read… um, sorry,' she giggled anxiously, 'um, what if the right person came along?'

Travis leaned back in the seat and looked left and right. The booths were completely private, apart from the staff collecting or delivering glasses.

He lunged forwards and grasped the sides of Madeleine's head, gently coaxing her face towards his waiting lips. She didn't resist, and soon, they were enjoying a long, passionate kiss.

'Maybe you just have,' he said as their faces parted.

'Do you want to come back to my hotel?' he asked. 'It's quite beautiful.'

'Yes… no, oh, ah…I can't. I have to get home for Mum.'

Madeleine now appreciated how it must feel to lose a winning lottery ticket.

Travis dipped his head and looked at her from beneath his sultry lids.

'Okay, how far away is home?'

'Twenty minutes in a taxi… what?' she said as the implication of what he was asking hit her like a double-decker bus. 'You really want to come back to my house?'

'Yes, I do. Really.'

'Oh my God!'

Madeleine bit the inside of her lip as she considered what Travis Yardley was putting on a plate – her plate. He *actually* wanted to go home with her. Did he mean to sleep with her? That's how it was coming across. She wouldn't object, my God! *I mean, how stupid would that be?*

The thoughts and questions raced around her floating head. Her mother would be asleep, and she had no neighbours to speak of, not for several hundred metres, anyway.

'Okay,' she said breathlessly.

'Good. Let's have another drink. Do you like champagne?'

Madeleine let out a stifled giggle. 'Yes,' she spluttered.

They did their best to enter the modern barn conversion on the edge of Hinton Charterhouse with the dexterity of a surgeon; however, neither of them succeeded, and they both spilt in through the door to giggles of "*Shhhhh*".

No sooner had the door closed than Travis had Madeleine pinned up against the side of the hallway wall, their lips entwined, their hands exploring one another's bodies with the frantic eagerness of young lovers.

'Not here,' Madeleine panted as she fought for her breath.

She took Travis by the hand and led him swiftly through the wide entrance hallway to a beautifully-appointed bedroom with crisp white sheets and a luxurious four-poster bed taking centre stage of the warm stone-clad room. Soft lighting caught the shimmer of delicate lace draped on either side of the bed.

'Perfect,' Travis commented in a low voice.

Madeleine walked him to the edge of the bed, sat down in front of him and hastily unbuttoned his shirt, quickly followed by the buckle of his jeans.

His clothes fell to the floor around his feet, and he grabbed Madeleine by the shoulders and encouraged her backwards onto the bed, straddling her prone body.

He kissed her mouth, neck, and earlobes and slowly moved down towards her chest, opening the buttons of her blouse with the gentleness of two people exploring one another for the first time.

He stopped shy of her breasts. 'I have an idea,' he said, inches from her skin.

'Yes,' Madeleine said, her body writhing with delight.

'You said you had always wanted to be an actress.'

'Yes.'

'Does *this* remind you of anything?'

Her eyes opened, and she stared at the wooden frame of the four-poster bed. 'The murder scene from the show?'

Travis let out a puff of air against her heaving bosom.

'You know, I don't actually rate Holly Delgado.' He raised himself to look at Madeleine. 'I've often wondered how much better it would be with someone different.'

He pushed his hands into the soft duvet on either side of Madeleine's head.

'Why don't you try?'

Madeleine giggled. 'But it doesn't end well for Gemma in the show.'

Travis sat up and leaned his weight back through his bottom, pinning Madeleine's legs to the bed.

He opened his mouth and tracked his eyes over her body.

'Now, something's missing?'

'Um, the knife… can't we just imagine that bit?'

'No, we cannot.'

He sprang from the bed and rushed out of the room.

Madeleine scratched beneath her ear, re-buttoned the bottom of her blouse and pulled her legs up into a sitting position, and hugged her knees.

As she waited for Travis to return, she did her best to sober up by attempting to focus on the small digital alarm clock on the bedside dresser.

12.17, or is it 12.11?

Looking over towards the door, she saw the shadow of Travis approaching silently in the semi-darkness.

'Gemma,' he said; his American accent stronger than before. 'You have been a nasty girl.'

'I'm Madeleine. I don't like this. Please stop.'

He grabbed her ankles and pulled her feet towards him.

Before she could respond, he was straddling her body, this time pinning her to the bed with the force of his thighs.

'Travis, I don't like this,' Madeleine whimpered.

'Shut up, bitch,' he said, slapping her face with ferocity. 'You've done me wrong, and now you must pay.'

He grabbed her throat and squeezed so hard that Madeleine could barely breathe.

'You have wronged me for the last time, Gemma.'

He released his grasp and raised both hands high above his head.

As Madeleine struggled to re-gain her breath, she caught the glint of steel between his balled fists. Instinctively, she tried to squirm away but his body weight fixed to the spot.

What are the fucking lines? She struggled to remember as pure fear gushed through her veins.

'No, Jesse…' she said, remembering the scene from the show. 'I–I promise—'

Travis smiled menacingly. 'It's too late for promises, bitch.'

He thrust the blade down with all the force he could muster.

HOW WAS DEATH DO US PART?

I love to hear feedback and reviews help other readers take a chance on a new author for the first time.

It need only take a moment of your time and be as short as you like.

Visit my Goodreads page at James D. Mortain,
or my Amazon author page at James D Mortain.

Thank you!

FREE EBOOK

THE NIGHT SHIFT

Join my ***CRIME SCENE TEAM*** and receive the compelling short story prequel to the *Detective Deans Mystery* trilogy for FREE.

By signing to join my ***CRIME SCENE TEAM***, you will receive your gift plus occasional news and updates related to my writing.

Don't just be a reader; become part of the team!
Visit www.jamesdmortain.com for more information.

No spam guarantee.
You can unsubscribe at any time.

ALSO BY JAMES D MORTAIN

DETECTIVE DEANS SERIES

STORM LOG-0505

eBook/Paperback/Audio

DEAD BY DESIGN

eBook/Paperback/Audio

THE BONE HILL

eBook/Paperback/Audio

DI CHILCOTT SERIES

DEAD RINGER

eBook/Paperback/Audio

DEATH DO US PART

eBook/Paperback/Audio

A WHISPER OF EVIL

eBook/Paperback/*Audio - coming soon!*

ACKNOWLEDGEMENTS

I owe a huge debt of gratitude to many people who have helped me create this book. To my excellent editor, Debz Hobbs-Wyatt. To my trusted advisers: Terry Galbraith, Phil Croll, Stuart Mitchell, Liz Wheeler and my wife, Rachael. Thank you for taking the time to read, digest and advise me on the earliest versions of this story.

As always, a massive thank you to my team of Advance Readers. You provide me with the 'safety net' that is so important to the publishing process. Your ongoing support is unbelievable and gratefully received.

Over the years, since my first book was published, it has been a pleasure to use the real names of competition winners who won the chance to see their name in one of my novels.

Many of these 'characters' have become integral parts of the ongoing storylines. And so, Nathan Parsons, Julie Foster, and Fleur Phillips thank you for once again allowing me to use your names in this novel - I'm pretty confident Chilcott is going to call upon you again! Also, to Penny

Fleming and Emily Chiba, two of my dear ex-colleagues from when I was a young man starting life in the working world. I hope you both approve of DC Penny Chiba!

In addition to the returning characters, I am thrilled to include more real-life names in this novel. And it's fair to say I've had a lot of fun with these. To my best mate, Richard (Richie) Allen and his lovely wife Leah Allen née Holman (yes, they got together in the end). To Trevor and Jane Hicks - hilarious company and great friends. And finally, to Debbie Williams, who made the mistake of asking to be in one of my books. Thank you all so much for giving me the freedom to create madness and mayhem in your names.

Finally, thank you to all my readers, some of whom have been reading my books since the start. You all keep me inspired to write. It is that simple!

Take care and best wishes,

James

ABOUT THE AUTHOR

Photograph Copyright of Mick Kavanagh Photography.

Former British CID Detective turned crime fiction writer James brings thrilling action and gritty authenticity to his writing through years of police experience. Originally from Bath, England, James now lives in North Devon with his young family.

James has a 'normal' day job, he is also a content writer for a luxury travel company, but is happiest creating fictional mystery and mayhem. Don't miss the latest releases by following James on Amazon, Bookbub and Goodreads.

You can connect with James on social media or by visiting his website a www.jamesdmortain.com.

Please send any emails to jdm@manverspublishing.com.

facebook.com/jamesdmortain

twitter.com/@jamesdmortain

instagram.com/jamesmortain

Printed in Great Britain
by Amazon